Layce Gardner

2011

Copyright © 2011 by Layce Gardner

Bella Books, Inc.
P.O. Box 10543
Tallahassee, FL 32302

All rights reserved. No part of this book may be reproduced or transmitted in any form or by any means, electronic or mechanical, including photocopying, without permission in writing from the publisher.

Printed in the United States of America on acid-free paper
First published 2011

Editor: Katherine V. Forrest
Cover Designer: Linda Callaghan

ISBN 13: 978-1-59493-247-2

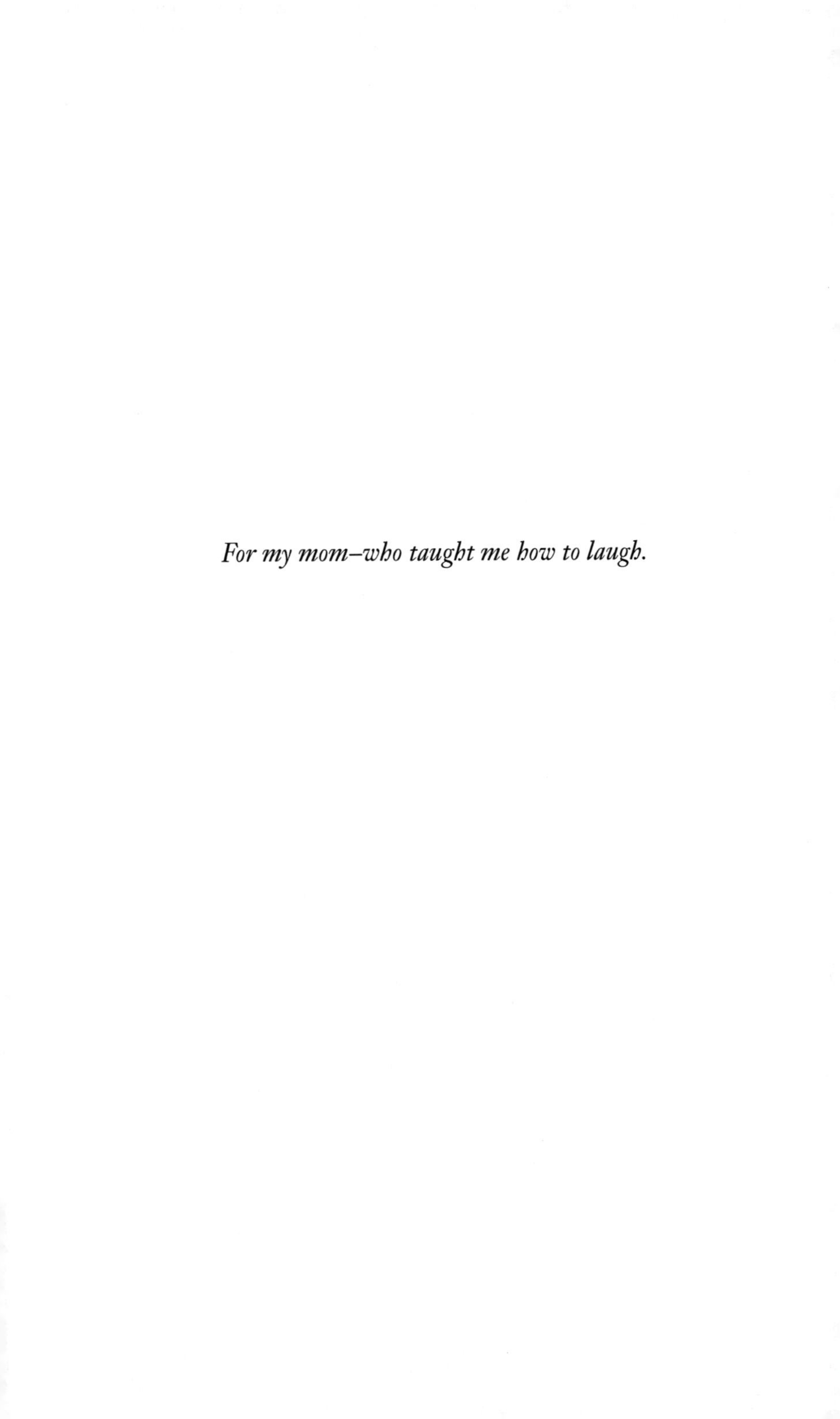

For my mom—who taught me how to laugh.

Acknowledgments

I am blessed to have a mother who's also my best friend. She's the funniest person I've ever met and she taught me how to laugh. My daughter, Emma, is the second funniest person I've ever met, and thanks to her I never stop laughing.

A big heartfelt thanks to my UberAgent and lawyer, Joan Timberlake. She's an agent, a lawyer, an editor, a mother, a pit bull and a friend all rolled into one.

And how lucky am I to get The Katherine V. Forrest as my editor?

Much big love to my cocoon of girlfriends who inspire me on a daily basis: Angie Bliss, Vicki Cheatwood, Saxon Bennett, Jeanne Magill, Laurie Salzler, Sherri Marler Jones Roper, Cherokee Lowe, Trica Farley and Erin Short. And Joey Pohl.

About The Author

Layce Gardner lives on the furthermost edge of the fourth corner of the world with Emma, Stanley, Darla Sue, Honey Bear, Beetlejuice and Asscat. Layce collects motorcycles, tattoos, I Love *Lucy* dolls, cows and female action figures. She loves pie and cheese and conspiracy theories. You can visit her website at Laycegardner.com or her blog at Laycegardner.wordpress.com

CHAPTER ONE

I'm a sucker for a nice pair of tits. And this pair ranks right up there with some of the nicest I've ever had in my face.

The stripper teases me a minute longer before pulling her tits away. I tuck another twenty in her g-string and she gives them back to me. Her long black hair blankets my head and shoulders and I use my teeth to tug on her nipple ring.

She jerks away, surprised, and offers me her ass instead. It takes a couple more twenties to get her tits back this time.

She's no fool. She plays keep-away from me for the next three songs. Three songs is how long it takes to empty my pockets.

Two grand, every cent I have, gone in the space of fifteen minutes. Did I mention I'm a sucker for a nice pair of tits?

"What's your name?" I ask when she bends down near me again.

"Ginger," she whispers.

"Ginger, what time you get off?"

"I'll get off right after you take me home," she answers with a bump and grind aimed right at my face.

I'm sure the bump and grind seems like a good idea. What Ginger doesn't know is that her answer gets me so excited I lean forward. Just enough that my nose smashes into her bump and her grind makes sure it's broken but good.

I gush blood all over me, all over her and all over the dance floor. I guess the smell of blood gets her all excited, because the next thing I know, she's pulling me by the collar out the back door.

I stand in the employee parking lot like a fool with two tissues shoved up my nose while she yanks on jeans and a T-shirt. She throws a leg over the back of a Harley Fatboy, fires up the engine and yells over the pipes, "Get on! You're riding bitch!"

Ginger makes me ride bitch for the next six months. I clean the house, do the laundry, mow the lawn, wash the dishes, I even re-shingle the roof. If I'm good, she lets me ride her Harley. If I'm really good, she lets me ride her.

I haven't been so good lately.

This morning Ginger finally drags home about ten o'clock. She's wearing her favorite T-shirt. It's red with big letters across her tits that read 'I like to fuck.' Talk about your red flags.

"Where you been?" I ask.

"Last time you stuck your nose in my business I broke it," she says, crawling into bed and turning her back to me.

I catch sight of that little birthmark on the inside of her thigh and my thinking gets all cloudy. I get in bed, reach over and caress her ass just the tiniest bit and she turns and slaps the shit out of me.

"What the hell?!"

"I'm tired of being touched," she snaps. "Everybody's always got their hands on me."

"Am I the only one who finds your T-shirt ironic?" I mumble.

She whips the shirt off over her head, wads it up, and throws it in my face. "You like to fuck so much, you wear it," she says, burying her face in the pillow.

"I think your idea of much and my idea of much are two different things," I say, crawling out of bed. I slip my jeans on over my boxers and a T-shirt over my wife-beater. I throw on my leather jacket and my boots. I have my trusty pocketknife in my front pocket, forty bucks in cash and my driver's license. I pat my jacket pockets because I don't go anywhere without my journal and my well-worn paperback, *Zen and the Art of Motorcycle Maintenance.*

I'm walking out of the room when Ginger leans up on one elbow and says, "If you're going riding, bring her back with a full tank."

I nod goodbye to her nipple rings and walk out the door.

There's just something about the vibration and rumble of a motorcycle that lifts my spirits no matter how low they are. I'm flying down the highway at eighty miles per hour with my feet only three inches off the ground, the rising sun on my back, and chasing my own shadow. Ain't nothin' sweeter.

I check over my left shoulder and swing into the passing lane. I open the throttle to ninety plus and breeze right by the semi-truck in the right lane. He honks at me as I whip by and I toss him a small wave before I edge back in his lane.

I'm not a speed-aholic, I just like to go fast. I laugh a little at that thought. I've met many a drunk who says, "I'm not an alcoholic, I just like to drink." Who knows, maybe I am a speed-aholic. Speed jolts me full of adrenaline and when I hear my heart pounding in my ears, I know I'm for sure alive. Besides, speed limits are just that—limits. Me and limits, we don't get along so good.

I like that ad that tells you to think outside the box. Life is too full of boxes as is. You watch TV, it's a box. You go on the computer, it's a box. Phones are boxes. A car is a box on four wheels. People go to work and sit in little cubicle boxes. Houses and offices and stores are just big boxes. When you die they stuff you in another box. A motorcycle is not a box. That's what I like about them. Riding a motorcycle is life outside the box.

I work on and rebuild old motorcycles. I find old pieces of junk and restore them. I don't just put them back the way they were, I make them better. It's not a great living, but it's living the way I want. And how many people can say that?

I have a car, too. It's a necessity of life. You have to haul something somewhere or it's raining, you have to drive a car. I own a 1976 black El Camino. I named her Hell Camino. She looks like a beater, but I rebuilt every little piece of her engine myself and she's pristine.

Two drops of cold rain splatter me in the face. I dump the throttle to sixty-five and scan the streets for any familiar landmarks. I really have no idea where I am. I'm not lost as far as general directions go, but still I don't know exactly where I am. I take the next exit and plan on working my way back on surface streets and that's when the rain blasts me from about three different directions all at once.

That's Oklahoma for you. If you don't like the weather just wait a minute 'cause it'll change. Right now half of Tulsa's sunny, but the half I'm unlucky enough to be in is like being under a waterfall. And when you're on a bike going sixty mph, it feels like a swarm of bees stinging you all at once.

I notch down the gas even more and the wind blows me three feet to the left. I lean into the wind, guide the bike back over and hug the white stripe before it throws me back to the middle of the road. I must look that toy, the Weebles. I keep wobbling, but I don't fall down.

I scour the road ahead looking for a way to get out of this battering. I slide into the nearest parking lot and, of course, it turns out to be a Walmart.

I kick the bike down right near the front in one of those spots where you're only supposed to park if you have a sick kid and you're getting them medicine, but who's going to argue with me over whether I have a sick kid or not? I unzip my jacket and hold the sides up, scrunch my head down like a turtle and run right through the double doors of Big Blue. I stand over by the carts and shake myself off like a dog.

Huddled directly across from me is a troop of green-clad Girl Scouts behind a folding table that's loaded down with boxes of cookies. All their little faces are shut down and miserable-looking. They all stare at me with their little lifeless eyes and this one Girl Scout, the biggest, boldest one, waddles over to me, looks me up and down and asks in a dead voice, "You a woman or you a man?"

I hold out the sides of my jacket, showing her my boobs, but she has the gall to look at my chest and make a face like she considers my wares negligible. Okay, so my boobs aren't even big enough to be called tits, but being insulted by a ten-year-old still pisses me off.

"Buy some Girl Scout cookies," she orders.

Now it's my turn to look her up and down and wonder when did little kids start getting so fat? If you ask me, she's not a very good advertisement for cookie sales. "Looks to me like you've been eating all the profits," I say low.

She sticks the toe of her brown loafer in the puddle around my feet and smears a streak across the floor. She cocks her head up at me and orders again, "I said, buy some Girl Scout cookies."

"Do you all take credit cards?" I ask, feeling guilty about my earlier remark.

She snaps her head back real sassy-like and does that neck roll thing that black women are so good at and says, "What'm I gonna do with a credit card? Swipe it in my ass-crack?" She snaps her fingers at me for emphasis.

I laugh. Good for her. She may be as wide as she is tall, but ain't nobody going to push her around.

I buy forty dollars worth of thin mints.

Ten minutes later the sun is beating down bright and I'm back on my way, forty dollars poorer, but cookie rich. I've no more than ridden a couple of miles before the floodgates open back up and water is gushing out of the sky. I'm in the middle of open country on the outskirts of town and there's nowhere to hide. Even the cows are circled together with their back ends pointing to the storm. Finally, I see a scraggly stand of trees alongside the road and figure I may as well hunker down there until the storm passes.

I ease the bike over under the trees, cut the engine and slip the key in my front pocket. I un-ass and peer through the sheets of water. Damn. I'm in the middle of a cemetery. I don't like cemeteries. Probably because there's always dead people in them.

I catch sight of a pole tent whipping in the wind about a hundred yards away. A bunch of people are herded under the tent, shoulder to shoulder, backs facing the wet. I un-bungee the boxes of cookies from the luggage rack, stuff them as best I can under my jacket and work my way through ankle deep mud all the way to the tent. The people all watch me approach with big eyes, but none of them dare say a word. I have to nudge and poke, muttering some polite 'scuse me's before I make some room for myself. I'm about a head taller than everyone else here, what's new, and a few people glance nervously at my dreadlocks. Which is exactly what I like about my locks; they give me a cushion of space around myself that most people are afraid to enter.

Well, this is about the last place I thought I'd be when I started out this morning. Teetering on the edge of an open grave, my boots sliding in the mud, clutching the damn thin mints under my jacket, with all these social-climbing, golf-playing, country club martini-drinking fat-asses ogling me like I'm the weird one.

I scan the crowd of faces and realize most of these people are my age, they just look way older. I don't get it. Why do women in the midwest hit thirty and automatically lose all sense of style? It's like hormones (or lack of) kick in and create an insatiable appetite for polyester flowers and capri pants. I pride myself on not having much fashion sense, but I don't have to read any fashion magazine to know that capri pants do not make fat legs look thinner. And somebody should pull these women aside and tell them that more makeup doesn't mean more beautiful. I once saw lipstick on a pig, but that didn't make it pretty.

I'm just wet and cold and pissed off. These people don't deserve shit from me. I remind myself that these people are actually out there running in the rat race. I'm just sitting on the sidelines watching. Besides, somebody they loved died and here I am making fun of their damn clothes.

I take a deep, ragged breath and try to think respectful thoughts.

I overhear snippets of the conversation whirling around me: 'Plop, plop, fizz, fizz,' 'Instant implosion,' 'Homecoming Queen.' A paunchy man about half my height leers at me and for a moment I think he's eying my boobs before I realize he's actually drooling over my cookies. I edge over and nonchalantly hide my cookies behind the closest large woman. I glance toward the sky, looking for a break in the weather and hopefully a break in my future.

And just like that...the rain stops, the clouds part and a golden spotlight of sunshine illuminates the most gorgeous woman I've ever seen.

Well, okay, not really.

It's still raining and the woman I left behind in bed is actually way more hot. But there's just something about this one... Maybe it's the fact that she has long red hair the color of hot copper pipes right after you weld them together. Or maybe it's her eyes which are more purple than blue like the color of pvc pipe glue. And her tits... She has them sitting right out there like a window display. (I have this weird thing where I nickname women's tits after famous couples in history. So, right away I name this pair Sonny and Cher.)

She's standing out in the open a good twenty yards away from everyone under the tent, getting soaking wet and paying no never-mind to the foul weather. She sucks a long, hard drag off her wet cigarette and flicks it like an ace into the nearest puddle.

Something about that little flicking gesture warns me she's a woman to be reckoned with.

Too bad she's a hooker. I think that because she's dressed like one. Not like a sleazy hooker, more like a hooker who takes pride in her work and respects the power of advertising. I'm thinking about how most hookers are really gay (so are strippers and playboy centerfolds. It's true.) when I realize I've been gawking at Sonny and Cher for the last fifteen solid seconds. And the Hooker's piercing me with her purple eyes like she knows the dirty thoughts I'm thinking.

I offer her a small smile, but she tilts her head to the side a tiny bit and squints at me. She's either nearsighted or thinks I'm weird.

The double-wide woman I've been hiding behind turns around in her wet, wedgy shoes, slips in the mud and starts to topple. She makes a tiny little squeaky noise in her throat, "Eee eee eee..." She holds her arms out to the side and makes those little circles with her arms that most people do when they're about to take a big fall. Her eyes meet mine and I recognize sheer panic. You know how you lean back in a chair on its hind legs and that split-second fear you have right before you fall over backward? That's what her eyes tell me. I have a decision to make: help her out or save my own butt.

I jump back and let her take the spill on her own.

She kerplunks into the mud, splaying flat on her back and splashing water up knee-high. She wallows around, heaving her considerable bulk from side to side, trying to gain some momentum to get up before a paunchy man grabs her by her flailing hands and hefts her back upright.

She leaves an angel imprint in the muddy ground.

I laugh. God help me, I laugh. I can't help it. Ever since I was a little kid, I get a kick out of people falling on their asses and I never grew out of it. I try to stifle my laughs by burying my face in my shoulder, but I end up snorting real loud and that just cracks me up harder.

Another peal of laughter joins in concert with my own and I look over to where it's coming from. The Hooker is laughing so hard she's actually slapping her knee with one hand and pointing at the fat woman with the other. I don't think I've ever actually seen somebody slap their knee when they laugh but, by God, she really is.

Our eyes meet and this sends us both into fresh bouts of laughter. The Hooker laughs so hard, she doubles over, grabbing both her knees. I stop laughing. Not because it's not funny anymore, but because when the Hooker bends over like that

Sonny and Cher strain against her tight shirt, threatening to make an early entrance and I completely forget to laugh.

"How dare you!" hisses a lady right at me, causing me to jump a little. "How dare you laugh at my sister's funeral!"

Oh, shit. Now I feel bad. "I'm sorry," I mumble to the hissing lady. And just to show my remorse and goodwill, I hold out my cookie boxes and offer, "Want some cookies?"

I hand the boxes over to couple of kids and they start ripping into them right away. I back away from the hard stares of the mourners, turn around and see the Hooker walking toward me.

Women who are so self-assured in their sexuality thrill me and scare me at the same time. The scared part usually comes first. So, I hook my thumbs in my belt loops and try out my John Wayne stance. That doesn't feel right and so I shift, hoping to strike a more *Rebel Without a Cause* pose.

The Hooker's high heels sink in the mud with each step and make slurping noises in the earth as she pulls them back out, but she doesn't seem to notice. She lifts her knees higher in the air and keeps on marching.

She stares straight at me and I get this eerie feeling that her stare is really a stab. I blink hard and look away. A spinning vertigo washes over me and I feel like I'm on a merry-go-round going much too fast. I inhale and hold my breath, hoping to God I don't faint when she finally sucks her way over to me.

When I open my eyes, she's standing right in front of me wearing a little smirk at the corners of her mouth and for a long, slow second I'm lost in her perfume and in her long, red hair and in the little rivulets of rain dripping into her cleavage. She's soaked through and through and cold, too, because her nipples are hard and aimed right at me. The logical part of my brain takes over and I say, "You're wet."

She laughs in a throaty, unsettling way, looks like she's about to say something, then takes it back. That's when I get what I just said. I didn't mean it that way, but I think that's how the Hooker took it.

I try to cover with a quick question, "You want a Girl Scout cookie?"

She flashes her eyes at me and looks away. I guess that's a no.

"I'm not a real Girl Scout," I blurt.

She lights a cigarette, mumbles something I don't quite catch, and hands me the lit cigarette with her lipstick marks on the butt. For some crazy reason I kind of like this and I put my lips right where her lipstick marks are.

The first drag off the cigarette scorches my throat. I don't usually smoke or drink or get high or anything anymore unless somebody hands it to me, but lately, it seems like people have been handing me lots of stuff.

There's an awkward pause and I take a few drags while pretending to watch the cattle graze on the cookies, but in reality I'm checking this woman out. She's obviously bored and you can tell she's somebody who doesn't deal well with boredom. She's got an entire animal print theme going on with her outfit, even the shoes, and I wonder what that means. Does it mean she has a wild side? Or does it mean if you get too close she'll eat you alive? She feels me looking at her and tilts her chin up at me, looking my face over real careful before looking away again. I get a brief flash of something familiar, but there's no way I'd have encountered this woman and not remember, so I just shrug it off.

Another drag off the hot cigarette and I blurt, "I *used* to be a Girl Scout. But I got kicked out for eating a brownie."

She looks at me a little startled and before I know what I'm doing, I just keep blathering on and on. "Sorry. Bad joke. You know that little mechanism between your brain and your mouth that keeps you from blurting? I don't have one." I take another drag. "I think they call it Tourette's."

She lights herself a cigarette and takes her time sucking the lipstick off her teeth. She still hasn't said a word. I'm starting to wonder if she even speaks English.

"Good fishing today," I cast out there.

She squints one eye at me through the smoke and I take a minute to savor the crinkles around her eyes before I jab my cigarette in the direction of the cookie-grazing mourners. I explain, "All the cattle are facing east. That means good fishing."

She throws her head back and laughs. Her laughter bubbles over from deep down in the well of her belly. She uses her whole body and every fiber of her being to laugh and it's so contagious, I join in, too, and I know there's nothing more delicious than this moment.

Her laughter finally dies down to a few short hiccups and sputters and she sets about to right herself. She sticks her hand down the front of her blouse and lifts and separates Sonny and Cher. She tugs on the front of her short skirt, but that doesn't help too much because now it's just riding up higher in the back and you can honest-to-God see some kind of animal print panties that look like they're being devoured. And even though the rain has finally stopped and the sun is peeking out from behind the clouds, I know I'm not going anywhere. I'm sticking around for the show.

I hope I didn't just say that out loud.

"What show?" she asks.

Thinking fast, I reply, "The...um, show, you know, the funeral services." Okay, so that wasn't thinking so fast.

Her lips twitch again and her eyes laugh at me like she knows she caught me in a lie and that I know that she knows she caught me in a lie. She ends up blowing a short puff of air through her nose in my direction. I don't know if she thinks I'm funny haha or funny weird.

I try again. "This may sound retarded, but...you look familiar to me."

Her gaze cuts a path from my boots to my face, she lifts one shoulder in a half-hearted shrug and looks away. Her words come out in a cloud of smoke. "No one would even know you're retarded if you didn't tell them."

Did she really just say that?

What the hell?

The merry-go-round I'm on screeches to a halt and shocks me back to reality where I know this woman is just another hooker and her hair is dyed and she's wearing purple contact lenses, not to mention her tits probably aren't even paid for yet.

"I'm going to pretend that you weren't just a bitch," I say with clenched teeth, because I swear to God, I'll deck this Hooker Bitch, I'll pick her up by her cheetah print panties and throw her into that open grave—a loud caw-like screech and a gust of Jean Nate blows this strange little woman right in front of us. She grabs the Hooker Bitch in a bear hug and talks absolutely nonstop: "Oh my God, Vivian, I'd recognize you anywhere. My God, how long's it been? Fifteen years? Oh my God, hug me back! Don't you remember me? Becky Sheldon! We were cheerleaders together! I was two years behind you in school!"

And to prove her point, Becky takes three steps backward, plants both feet and claps her hands to her thighs. "Ready, Okay!" she yells. What follows are some strange contorted moves that were probably titillating when she was fifteen years younger, but now just look fuckin' strange. This woman who calls herself Becky spells in her loudest voice: "Gimme a C! Gimme an H! Gimme an A! R! G! E! R! S!

The Hooker Bitch stumbles a few steps back and bumps into me. She shakes her head at Becky. "I'm sorry, you've got the wrong person. I don't even know how to spell Chargers."

Oh my God, that's how I know this woman! Vivian Baxter the cheerleader from high school about a billion years ago. I got kicked out of pep club because of her. Well, her and the other cheerleaders. I'd already gotten kicked off the basketball team for smoking pot in the locker room and was pushed into the pep club reject pile. I'd entertained myself by picking ice out of my pop and tossing it at the cheerleaders while they did their stupid cheers on the floor in front of us. I scored a lot of three-pointers, right down their little sailor suit tops. All the cheerleaders were mad as hell and sent their little homely wannabes out into the pep club bleachers to spy and that's how I got nailed. Fat Julie Randall ratted me out. When Julie told Vivian she saw me throwing the ice, Vivian snuck up behind me in the bleachers and dumped an entire pop down the back of my shirt. I got kicked out of pep club, but Vivian didn't get squat.

So this is what happens to cheerleaders after high school.

"Vivian, you're so funny," Becky says, "Where have you been all these years? God, girl, we are going to have to get together. Let's do lunch tomorrow!"

Then the strangest thing happens. Vivian the Cheerleader grabs me by both elbows, leans in close enough that I can feel

Sonny and Cher pressing against me and whispers right under my ear, "Please, God, I'll give you anything. Just get me out of here."

I wonder if her anything means the same thing as my anything.

This is one of those what-if situations that are always and forever getting me into trouble. On the one hand, I know this woman is bad news and I'll probably either end up in jail or with another tattoo, but on the other hand, I know I can't spend the rest of my life wondering what could've happened—if only.

"What time is it?" I ask a little too loud. "Oh my God, it's time for your meds!" Vivian the Cheerleader looks at me with surprise. I'm even surprising myself with this little Oscar-winning performance. I grab her by the arm and pull her none too gently through the mud toward the Harley. I yell over my shoulder to a very stupefied Becky, "I'm sorry but my emotionally incontinent and developmentally disabled sister has to get back to the home before they report her missing again!"

Vivian the Cheerleader's eyes burn a hole in the back of my head and I suppress a smile as I add, "We let her dress herself today, sorry 'bout that!"

Vivian the Cheerleader jerks her arm out of my grip, rips off one of her muddy shoes and whacks me in the back of the head with it, pointy end first.

"Shit! That hurt!" I grab the damn shoe out of her claw and heave it about fifty yards away. "Are you fuckin' nuts?"

"That's a Jimmy Choo!" she yells, hobbling off to retrieve it.

"No, that's a weapon!" I shout at her back.

I watch her plod off to get the shoe, slipping and sliding in the mud, clutching her big red bag like a life preserver and I've got to admit I admire her pluckiness. What is it about cheerleaders? You could be down by fifty points, but they're still jumping around, doing splits and backflips like there's still hope. I shake my head and watch her trudge through the mud. She stops, pulls the panties out of her crack and scans the mire for her shoe. I catch myself smiling way too big and that's when I smash face-first into the darker side of myself. I hate cheerleaders. I love cheerleaders. I hate them. I love them. Lord help me, I am going to love hating this particular cheerleader.

I must admit I'm not too proud of what I yell at her next. "Listen, if you'd rather stay here with your shoes and do some cheers with Becky, I'll understand. I'm sure you and Becky have a lot of catching up to do."

That does it. She does an about-face, takes off her remaining shoe, and marches back toward me. Without even so much as a glance in my direction, she brushes right by and swings a leg over the back of the Harley.

Believe you me, short skirts are not meant for motorcycles.

Vivian the Cheerleader looks up at me seductively and with saccharine dripping from her smile says, "We going? I believe I'm late for my meds back at the group home."

CHAPTER TWO

This is turning out to be a not-so-boring day. The sun has come out, the breeze is warm, and I'm riding a bike with a babe behind me. The grin plastered to my face gets even bigger when I pass a couple of good ol' boys in a primered truck and they stare at us open-mouthed. I know, I know, don't you wish you were me? I don't know what Vivian looks like back there behind me, but I'm pretty damn sure she's got enough skin showing that those boys are sweating pretty hard.

Her knees press into my sides and her fist is gripping the waistband of my Levi's. I adjust the side mirror so I can take a peek at her without her knowing. She squints into the wind and her hair blows about a mile behind us. The tops of her tits jiggle in time with the motor and I like that. I don't think she's ever ridden a bike before, judging by the death grip she has on my pants, but I think she's discovered that a big rumbling, vibrating machine between your legs can be inspiring in more ways than one.

I flip out the cruise pegs with the toes of my boots, stretch out my legs, lean back against Vivian and just stay in the now. Because right now is pretty damn good.

We zip past the airport on our right, then the zoo on our left and I'm starting to get a little un-lost, though I have no idea how to get where we're going or even *where* we're going. I try not to think about it because that's one of the joys of riding. To most people the road is a way to get somewhere. To me the *road* is somewhere.

Vivian thinks she's being sneaky, but I know exactly what she's doing. She arches her back and leans forward a little. I look in the mirror and see that she has her eyes closed and is biting her upper lip. She squirms in the seat and I feel her tense and shudder against my back, then relax. A biker babe has been born.

I level with myself in my head before I get too carried away with this cheerleader who has her hand stuck halfway down the back of my pants: I know Vivian's straight. I just hope she's not straight *and* narrow. She wouldn't be the first straight woman I ever had a good time with. So, I promise myself that I'm going to keep my hands in my pockets and just go along for the ride because you never know what little detours life will take. Plus, as long as I'm being honest with myself, I have a big time thing for redheads and straight women. I have to stop thinking about it or I might let the vibration get to me and that could be deadly.

I have about five minutes of numbing bliss before Vivian sticks her arm out to the right and punches the air with the heel of her shoe. She leans forward, sets her tits on my shoulders and yells over the engine, "Pull over there!"

I guess I've been in one of those driving fugue states where you just automatically go somewhere but can't remember how you did it. I look to where Vivian is pointing her shoe and it's none other than The Glitter Box.

"You don't wanna go there!" I yell back, "That's a titty-bar!"

She snaps the elastic of my boxers, hard, and yells again, "Pull over there!"

Then I understand. I pull into the gravel lot of the strip club and kill the engine. I hold the bike upright with both my feet planted on the ground so she can climb off first. I watch my side mirror in silent amusement as she tries to keep her skirt down and get off the back of the bike at the same time. Finally, after a few false starts, she gives up and just throws her leg off over the sissy bar and flashes anybody within flashing distance.

I kick down the stand, take off my sunglasses and throw my leg off the bike. "Are you late for work?" I ask.

"What did you just say?!"

I can't tell if she's deaf or pissed. I decide to try for deaf. "I said, do you work here? Are you a stripper or something?"

I'll be damned if she doesn't do it again. She takes her last remaining shoe and smacks me upside the head. I could've ducked it. I saw it coming. But I just couldn't believe she was actually going to whack me with a shoe again.

A small spark of anger flashes behind my eyes. "You've got to stop doing that!" I pry that damn evil shoe from her hand and throw it toward the Dumpster at the side of the parking lot. To my surprise it actually lands *in* the Dumpster. I take a deep breath, blow out the fire and offer calmly, "You're not going to have any friends if you go around hitting them in the head all the time."

"That's my last Choo!" she yells, running barefoot for the Dumpster. "The real fuckin' thing! Do you have any idea how much those cost!"

"Yeah, well, I'm out forty bucks on Girl Scout cookies. So, what? Suck it up."

She's not about to let it go. She climbs the side of the Dumpster and fishes out her shoe while yelling, "A thousand bucks!" She turns back to me and emphasizes each word with a poke of her shoe, "One. Thousand. Fucking. Dollars!"

Shit, is she real about that? A thousand dollars for something you can't even walk in? They must've been made out of real leopards or something. I'm astounded. I watch her walk back toward me picking her panties out of her crack before I say, "Do you know how many pairs of panties you could've bought for that much money? I mean real grown-up panties. The kind that don't crawl up your ass every time you move."

She stands dead-still for a moment and even squints at me a little. Then she actually cracks a smile. She flaps her hand in the air like she's dismissing a bad thought, and punches me in the arm the way all straight women do when they're imitating somebody macho, and says, "C'mon, I'll buy us a drink."

She opens the door for me (still being macho, I guess) and I enter the darkness. My boots take turns making sticking and un-sticking noises as I walk up to the bar in the back of the room and I don't even want to imagine Vivian's bare feet.

I sit on a stool, spin around and look the place over. It hasn't changed much since the last time I was in here. Same smell of cigarettes, booze and sex, same flashing colored lights cutting though the dark, even the same tired girls gyrating around the poles on the raised platform in the center of the room.

Every time I walk in here it feels as if my I.Q. drops about fifty points and even before I've taken a drink my senses dull. There's so much raw sex vibing in the air I swear I can taste it.

Tawny is dancing at the front of the stage. Tawny is Ginger's ex-girlfriend and she's always hated me. She probably can't wait to get off the stage and call Ginger with the news that I'm here with another woman. I watch her shake her tits, but she's had so many do-overs that everything except her tits shake. A 6.5 on the Richter couldn't even make them jiggle. Personally, I think her money would've been better spent on a treadmill or one of those ab crunchers. I'm not usually that cruel about women, especially about their bodies, but I make an exception for Tawny who dances like she needs an exorcism.

Tawny grabs some poor trucker by the ears and pulls his face smack-dab between her girls, Pebbles and Bam-Bam. Her eyes shoot poison darts at me from over the top of his balding head. I give her a wink and my best go-to-hell smile before spinning back around.

Vivian stands beside me with her purse hanging off her shoulder and with a discerning expression, she looks around the room. She wrinkles her nose in Tawny's direction before sitting down. I gloat a little bit over that snub.

The bartender throws a damp cloth on the bar in front of us and wipes it down, leaving behind a smear of sticky wet circles. He's a big, mean-looking guy with full tattooed sleeves and a clean-shaven head. He's several inches taller than me and about two hundred fifty pounds of glistening muscle. He has Dixie tattooed across a broken heart right over his left pec and if you ask him why he'll tell you that's his name.

I like Dixie a lot. He protects the dancers (he calls them Dixie's Chicks) from the low-life, and he always tops off my drink with a little extra. Plus, he's an old movie buff, so we have that in common.

He greets me with our usual game, "Hey, look Mister, we serve hard drinks in here for men who want to get drunk fast..."

I pick up where he left off, "...and we don't need any characters in here for atmosphere." We give each other a knuckle bump and I add, "*It's a Wonderful Life*."

"Frank Capra. Nineteen forty-seven," he says, giving me one of his rare smiles. "How's Ginger?"

"You'd know more about that than me."

He purses his lips and nods sympathetically. "Haven't seen your face in a while," he says. "You been working hard?"

I dip into a bag of clichés and say the first one I pull out, "Hardly working, Dix, hardly working. I'll have the usual Jack and Coke, light on the Coke and..." I jerk my thumb toward Vivian, "give her something fancy with an umbrella in it."

"No umbrellas anymore," Dixie says. "I can't put pokey things in the drinks after the last incident."

I laugh. "Make that two Jacks then."

"I can order for myself," Vivian says testily, sitting on the stool beside me and setting her shoe on the bar in front of her.

Dixie pauses in his wiping, waiting for her order. Now that she has his undivided attention, Vivian leans forward, resting her tits on the counter, and scans the rows of bottles in front of the mirrored bar back. Dixie's seen enough tits that he doesn't even glance at hers. I would look straight at them, but the reflection in the mirror provides a better view.

Finally, Vivian straightens up and says, "I'll have a Jack, straight up, on the rocks."

It must be my ears, but I could swear she just said that with a British accent.

Dixie rolls his eyes and begins pouring. "You want those on Ginger's tab?"

I frown. "Better not."

Vivian swings on her stool to face me. "Come here often?" she asks, like she thinks this is a truly amusing remark.

"Not for a while," I say truthfully. "One time when I was here a dancer broke my nose."

Vivian grimaces. "What the hell did you do to deserve that?"

"She didn't hit me with her *fist*," I halfway explain, hoping she'll get it on her own.

She doesn't. She looks at me blankly, props one elbow on the bar and plays with a strand of her hair.

I try again, "Let's just say that I learned to ask before I stick my face somewhere it doesn't belong." I wonder if she got it this time.

She wraps her hair around and around her index finger. She nods and says profoundly, "Oh."

I'm still not sure she got it.

Dixie tosses down a couple of napkins and places our drinks in front of us. Vivian scoots a twenty his way. She takes a swig of her drink and swishes it around in her mouth like it was a fine French wine, sets it down with a purpose and asks, "So...you're a *patissier*?"

"A what?"

"A pastry chef," Vivian explains like I'm dumb.

"A pastry chef? What gave you that idea?"

"The cookies? The funeral?"

"Oh, the cookies. No, I'm not a pastry chef." Just the thought makes me laugh.

"I was being sarcastic," she says.

"Oh," I reply. "You sounded so serious."

"What *were* you doing with a bunch of Girl Scout cookies?"

"Community service," I explain. "It's part of my parole agreement."

She arches one eyebrow just the tiniest bit, then turns and takes her time looking at herself in the mirror behind the bar. She pushes and prods at a few imaginary places on her face that only she can see. "I look like hell," she finally says.

"Not really," I say.

"Well, thank you, I guess," she replies dryly, then adds, "*You*, however, do look like hell."

"I didn't mean that. I meant 'not really' about the parole thing. I was just being sarcastic."

She laughs. "No parole then?" she asks.

"No."

"Prison?"

"Nope."

"Damn," Vivian sighs. "Just when I thought things were gonna get exciting."

"You know..." I start in, "My name's Lee. Lee Anne Hammond. From high school? We were in the same grade. I know you probably don't remember me, being Miss Basketball Queen and all, but..."

"Football Queen not basketball," she says disgustedly like there's some kind of huge difference between the two. "And I know who you are, all right," she continues, her face lighting up. "I paid you five dollars to swallow a live guppy in biology class."

"Goldfish, not a guppy," I say disgustedly because there is a huge difference between the two. I swell up at the memory. "And the whole class chipped in. I made over a hundred bucks for that stunt."

It was my fifteen minutes of fame. I sat in the back row of biology class and Vivian was in front of me and to my left. That day the teacher handed out live goldfish to all of us and we were supposed to dissect them and look at their wet little insides. Vivian got her fish first, pinched its tail between her fingers and turned to me. She straight-armed the fish directly into my face and said loudly so the whole class could hear, "I'll give you five bucks to eat this!"

The whole class laughed and Vivian and I engaged in a stare-down. I reached out and grabbed her wrist and held it steady. I knew my grip was hard enough that it probably hurt, but to her credit, it didn't show on her face at all. I mouthed the words 'Eat me' so only she could see. She laughed out loud and tried to pull the fish out of my face, but I kept her hand from moving. I didn't know why she picked on me, but she picked on the wrong gal.

"A hundred bucks," I said. "A hundred bucks, I'll eat it *and* I'll like it."

The whole class chipped in and pretty soon my desk had a pile of crinkled bills on it. Even the teacher opened his wallet and added a ten-spot. I held Vivian's hand above my head and opened my mouth right under the dangling fish. She dropped it in. I swallowed. I swallowed again, harder. I felt the fish wiggle its way clear down to my belly.

Vivian led the class in applause and I wallowed in the moment, but secretly I couldn't wait till the bell rang so I could run to the girls' room and heave.

It wasn't until much later in the day that I realized Vivian didn't ever add her five dollars to the pile.

I sigh and shake my head at the memory. "I still can't believe I ever did that," I say to Vivian. "And I can't believe you remember it."

"Worth every cent," Vivian exclaims, laughing loudly.

God, I love her laugh. I love it so much, I decide not to tell her she still owes me five dollars.

"It's not the worst thing I've ever had in my mouth," I say.

"Oh my God, honey, me neither. Meeeee neeeiiiitttthhher."

Her laugh is catching and the next thing you know, I'm laughing, too, and I find myself not really minding the lumps on my head.

I've got saddle sores from sitting on this barstool. How many drinks have I had anyway? Nine? Ten? Vivian will not shut up. I think somewhere along the third or fourth drink, she swallowed her own little brain/mouth mechanism.

I stand up and lean on the bar, flexing my butt while she

babbles, "I wasn't stalking her or anything. I just think Princess Di and I had a lot in common. So, one morning I had an epiphany. I woke up in my trailer crammed full of Franklin Mint Princess Di collectibles and thought, 'Why? Why her and not me?' I'm prettier than her even, but she got the prince and not me. Ten minutes later I booked a one-way ticket to England and packed one suitcase full of clothes and one suitcase full of my favorite shoes and flew five thousand miles to meet my destiny. I mean, really, what did Di have that I don't? Or Lana Turner, for that matter. All she did was sit on a barstool in some drugstore and get discovered and, God knows, she's not the only one who can fill out a sweater."

I signal to Dixie for another round and look back to Vivian. I watch her full red lips move around her constant stream of words.

"So I get to London and rent a room from this little Korean woman named Tulip, but her real name is Esther and she's a dominatrix who specializes in pony play, and when she sees how many great shoes I have she gives me some of her crush customers. All I have to do is wear my heels and stomp on fruit. I did so good at that she handed over some of her trample clients. I just put on my heels and walked up and down their backs."

If she doesn't whip out a tit or something soon, I'm going to fall asleep.

"Esther was Korean by blood but she was adopted and raised by Jewish parents so I don't know if the Korean part really counts," she says. "She made a really good living by sitting on men like they were a horse and slapping them on the ass, saying 'Giddy-up!' It may sound kind of weird, but fer chrissakes, Ann-Margret wallowed around in pinto beans and chocolate for that movie *Tommy* and got famous so I guess a little fruit stomping won't hurt me any." She pauses to light a cigarette off the red embers of her last one.

I bet she has pink nipples. But you never can tell. Ten to one though, she does.

"There was this old Italian guy with a Marlon Brando complex who would bring me to Rome for weeks at a time and make me feed him spaghetti in the bathtub and I let him call me Mommy. He introduced me to my Prince Charles. He's not really a prince, but he's big, really big, and his name was Charles Townsend so I called him Prince Charles. He paid me enough that I didn't have to walk on backs anymore. I went over to his mansion every Thursday night and wore little French maid outfits and he told me he loved me and was going to marry me, but the reality is those English never get divorced because the Pope won't let them and even though his poodle of a wife is always off fucking the real French maid, I'll always be just his mistress."

She stops for air and before she can get started again, I interject, "I've never met a real live mistress before."

She doesn't miss a beat. "It's kinda boring, really. But the pay's not bad. And he wasn't asking me to do anything I wouldn't have done for free anyway."

"Are you here, Lee? It's Ginger."

I pull my eyes away from Vivian's tits and see that Dixie is holding the bar phone with his hand over the receiver.

"No," I say, while simultaneously Vivian says, "Yes," and snatches the phone out of Dixie's paw.

I gesture emphatic no's and make slash marks across my throat, but Vivian just smiles and whispers, "I can take care of this." She spins on the stool, putting her back to me and plugs one ear with her finger. "'Ello?" she says into the phone with her best British accent. "To whom am I speaking? No, it's not. She is rather inconvenienced at the moment, may I give her a message?"

Vivian spins back around, lays the phone on the counter and gives me an innocent shrug. "You have some really rude friends."

"Shit," I say. "Listen, I really need to get out of here." I straighten up and turn toward the exit only to find myself tit-to-tit with Tawny.

"Going somewhere?" Tawny asks, taking another step toward me. Her torpedoes back me into the barstool and sit me down hard.

"Nope," I say, moving my face out of their line of fire.

"Nice shoes," Vivian says, looking right at Tawny's huge tits. "Where'd you buy 'em?"

Tawny aims her torpedoes at Vivian's nose. Vivian doesn't flinch. "You a dancer?" Tawny asks.

Vivian laughs like it's the most absurd thing she's ever heard. "Honey, aren't we all dancers? The only difference between you and me is that I make a lot more money."

"Is that so?" Tawny replies with a sharp edge.

Vivian stands and grabs Tawny by the wrist. "Let me show you a trick or two," she says, pulling Tawny toward the dance floor.

Oh shit, oh shit. This cannot be happening. I follow behind, a long ways behind, 'cause when the shit starts flying, I don't want to be splattered.

Vivian hops up onto the stage, slinks to the middle and closes her eyes like in a trance. The other dancers stop their routines and look at her sideways. It's going to get bloody.

Vivian starts to move. Slowly, ever so slowly, then with assurance and control she picks up the tempo. In that instant, I take back everything I ever said or thought about Ginger being the best dancer I've ever seen. Ginger can't hold a candle to Vivian.

The other strippers, Tawny included, have the good sense to back away and just watch.

Vivian doesn't just move with the music, Vivian *is* the music. She moves in the musical notes, around the notes, over the notes, under the notes, slides and rides the notes like only a woman who knows her own body can. She doesn't take off one bit of clothing; she doesn't shove her tits in anyone's face; she doesn't rub up against the pole; and yet, somehow, she's the sexiest thing I've ever seen.

And I'm not the only one who thinks that.

The whole place, the men, the other dancers, are mesmerized into a stupor. When the song ends, I'm completely whipped and drunk on something stronger than Jack.

All the men sitting around the floor dig in their pockets and hold out fives, tens, twenties. Vivian walks amongst them, accepting their money and smiling seductively. If a man tries to stick the money in her skirt or her shirt, Vivian grabs it before he can. When she's made the rounds, Vivian has a stack of bills in her hand two inches thick. She walks up to Tawny and sticks the wad of money between her tits.

"There you go, doll," Vivian says sweetly. She turns and struts up to me, saying, "Let's get out of this place."

"Sure," I say, turning for the door. I wobble left, then right and Vivian reaches out and grabs my belt buckle, holding me steady.

"You sure you can drive?" she asks.

"Hell, yeah," I answer with a lot more confidence than I feel.

"Good," Vivian says with a laugh. "'Cause I'm drunk off my fuckin' ass."

I suck in some cool night air and try to shake the soggy cobwebs from my head. I blaze the trail into the parking lot, heading toward the spot where I parked the bike. Vivian follows in my footsteps, walking like she's playing a game of Mother-May-I. Three baby steps, one giant step, one step back, two tiny steps to the side...

I stop dead. I shake my head. I rub my eyes with my fists like some Merrie Melody version of "I can't believe what I'm seeing."

Vivian bounces off my back. "What is it?" she slurs, looping her arm through mine and almost pulling me off balance.

"I can't believe what I'm seeing," I say, the fear already settling in.

"What?" she asks again, scanning the pavement around our feet for anything unusual.

"I mean...I can't believe what I'm *not* seeing."

"I don't see it either," she chuckles. "What exactly is it that I'm not seeing again?"

"The bike," I reply, instantly sober. "I parked the bike right here." To prove my point, I stamp my boot right where the bike used to be.

"Weeellllllll," she slurs, "fer chrissakes. Where'd it go?" She looks around the parking lot like it's just playing hide-and-seek or something.

A cold fist of fear punches me in the gut. There's no way, no fuckin' way.

Vivian perks up and stumbles off. "No problem. No problem at all. I'll just ask this nice young woman in the El Camino for help."

I follow Vivian's trajectory and see she's headed for Hell Camino. What the hell is my car doing here? I thought I rode the motorcycle. With Vivian on back. Did I? Or did I...?

I squint. Sitting in the cab of Hell Camino is the silhouette of a woman. Vivian is already at the car and tapping one fingernail on the passenger window. All the puzzle pieces snap into place.

Oh my God, no! I scream. Or maybe I just scream it in my head because I feel like I'm all tangled up in one of those nightmares where your legs are paralyzed and try as hard as you might you can't run away from the monster.

I finally find my legs, but my brain's lagging about two seconds behind. "That's Ginger!" I yell, "Viv, don't—!"

Too late. The silhouette leans back and kicks open the passenger door. The door slams into Vivian—and Vivian is airborne for a few slo-mo seconds before she hits the pavement ten feet away with a sickening thud. Legs splayed, skirt bunched up, she lays on the ground, not moving.

After what seems like an eternity, Vivian leans up on one elbow and mutters, "Goddamn...that's gonna hurt tomorrow."

Ginger jumps out of the passenger side of the car, wearing a skimpy halter top and those Daisy Mae jean shorts I love on her so much with cowboy boots. Her belly button ring catches the neon lights of the bar and winks colors as she struts toward me. She looks really hot. I quickly throw that thought away because it's just not going to help me at all right now.

Ginger's boots crunch menacingly all the way over to me. She steps in close, too close for comfort. I take a small step back and glance over at Vivian who's still sprawled on the ground, but is now busy digging through her big red purse. I hope she's got a gun in there because I have a really bad feeling gnawing at my gut.

"Listen, Ginger..." I say, clasping my hands together in a pleading gesture. "Your bike is obviously stolen. But it's no big deal. Really. We'll turn it in to the police and I'm sure they'll find it."

"I moved my bike," Ginger says in a voice so eerily calm it send chills all the way through me.

Yep, she sure did. I don't know how I missed it before, but there it sits on the other side of Hell Camino.

"Ginger... Let's talk about this, okay?" I whisper feebly.

"Okay," Ginger says. "Let's. Talk." She starts at my belly button and walks her fingers right up my stomach, across my chest, and doesn't stop until she tweaks my right nipple. "Let's talk about how you stole my bike out of the garage this morning."

Another tweak.

"Let's talk about how I don't know where the fuck you are all day."

Tweak again. Now she's really getting wound up.

"Let's talk about how I find you back here, drunk off your fuckin' ass!"

I cover my boobs with both my hands.

"Or why don't we talk about that slut you're panting after like some damned dog in heat!"

"Hah!" Vivian barks and pulls a cigarette out of her purse. So much for the gun.

"Ginger, baby..." I put my hand on her hip and make one seriously big mistake when I say, "Let's, uh, go back home and work this anger out in a more, uh, productive way."

Ginger doesn't even pause to think about it. She throws a roundhouse punch straight to my nose. And this is no girlie pseudo-macho punch either. This is the real McCoy. The next thing I know, the gravel is biting my ass, my nose is spurting blood, and Ginger is peeling out of the lot on her Harley.

"Who the fuck was that?" says Vivian, standing and dusting off the back of her skirt with a lit cigarette clenched between her teeth.

"That's the second time she's broken my nose," I sputter, sitting up.

"She has absolutely no sense of style. That Dukes of Hazzard's thing is so nineteen eighties."

I roll onto all fours, trying to make it back upright.

"Why didn't you hit her back?" she says, demonstrating what I should've done by swinging her big-ass red purse in a high arc that almost sends her back to the ground.

I don't answer. I'm too busy bleeding to answer.

"God, what a pussy you are," Vivian says disgustedly, kicking chat in my direction.

For some odd reason, I feel it necessary to defend myself. "I'm not going to hit a woman."

"You *are* a woman," she says. "You can hit another woman. It's allowed."

"Where's that written? The cheerleader handbook?"

"Yes, it is," she says, sounding really, really serious. "It's in Chapter Eight right before 'A Wonderbra is a girl's best friend'."

"Well, then, that explains it. I only read as far as Chapter Seven."

Vivian lifts herself into the passenger side of my car, crawls across the seat oblivious to the fact that her ass is in the air for the whole entire world to see, and situates herself behind the wheel. The engine roars to life and she backs up the car, slams it forward, back again, forward again—I don't know what the hell she's doing—the passenger door flopping open, closed, open, closed...

"Hey! That's my car!" I yell.

Vivian slams on the brakes, hangs one arm up over the back of the seat and says, "May I suggest if you ever want to see your car again that you get in."

I take off my leather jacket before it gets all bloody and throw it in the bed. I strip off my T-shirt and wad it up under my still-bleeding nose. I climb in, lay my head back on the seat and stare straight up at the ceiling.

Vivian looks at my wife-beater and snorts through her nose. She rolls down her window, throws the car into drive and peels out. She ignores every stop sign and stop light and I don't think she even knows where the brakes are.

I close my eyes and concentrate on not throwing up.

She squeals to a stop at the Redman Motor Lodge. There's a bright orange and red neon sign of an Indian in war gear and full headdress blinking on and off, on and off. Near the motel office is a life-size concrete teepee and it's outlined in little blinking lights of its own.

Vivian hops out of the car with her red bag and shoe, kicking the door shut behind her. I straggle out and collect my jacket from the back, still holding my head back and trying not to drip all over the place.

Vivian ambles over to room number seven and is talking nonstop again. I only catch tidbits of what she talking about: "Di and I could've been such good friends. She was like the sister I always wanted. My brother was like my sister except he always borrowed my sweaters and stretched out the shoulders. Di wouldn't have done that. We're the same size."

She opens the door and flips on the lights. There's one bed and plenty of cheap decor. The curtains and bedspread match each other with a cowboy bull-riding motif. Above the bed is a huge painting of a dream-catcher with a howling coyote sitting under a full moon. Another painting of a big, sad-eyed Palomino stares at us from over the chest of drawers. They're both bolted to wall. A wagon-wheel table and barrel chairs round out the western theme.

I plop down right on the bed and lay my head back on the pillow. I close my eyes and will myself to stop losing bodily fluids. I hear Vivian rummaging around the room and the door opens and closes. She's gone.

I have time to think about this situation. I never have any problem getting women into bed, it's keeping them afterward that I have a problem with. I'm thinking I'd like to keep this one around for a while. I don't know why exactly. Except for the fact that she's surprising. I never know exactly what she's going to do next. I like that. Maybe if I don't sleep with her for a while, she'll stick around. I'll let her make the first move. I won't do a damn thing until she does. I just hope she does it soon.

The door opens. The bedsprings squeak beside me. Vivian presses a towel full of ice to my nose.

"Thanks," I say.

She gets up and pulls my boots off and sits them on the floor at the end of the bed.

"Thanks," I say again.

She quietly disappears and leaves me to my misery. I wonder what Ginger's doing right now. Probably throwing all my stuff out on the front lawn and burning it. No, she's probably not, that would mean too much work.

I hear the shower turn on in the bathroom and Vivian talking to herself.

I wonder if she's a crazy person? I mean really crazy, like certifiable. Maybe she's just drunk. Her taking a shower is a plus in my direction, right? It means she wants to make love, but wants to be clean first, right? Hell, I don't know.

I ease out of bed and tippy-toe over to the bathroom door. Normally, I don't do stuff like this. I don't eavesdrop or pry, but if she's truly crazy I'd like to know about it before I wake up and she's standing over me with a butcher knife.

I press my ear up against the door. She's talking to herself all right, but I can't make out what she's saying over the noise of the shower. She's quiet for a moment and just as I start to tippy-toe back to bed, I hear her. She's crying. It's unmistakable. She's crying pretty damn hard, too.

I back away, sorry now that I invaded her privacy. I squirm out of my jeans and slip under the bedcovers. I wonder why she's crying. She doesn't seem like the crying type.

I touch my tender nose and even that slight pressure brings tears to my eyes. Great. We're both going to be crying all night.

I hear the bathroom door open and I quickly slide to the right side of the bed. I'm right-handed so my right hand is my tittie-dominant hand. I'm just thinking ahead here. I like to be prepared.

When Vivian walks back into the bedroom, she's wearing a too-big, old OU T-shirt and panties and that's it. The T-shirt has a big rip under her right arm and I catch a quick glimpse of her right tit as she sits on the other side of the bed and slides under the sheet.

Pink nipples. I knew it.

I breathe in deep and easy, smelling her newly clean scent. We lie on our backs next to each other and her electricity lights up the dark. I listen to her breathe and am reconsidering the whole let her make the first move thing when she whispers softly, "If you were a man..."

I hold my breath.

She continues, "...you'd have already left by now."

She turns on her side, pressing her butt against my thigh and is snoring lightly before I breathe again.

CHAPTER THREE

Something tickles my nose. I snort and it disappears. Tickling again. I open my eyes. Long red hair caresses my face. I wipe it away and turn my head to look. Vivian looks so angelic in her sleep. Except for the snoring part.

I slide out of bed and get my journal out of my jacket pocket. Writing when I first roll out of bed before my brain wakes up is the best time. I mean to write about Vivian, but when I get started I wind up thinking about Lori Spangler instead.

Lori had red hair, too, and she was the beginning of my red hair fetish. She was the prettiest girl in seventh grade and me and every other boy in our class had a giant crush on her. She's the reason I got up early on a Sunday morning and put on my best pair of jeans and ironed the wrinkles out of my shirt and laced up squeaky shoes and left the house without waking anyone up. She was the reason I walked through the doors of the First Baptist Church because if Lori wanted to personally introduce me to Jesus, that was fine with me.

A couple of old ladies with matching flowered dresses and huge hats perched on their hard nests of hair patted me on the shoulders and pushed me in the direction of Sunday school.

I clomped down the steep stairs and into the basement feeling like I should've worn a dress, except for the fact that I didn't have one, and I took a bath that morning but still felt dirty.

I stood in the doorway and shoved my hands in my pockets. What the hell was I thinking? Baptists don't have ragged, bitten fingernails and bruises and scabby bug bites. I was just about to turn and race back up the stairs when Lori saw me and waved from across the room.

Her pretty dress rustled when she walked and I could smell her fruity perfume from ten feet away. When she smiled at me, my throat froze shut.

She politely held out her hand. "Welcome." She smiled. I gave her a limp handshake and made my mouth into a smile that I hoped looked easy.

"I'm Lee Anne," I introduced myself.

"I know that, silly," she said. "Wanna sit by me?" Before I could answer, she pulled me in the direction of two empty chairs and sat down beside me.

That's how I knew there was a God.

The Sunday school teacher was a cranky-looking old woman with wrinkles all over. Even her panty hose were wrinkled and baggy. It was like she used to be five times bigger before she deflated inside her own skin.

Lori and I sat in the back, sharing a Bible. We pretended to study the words of Jesus written in red, but instead we played hangman and drew goofy pictures of the teacher. Lori giggled and poked me in the ribs with her elbow and I giggled and poked back.

Every time Lori looked at me with those green eyes of hers my heart swelled up like a tight balloon and if it weren't for my ribs, it would've floated right up in the air.

Lori whispered in my ear, "Wanna come to the slumber

party Friday night? It's just us girls here in the basement. It'll be fun."

Her hair was in my face, but I didn't brush it away. I took a deep whiff of her scent, memorizing it for later. "Sure," I said, acting like I didn't really care but why not.

Friday night took forever to arrive. I showed up at church early and Lori showed up late. She was so popular that I didn't get any alone time with her at all. So, I made do with junk food instead. I shoved the popcorn and potato chips in my mouth with both fists. The other girls just nibbled, but I'd never gotten to eat so much shit at one sitting in my life, so I took full advantage of it.

We all sat around in a big circle on the basement floor on our sleeping bags. Lori's mom brought me an extra one since I didn't have one. It must've been Lori's big brother's sleeping bag because it was camouflage, had some dog hair stuck to it and smelled like gym socks.

My pajamas were just a big old T-shirt and panties. I never bothered with pajamas. I just went to sleep in whatever I happened to be wearing at the time. Sometimes I even slept in my shoes if I was wearing them to begin with. That way if I had to run, I didn't have to get dressed first or take a chance on being half-naked. All the other girls had cute little store-bought pajama sets or nightgowns. I felt like shit warmed over compared to them until Lori said in front of the other girls, "I wish I was as pretty as you, Lee Anne. You can wear anything and look great."

The burn started in my cheeks and worked itself all the way down. "Thanks," I mumbled.

All the girls started in talking about Ray or Jeff or Brian. Who they wanted to go steady with, who they had a crush on. I just kept quiet and ate more chips.

"When Ray kisses me he slobbers all over. I swear his spit drips down my chin after," said Janet.

"Ooooh," everyone squealed.

"How can you stand that?" asked Tracy.

Everybody laughed and they all talked at once about the way their boyfriends kissed and they giggled and screamed.

Lori's mom opened the door and peeked her head inside. "It's midnight, girls, time for lights out."

"Noooo," they all said at once.

Lori's mom flipped out the lights. "Sleep time," she said. "We have a lot of activities planned in the morning. You girls need your beauty rest." She shut the door and left.

Everybody made getting ready for bed sounds and a couple of the girls across the circle from me whispered and giggled still.

"I have an idea!" Lori whispered. "Let's practice kissing!"

Everybody clapped their hands and laughed and I felt a weird energy in the air, and that's when I knew this was why we were all there. This was the part of the night they'd all been waiting for.

"Who're we gonna practice kissing on?" somebody asked.

I was wondering the same thing.

Lori sat down next to me so close our thighs touched. She whispered through the dark, "Lee Anne has volunteered to be the boy. Right, Lee Anne?"

"Yeah, okay," I said. I hoped I didn't say that as scared as I felt.

"I go first," Lori said.

"Two minutes," some girl said. "Two minutes apiece, then Lee Anne tells who's the best kisser out of all of us."

I didn't even have enough time to let the scared sink in good before Lori pulled me to her and touched her lips to mine. I closed my eyes and concentrated on kissing her back. She tasted like popcorn and mint gum. She opened my lips with her own and put her tongue in my mouth. I tasted her tongue and pressed into her harder. My hands wrapped around her waist and squeezed tight.

Two minutes was over long before I was ready for it to end. Just when I was getting the hang of it.

Another girl took Lori's place. And another took her place. And another. Sixteen minutes later I'd kissed each and every one of them.

"Who's the best?" one girl asked.

"Yeah, Lee Anne, who kisses best?" they demanded to know.

"Lori," I said. "Definitely Lori."

Lori reached out into the dark between us and found my hand. She raised it to her mouth and pressed my knuckles to her lips.

If I'd been a little quicker on the uptake, I'd have declared it a tie and demanded a tie-breaker.

Later, I'm all tucked inside the sleeping bag on the cold linoleum floor in that half-sleeping state where I still felt the ghost of Lori's lips on mine and my body was buzzing from it.

"Ssshhhh," Lori said right next to my ear. She slowly and carefully unzipped my sleeping bag and crawled in with me, pressing her warm body up next to mine. Our lips found each other and she guided my hand to her chest. Her boobs were small and hard and when I touched her nipples she squirmed her hips against me.

She rolled over onto her back and pulled me on top of her. I kissed her lips and her neck and her ears and she grabbed my butt with both her hands and rubbed against me, making little whimpering noises in the back of her throat.

That night, I found salvation in the house of God.

And I've had a thing for red hair ever since.

I stow my journal back in my jacket and jump in the shower. I let the pinpricks of hot water hit my sore nose, kind of hoping the sharp needles of pain will take away from the throb in my head. My mind is still dancing with thoughts of red hair and Lori/Vivian and I get an overriding urge to touch myself. I lather up my hands and slip one between my legs.

I close my eyes and Vivian surprises me by stepping into the shower naked. She turns her back to me and lifts her face to the stream of hot water. I rub soap all over the front of her and she responds by pressing her ass into me.

That's when the real Vivian swings open the door and walks in, startling me. I jump pretty good and even though I don't think she can see me through the flowered shower curtain, I pretend I was washing under my arms the whole time.

I hear her peeing about six inches away.

"How's your nose?" Vivian asks in a voice full of sleep and sand.

She sounds genuinely concerned, so I answer honestly, "Hurts some. But I don't think it's broken. I think it just popped back in place from the last time."

"You got any plans today?"

"No."

"You do now," Vivian says. She flushes the toilet and my water is instantly scalding hot.

"Holy shit!" I exclaim, jumping backward. "That's hot!"

"Do ya good," she says on the way out, closing the door behind her.

By the time I walk out of the bathroom, fully dressed in my day-old jeans and bloody T-shirt, Vivian has somehow managed to pull it all together and look pretty fabulous in a new outfit. I don't know how she managed that so fast. Must be all the cheerleader training. She's wearing the same kind of ensemble, just a different animal print (zebra or maybe tiger. Hard to tell, but it does have stripes) and another pair of stabby shoes. Her tits are kind of heaved up and out like the prow of a Viking ship. She's putting on lipstick in the mirror and that's a pretty good signal that we're not thinking the same thing at all.

"Guess I'm ready," I say lamely, sitting on the end of the bed and pulling on my boots. "What're we going to do?"

"You can't wear that shirt," she says, smacking her lips on a tissue. She roots around in her suitcase, finds what she's looking for and throws it at me. "Try one of mine on."

I look at what she threw at me. I hold it up and examine it from every angle. What is she, nuts? Has she not been paying any attention at all?

"I can't wear this," I say. "It's not even a whole shirt. Just pieces of a shirt. Not even the best pieces."

"It'll look great on you," she replies. "Less bloody, anyway."

"This won't even cover up my sportsbra."

"God, you're so helpless. You don't wear a bra with that. The support is built in."

I turn it over in my hands. "Where?"

"Put it on," she orders.

I hold this thing she calls a shirt up in front of me and look in the mirror.

"That's the back. Turn it around," she sighs.

Now she's tapping her foot at me and I'm getting nervous because I remember how lethal she can be with footwear so I disappear back into the bathroom. I strip off my T-shirt, wife-beater and sportsbra and look at myself in the mirror. My boobs are actually okay, just smallish. I press them together with my palms and hold them up as high as I can. That kinda hurts, but it's the only way I can create cleavage.

I throw her shirt over my head and pull it down. It's tight. Way too tight. I look in the mirror again. Yep. The shirt's so tight, what boobs I did have are now mushed down to oblivion. I roll my eyes at my reflection and head back to Vivian.

When I walk in the room, Vivian looks right at my chest and knits her eyebrows. I turn beet red from head to toe.

"I really really really feel uncomfortable in this."

"You don't look half bad," she says.

"Which means I don't look half good either. I couldn't find the support."

"You just need to poosh them up some," she says.

"Poosh?" I ask. "Did you just say 'poosh'?"

"Poosh 'em up some," she explains, cupping her own tits up high as an example.

"My boobies don't poosh."

"Boobies?" she laughs. "Did you just say boobies? Four-year-olds have boobies. Grown women have tits."

"Some grown women do," I retort. "Some don't."

"Oh, for chrissakes, you have tits. You've just been binding them down for too long." Then she actually sticks her hand down the front of my shirt, cups my boobie in her hand and pooshes it up. "See?" she says, already pooshing up the other one too. "*Voila*! Tits!"

I look at myself in the mirror. She's right. I have cleavage. The shirt is squeezing them high and hard and I actually kind of have tits.

Here comes her hand again. "Now if you can just make your nipples hard—"

"Stop it!" I yell, slapping her hand away. "Don't do that unless you mean it."

She laughs and flops down on the bed. "You amuse me," she says, "you truly amuse me."

"Well, I'm happy you find me so amusing," I say. "What're we getting ready to go do?"

"Go eat," she says and rolls off the bed with a peppy bounce. She walks to the window and peeks her nose through the curtain, looks around, closes it and heads to the door. She flings it open and steps outside, blinking in the hot sun.

She stops and scans the parking lot. "Which El Camino is yours?"

"IHOP is my favorite sit-down restaurant in the whole entire world. Endless coffee, six different types of syrup, you can even get pancakes shaped like Mickey Mouse's head if you want," I ramble while Vivian fixes her lipstick in my rearview mirror.

I score a parking spot near the front of the restaurant and get out of the car. I'm at the front door before I realize Vivian is still in the car. Now she's using the rearview mirror to put on mascara. I cross my arms. I tap my foot. I count to twenty and back again. If I had a watch I'd look at it. I finally get tired of waiting and go on in.

Inside smells like pancakes and bacon and syrup and coffee and old women's perfume. I love it. I could just wallow in the smell and rub it all over me. If somebody would bottle this smell, I'd buy a whole case of it. *Eau de IHOP.* It reminds me of my grandma, my mom's mom. I only met her a few times and she died when I was six, but I remember her smell. She told me once that when she was a girl she couldn't afford perfume, so she would dab vanilla extract behind each of her ears. She said it drove the boys nuts and virtually guaranteed that she'd get her ears cleaned every date.

A cute little brunette waitress with cat eye glasses and naturally pouty lips looks from my tats to my tits and up to my face. "Just one?" she asks.

"No, two. She'll be here in a minute."

The waitress grabs two menus from the podium and says,

"This way." She guides me to an empty booth halfway back. I scoot in and pick up the menu. "Pot of coffee, please," I order.

"Just be a minute," the waitress says, her eyes lingering on my tats.

She flips her hair and walks off toward the kitchen. I'm checking out her swing when Vivian opens the door and walks in. I wave at her and she starts toward our booth with a swing that puts the waitress's to shame.

Damn. I haven't seen her for all of five minutes and I get that little shock of how sexy she is all over again. As she passes by each table, all the men turn their heads and follow her with their eyes. She doesn't seem to notice the stir she's causing. She's probably used to it.

Vivian hovers over me and orders, "Switch me sides."

"Why?"

"I don't like having my back to the door," she answers.

"Okay, whatever..." I slide into the opposite side and Vivian scoots into my warm spot.

"You know what you want?" I ask, pushing a menu across the table to her.

She flicks the menu away with a swish of her hand. "Pie. Lemon pie."

The cute waitress delivers our coffee and I order pie for Vivian and a country breakfast and Mickey Mouse pancake for myself. This time when the waitress walks off I look at Vivian instead. She takes the sunglasses off the top of her head and puts them on while I pour our coffee. I watch her dump about ten packets of sugar in hers before taking a sip. She peers around the restaurant through the brown lenses. I can't see her eyes and I hate that. It's so hard to tell what someone's thinking when you can't see their eyes.

I drum my fingers on the table and when it becomes all too apparent that Vivian isn't going to say anything, I try to make conversation. My social skills leave something to be desired and I hate small talk, so I try to lead off with something a bit more meaty. "So...you're a mistress for a living. And you came back here for a funeral?" I ask.

Vivian doesn't answer or even give any indication that she heard me.

"How long are you staying? In Tulsa? In the U.S.?"

That question goes unanswered, too.

"What did you do right after high school? I mean, you didn't go straight into...your current occupation, did you? Did you go to college?"

No response.

"I didn't go to college. But I did get the reading list for all the classes from OU. Read all the books twice. I guess you could say I have a virtual master's degree by now."

At this point, I still don't know if she hears me or not, so I throw a weird question in just to see if she's listening: "How old were you when you lost your virginity?"

"Eighteen," she says, still not looking at me. "I have a Master's in English Lit from OU, which qualifies me to do absolutely nothing, and I'm going to be in the States until I leave." She pulls her glasses down to the tip of her nose with her index finger and looks at me over the rims. "How long have you been out of prison?"

I gulp hard, burning my tongue on the hot coffee. I grab for my water and gulp that too hard, also.

Vivian pulls a business card out of the depths of her cleavage and places it on the table between us. I only have to glance at it to know what it is.

"Your parole officer's card was in the visor."

I pick up the card and without looking at it, put it in my back pocket. Now it's my turn to not look at her.

"You don't have to tell me about it," she says, pushing her glasses back up. "I don't really care. I just think it's weird that you lied to me is all. And, perhaps, symptomatic of something deeper if you're going to lie about little shit like that."

"Sorry," I say. "People just tend to freak a little when they find out I was in prison. Lying about it's become a habit."

The waitress brings our food and places all my plates around me and Vivian's little pie plate in front of her.

"Nice tats," the waitress says to me. She reaches out and runs one light finger over my tribal flame. "Who did 'em?"

"Prison," Vivian cuts in. "She got them in prison."

The waitress takes a step back, forces a gritted teeth smile at Vivian, then turns and walks like she can't get away fast enough.

"A year and a half or so. I've been out a year and a half," I admit.

Vivian leans forward and rests her tits on the top of the table, and I try not to stare directly at them. Now I wish I'm the one who had on sunglasses.

"Listen, Lee, if we're going to do this thing, then we can't be lying to each other. Understood?"

"Thing?" I take a quick sip of water. "What *thing*? I mean, I'm not saying there won't be a thing, but do we have to call it a thing right now? I just met you."

Vivian shakes her head a tiny bit and crinkles her nose in thought. "Let's just call it an adventure. You wanna go on an adventure with me, don't you?" She takes away her tits, adding, "I mean, unless you have something better to do."

Adventure. I guess that's a good way to look at it. I glance at Sonny and Cher and hear myself say, "Sure."

"Okay then, it's settled. Let's don't lie to each other anymore." She takes a bird-size bite of her pie and says, "Seventeen."

"Seventeen what?" I say with my mouth full of pancake.

"I was really seventeen when I lost my virginity. I just wanted you to know what it felt like to be lied to," she says.

"You're right. That really stings," I say with maximum sarcasm.

We're quiet for a long time. I shovel as much food as I can in my mouth, hoping to soak up all the excess alcohol left in my system. Vivian, still looking around at everyone else, just plays with her pie.

"Aren't you going to eat?" I finally ask.

Vivian doesn't respond.

I stab part of my pancake with my fork and hold it across the table to her, asking, "Wanna eat Mickey's ear?"

"I'm a vegetarian," she replies dryly.

"Vegetarianism implies a healthy lifestyle. Lemon meringue pie does not."

"If you want a bite of my pie just ask," Vivian says flatly.

"Can I have a bite of your pie?"

She pushes the plate toward me.

I stab a big forkful of pie and I guess I underestimate the size of the bite I'm about to take and half of it falls off my fork and ends up in my new cleavage. Vivian quickly leans across the table and scoops up the meringue with her finger and pops it in her mouth.

Wow. What the hell was that? I look around and see that every man in the whole restaurant is staring at us open-mouthed.

"Men are staring," I whisper.

"Uh-huh," she agrees.

"Well, I don't like it when men stare at me," I explain.

"They're not staring at *you*. They're staring at your tits," she explains back.

"My tits *are* me."

"Don't be so naive," Vivian says. "Your tits aren't you. They're just garnish."

She reaches deep into her big red bag and pulls out an aspirin bottle. She opens it and scatters a few different colored pills across the tabletop. She picks out a blue pill, swallows it and puts the rest back in the bottle. I don't ask.

I eat half the pie in silence while Vivian tears her paper napkin into tiny little confetti pieces and nervously looks around. Something's going on with her, but I haven't known her long enough to know what exactly.

"You mad at me?" I ask. "I said I was sorry."

"Don't be such a girl," she says.

"I am a girl, though, you know."

"You don't have to act like it. Talk about something else. Anything, just talk."

Okaaay. She's so nervous and fidgety that I hope whatever pill she just took kicks in quick. If she wants me to talk, so be it. Rambling is what I do best anyway. So, ramble I do. "I like IHOP. I'd have to say it's my favorite. No matter where you are, there's an IHOP and the food is always good. I like that kind of knowing. You walk into an IHOP you know exactly what you're getting."

I pause for a bite.

"Uh-huh," she mumbles, not looking at me.

I swallow and ramble on, "I love to ride my bike to out-of-the-way places. Just head out on a county road with no destination in mind and just see where I end up. You know? You find some of the best eating places that way. I love those small town greasy little diners that're tucked back out in the middle of nowhere, don't you?"

"Uh-huh."

"I like to ride and just end up in some little town in some little diner where all the locals gather. I like to eat with the cowboys, farmers and those big-haired, big-boned women. I like to hear them talk and smoke and spit. I like to see their bellies dance when they laugh. I like to guess what they do for fun, and I like to overhear what makes their lives worth living. I like it that the old men always call me ma'am and never mistake me for a man even though I'm wearing hats and tats and boots. They know a woman when they see one. I just love the people I come from. Don't you?"

"Sure," Vivian says.

I shake my head and take another bite of pie. "I can't believe you were over there in England. Why'd you ever wanna go there? All those bad teeth. I can't understand what they're saying half the time between those bad teeth and that accent. You know what's weird? Listening to a black person speak with a British accent. It just sounds wrong. And when men speak with a British accent they sound like sissies. I mean, music aside...I love the Beatles and the Rolling Stones as much as the next person, but England's full of wimpy guys. Why, just one ordinary Oklahoma farm woman could single-handedly beat up ten of those English boys. And outdrink 'em, too. My grandma lived through the Great Depression and the Dust Bowl at the same time. She drank moonshine that she made in her barn and she slaughtered her own food. She could've won that Revolutionary War all by herself. For instance," I say, pointing my fork at a very proper looking man in a dark business suit, "that man there with the sissy accent. My grandma could eat him for breakfast and still be hungry."

Vivian follows the trajectory of my fork point over her right shoulder and sharply inhales. I don't even have her pie finished, but she slaps a twenty on the table and harshly whispers under her breath, "We're leaving. Now."

"But I'm not finished," I mumble with my mouth full.

"That's why you should always eat dessert first. Now put your fork down."

I do.

"Nonchalantly," she admonishes, putting a period at the end of each syllable.

I pick the fork up again and ease it back down to the table, resisting the silly urge to whistle.

"Follow me." She holds a menu over her face and cuts elaborate zigzags around the tables until she's out the front door.

As soon as we're out the door, Vivian snatches the keys out of my hand.

"Hey!"

"You drive like an old woman," she says, opening the door and sliding behind the wheel. "Get in!"

I manage to hop in the passenger seat a split second before she squeals in reverse. She slams the car into drive and burns rubber tearing out of the lot. I slam the door shut just as she turns onto the main road.

"What the hell, Viv?"

"Light me a cigarette," she orders. "I can't drive without a cigarette."

Vivian screeches my car into the Redman Motel and whiplashes up alongside room number seven. The door is partially ajar and the lights inside are on.

"Shit. They've been here," she whispers.

I take her cue and whisper back, "Who? The maid?"

She flicks her cigarette out the open window and says quickly, "The less you know, the better. You have a gun?"

"Noooooo," I answer. "You're scaring me, Vivian."

"You have a knife?"

"Sure," I say. I dig deep into my right front jeans pocket and pull out my pocketknife with the red maltese cross.

Vivian looks at it and rolls her eyes. "Not a pocketknife, goofball. A *real* knife."

"This is a *real* knife. A *real* live pocketknife."

Vivian sighs through her nose and slips off her stiletto heels. She hands me one shoe and grasps the other by its toe. She quietly gets out of the car and creeps up to the door barefoot, wielding her shoe like a deadly instrument. She flattens her back against the outside wall.

I roll down my window and whisper as loud as I can and still be whispering, "I think you've seen too many action movies."

She puts her finger to her lips and hushes me. Then in one swift motion, she turns, kicks the door wide open and assumes a fighting stance with her shoe held high. She looks around and then disappears inside.

I wait a few tense moments, tapping the toe of her shoe into my palm, then just as I'm starting to get really worried, Vivian sprints back out of the motel room with an armful of clothes. She throws them through my window, dumping them over my head and dashes back inside.

I mostly unbury myself just in time for her to throw more clothes through my window. She hauls ass back in the car, slams it into gear and is out of the lot before I can even get her panties off my head.

God, this woman drives like she talks. Ninety miles an hour and in five directions all at once. "You're on the wrong side of the street!" I scream, jerking the wheel to the right.

"Sorry," she says, "habit. Light me a cigarette, will ya?"

This woman is nuts. Truly nuts. I mean, I thought Ginger was nuts but this woman—I light a cigarette and stick it between her lips—takes the proverbial cake.

"Can I drive?" I ask hopefully.

She swerves around a slow-moving car in front of us. No signals, no looking, just pure swerving.

"Is this the adventure you mentioned before?" I ask.

"This is it," she says, clenching the lit cigarette between her teeth.

"I should've known."

"What'd you think I meant?"

"I dunno," I say. "I was just hoping..." I catch myself and change thought direction, "it wouldn't involve pointy shoes and car chases."

Vivian barely taps the brakes, jerks the wheel hard to the right and careens into a Kum and Go. She brakes just a couple of feet shy of the plate glass window.

"Go in there," she points at the convenience store's door with her chin, "and get some more smokes and a pop."

"What, you don't want me to take your shoe and rob the place while I'm in there?"

She tilts her chin down and looks at me over the top of her glasses like I'm not funny at all. She fishes a twenty out of her cleavage and hands it to me. "Get yourself something, too."

I twist around and look over both shoulders and out the back window.

"What the hell're you doing?"

"Looking for the camera," I explain. "You're with some reality show, right? Where you get people to do weird stuff and film it?"

Vivian grips the steering wheel with both hands and says very, very seriously, "This is real life, Lee. Real. And there's some real money in it for you, too. If you just go get my POP AND CIGARETTES!"

"Okay, okay." I give in, opening the door.

Inside the store I saunter over to the pop machine and fill a large cup with ice and Dr. Pepper.

Why do I always hook up with the bossy ones? Why do I always *let* them boss me around? That's the question. Maybe it's the shoes. I should stay away from women in spikey heels. Bossy women wear high heels. Or maybe it's because the heels cause so much pain it makes them bitchy. I don't really know. The only time I ever wore heels was at Junior Prom. They made me six foot two and my date was only five eight. He was an identical twin, I remember that. He sauntered up to me in the hall between classes and asked me to the prom. I said why not and he just walked away. He didn't even say his name. And to this day I don't know which twin I went to the prom with. And the fumbling almost-sex was nightmarish. I once saw a veterinarian stick his gloved fingers up a cat and it screeched bloody murder. The twin probably grew up to be a vet.

My teeth feel as if they're wearing sweaters, so I stop in the toiletry aisle and grab a toothbrush, toothpaste and mouthwash. I get the little traveling miniature ones 'cause I like things when they make them tiny. Plus, they fit in my jacket pockets.

This weird kid with a purple mohawk, like maybe sixteen years old, is checking me out. He tries to impress me with his jailin' jeans and he actually grabs his baggy crotch and licks his fuckin' lips at me. What the hell? I have tattoos older than him. Suddenly, I'm in a really foul mood and I hate this tit-showing shirt.

I throw the twenty on the counter and pay for all the shit. The mohawk kid walks up beside me and tips his head at me in a hello gesture.

"I can see your ass crack," I say to the little pockmarked pervert, grab my change and walk out the door.

And I am so not prepared for what isn't there.

"Shit!" Oh, shitshitshitshitshit, I yell repeatedly inside my head. She's gone. She's fuckin' jacked my El Camino and taken off. I throw the Big Gulp where my car used to be. That wasn't such a good idea. Splashback hits me right in the face.

The little mohawked pervert walks up behind me. "Need a ride?" He grins and gestures to his VW bug.

I grab the waistband of his baggy-ass jeans and pull up as hard and as high as I can. He drops his pop and grabs his crotch at the same time. I walk him on his tippy-toes to his VW and shove him headfirst through the open window.

Okay, I don't really do any of that. But I do *think* about doing it.

The kids just shrugs, gets in his car, turns the radio up full volume and leaves. I sit on the curb and fumble open the cigarettes I just bought. I shake one out of the pack and light it with shaking hands. My brain is spinning. Calling the cops is out. Calling Ginger for help is definitely out. This figures. I should've seen it coming. Women like her always do this to me. Lead me on, then jerk me off. What the hell am I thinking about? It's not her I'm missing. It's my car I'm missing. Isn't it? She's probably just getting back at me for the high school ice incident. This is her payback.

I brush my teeth and gargle. The only difference between me and that homeless guy walking by is that I still brush my teeth. Even if it is in a parking lot, sitting on a curb. I don't have a home and I don't have a car either. Last time I was homeless was because I actually ran away from home. My mom had left me and my stepfather and not long after that I left the bastard, too. I'd break into Chopper's shop to sleep at night.

Chopper was my mom's third husband. He was a biker, the real deal. He rode a chopped down Harley with big ape-hangers. He had a handlebar mustache and long hair that he wore in a braid. He had naked ladies tatted up both arms. He wasn't my dad, he was better. I hung out at his motorcycle repair shop when I was a kid, and even after my mom kicked him out, I would sneak over to his shop and he'd let me watch him work.

I haven't seen Chopper in years. I wonder if he still owns the shop and if I can sneak in there tonight to sleep.

Fuckin' Vivian and her fuckin' tits.

I crush out my third cigarette on the sole of my boot and suddenly, there's a squeal of brakes and the smell of burning rubber and this putrid little metallic green Pinto lunges to a stop just inches away from my toes. The Pinto's passenger door flings open and Vivian smiles at me from behind the wheel.

"Need a ride?" she asks.

The longer I sit here silent, watching her smoke and drive, drive and smoke, the madder I get. It's like everything in the past year has been leading up to this one point, to this one second in time when all it takes is just one more bitch to make me lose it.

Vivian is on another talking jag. "So I just walk around the lot looking for an unlocked car. One row over, *Voila*! I get this beauty! Unlocked with the keys still in it, can you fuckin' believe? Who in this day and age leaves their keys in the car? Sometimes I wish stupid hurt. Then maybe there wouldn't be so much of it, you know?"

"Where's my car?" I ask a full notch below calm.

"Oh, it's safe," she exhales.

I want to choke the casual right out of her and I don't care how much jail time I'd be looking at, it'd be well worth it. I unclench my teeth long enough to ask, "What do you call safe exactly?"

"Walmart parking lot. In the employee section. Nobody'll even know it's abandoned for days."

I explode. "Stop the car!"

"You didn't happen to get any baby powder, did you?"

"I SAID STOP THE CAR!"

She does. She stops so quick and looks at me so concerned... that I forgot what I was going to say. I grip the dashboard with both hands until my knuckles turn white.

"Do you have some anger issues we need to resolve?" she asks.

I jump out of the car. I need to breathe and Vivian is sucking up all the air inside that little Pinto. I take off stomping down the side of the highway. Vivian obviously never watches the animal channel. She's never seen what dangerous animals can do. Especially snakes. Especially snakes that've been poked once too often. Don't poke a snake, everybody knows that. Vivian has no idea what she's doing, she just keeps pokin' and pokin' and pokin'.

She guides the car slowly up next to the right-of-way alongside me.

"Get back in the car, Lee," she says.

I inhale some more air, and bend and look though the passenger window. "I need to know..." I say, "...I need to know a few things."

"Okay," she says. "But first I need to know...did you get any baby powder? My bangs have lost their fluff."

"No, I didn't. And here's your change back." I throw it into the front seat. "I need to know why you jacked my car, where and why you got this piece of crap, who you're running from and where you're running to."

"Well, I already told you where your car is. What're the other questions again?"

"I need to know if this is something illegal. You know, something I can't get mixed up in."

She drums her fingers on the steering wheel, then looks at herself in the rearview mirror and fluffs her bangs. "Depends on what your definition of illegal is."

"Don't poke me," I mutter. "Who the fuck is chasing us?"

She turns and looks directly at me. Is she pouting? Her lower lip is pooched out a little and twitching, and I'm thinking she's about to cry or some goofy shit like that. "A boyfriend, okay?" she answers with a hitch in her voice. "An ex-boyfriend. And, believe me, I don't want him to catch me." A couple of fat tears slide down her face.

Damn. I can't stand to see a grown woman cry.

I straighten up and hang my hands off my hips. A couple of cars zoom by and I watch them disappear over the horizon. We're surrounded by pastures. Pastures and cows, cows and pastures.

"Lee?" Vivian sniffles. "What've you got to lose? Where were you going anyway?" She leans through my window and tugs on my jacket. "I can't...I don't want to be alone anymore. And you're kinda alone. I just thought maybe we could be alone together."

God help me, I take a deep breath and climb back in the car.

"Good line, huh? I saw that in a movie once," Vivian says lightly, pulling back out onto the highway and pushing the little Pinto harder than it's meant to be pushed. "Fasten your seat belt, you're in for a bumpy ride," she adds.

CHAPTER FOUR

Crickets, bullfrogs, and the hum of locusts and june bugs make my ears vibrate. Anybody who ever said the country was quiet is just plain wrong.

All five feet eleven inches of me is stretched out across the hood of the tiny Pinto, the warmth from the engine seeping into my very bones. This is pure heaven. I feel as if I'm levitating and there's nothing more important at this moment than studying the blanket of dark sky and making dot to dot connections with the stars. If there's anything that feels better than this, I honestly don't know what it is.

I look over at Vivian lying on the hood next to me. If anything she looks better than she did in high school. Life can surely take some strange turns. She wouldn't have been caught dead with me fifteen years ago. Now we're more on equal footing. We're both stoned out of our gourds and neither one of us has anything except the clothes on our back (and in the trunk of the Pinto).

Vivian sucks hard on the joint before passing it back to me.

I take a toke and hold it in until I can't stand the burn any longer. "This is perhaps..." I completely forget what I was going to say, then I grab the thought again and run with it, "...the best high I've ever had. I mean, it is really, really, really..." Why do I keep forgetting what I want to say? "... good."

"Enjoy. 'Cause that's the last of it."

I crash back down to earth. "Well, you just pissed on a perfectly good high," I say.

Vivian takes another toke—"I smuggled it over here in my girlie hole."—and passes it back.

It takes every ounce of my self-control not to sniff it.

She exhales and continues, "The guy I got it from is young. Good-looking. Fantabulous sex. This one time—"

"Good for you," I interrupt, not wanting to hear about her sexcapades with men. I change the subject. "You know, I've never even seen this alleged spooklight. Every time I've ever come out here, I wait and wait, but it's a no-show."

"I've seen it," she says. "I've definitely seen it. It's just this little ball of light bouncing down the road. Like those old sing-along cartoons, follow the bouncing ball. This one time I was parked out here with the cute guy who worked at Reasor's, you know the one with the sideburns, and this little ball of light bounces down the road, right into the car and right out again. Scared the bejeezus outta the guy." She takes another slow drag and holds it in. "Saved my virginity." She exhales slowly. "If it weren't for that spooklight I'd probably be married to Lloyd with sixteen kids and raising them on a bag boy's salary."

"Nah," I say, taking the joint from her. "He's probably been promoted to checker by now."

"Nice scar," she says, running her finger lightly over the thin white scar on my forearm. "That hadda hurt."

"I don't remember," I reply a little too quickly, pulling back.

"On cop shows they'd call that a defensive wound, right there on the arm like that."

"I don't remember," I say again, "I was just a kid when it happened."

"Oh," she says and adds pointedly, "I thought maybe it happened in prison."

I look at her. "Nothing happened in prison. It was like the same day over and over again, every day."

Vivian pulls a lipstick out of her cleavage and adds another coat.

"How much stuff you got tucked away in your cleavage? You're always pulling different shit out all the time. It's like a magician's hat or something."

"What were you in for?" she asks, putting the lipstick back down her top.

"Guess."

"Shoplifting makeup from Walmart."

"No," I answer quickly, "and quit laughing, it's not that funny."

Vivian taps her fingernails against her chin. "Let's see..."

But before she can guess, I offer up, "I wore white after Labor Day."

"Ooooh." She smiles. "I hope they didn't go too easy on you."

I grumble, "Twelve years."

"You deserved it." Vivian sighs contentedly, putting her hands behind her head. "I just adore women in prison movies."

"Can we change the subject?" I ask.

"Sure." Silence for a while. "You want I should give your parole officer a blow job so he'll go easy on you?"

"It's a woman. And my parole ended last month."

"I don't like blow jobs anyway," she says. "It just bothers me that they're called blow jobs and you don't really blow."

"Yeah, blow jobs suck," I say, happy to just be onto a different subject.

"You ever have sex with anyone from high school?"

I ponder. I have a cheerleaders-are-a-bitch story, but no way in hell I'm telling that one to Vivian. "Do hand jobs count?" I ask.

"They do when you're fifteen," she pronounces.

"Then I slept with three guys from school," I say. "When I was a sophomore, Clint Green and I used to park in the school's parking lot and feel each other up."

"Really?"

"Kinda freaked me out. His dick felt like a chicken neck."

Vivian laughs. "They all feel like chicken necks."

"And I let one of the Hampton twins feel me up on the dance floor at Junior Prom."

"Which one?" she asks.

"I don't know," I answer truthfully. "It wasn't a very good experience. He kept shoving his finger up my butt."

"On purpose?" she asks.

"I don't think so."

"Who was the third?"

"You probably don't remember him. We had first period speech together. I just walked up to him and whispered in his ear, 'What're you doing tonight?' He said, 'Nothing.' So I said, 'You are now. You're doing me.' I showed up at his house that night and he took me to the garage and we did it in the backseat of his daddy's Town car. It was awful. He just like pounded me for ten minutes, my head banging against the door. When it was over he spewed some kind of grape liquor all over me. I had a headache and smelled like grapes for two days."

"What was his name?" Vivian asks.

"I don't remember his name. He played football, I remember that. He was tall, kinda cute, blond."

She sits up and looks at me. "Joey?"

"That's it," I say, "that was his name. Joey."

She sits straight up and stares me down. "You fucked Joey *Hanes*?" she demands.

"Yeah..." I say apprehensively.

"Goddammit!" she yells. "I wanted him so bad and he wouldn't give me the time of day! Goddammit! I was throwing myself at him and all the time he was fucking *you*?"

"Well, you don't have to be mad about it," I say. "And it wasn't all the time."

"I can't believe this shit," she bitches. "I was the cheerleader not you."

"Look at it this way. I saved you from getting thrown up on."

There's a weird vibrating sound. BZZZZZ. I hear it again. BZZZZZZ. It's Vivian's tits. She sticks her hand down her shirt and pulls out her phone. She looks at the caller ID then sticks the phone back from wherever she got it.

"Boyfriend?" I ask.

She sighs with an exaggerated roll of her eyes.

I shake my head. I can't believe I'm jealous of a phone call. A phone call she didn't even answer. Plus, she's lying here with me, not him. Maybe I should make my move now. Maybe I should just grab her and pull her to me and lay one on her right now.

Vivian derails my thought train by sitting up Indian-style and asking, "Ever been to France?"

"No," I giggle, "but I've been to Funkytown."

"Really? What's it like?"

"Not as fun as Margaritaville."

She laughs, accepts the joint from me, licks two fingers and snuffs it out. It disappears back down into her magic hat. No telling what else is down there. Maybe if I wait long enough a rabbit will pop out. I giggle again.

"Frenchmen are really weird, but for some reason they just love me," she says. "They think I'm smokin' hot."

"Well, you may be smokin' hot, but I'm smokin' pot. So there. I win." I laugh at my own joke, but Vivian just looks at me like I've lost it.

She continues, "I met this one Frenchman, Oliver, who was a narcoleptic and fell asleep right in the middle of it."

That mental image makes me laugh even harder.

"I gave him my phone number. Then he starts calling me. I can't speak French. He can't speak English. All he says is 'Hallo, Vivvi, Hallo.' And I just say, 'Bon jour and fromage.' "

Fromage. That's funny. Fromage is like the funniest thing I've ever heard in my whole entire life.

"Sometimes when he calls I teach him to sing stuff like 'Beans beans, the musical fruit' and 'A horse is a horse, of course, of course.'"

I'm laughing so hard by now I think I'm going to pee

my pants. I'm floating outside of my body, hanging up there somewhere in space and looking down on us. I can't believe that's me down there, doubled-up and laughing. Laughing my ass off on the hood of a Pinto parked out at the spooklight with Vivian the Cheerleader from high school.

"I think I just peed my pants," I wheeze. "I can't believe I just peed my pants in front of a cheerleader."

"I'll buy you some more tomorrow," she says, lying back against the windshield. "I've got tons of money."

"Where is all this money?" I ask. "Down your shirt?"

"Not yet," she says, leaning up on one arm and grinning at me slyly. "You know where I can get a shovel?"

"I can't believe I'm doing this. I can't believe I'm doing this. I can't believe I'm doing this," I chant out loud to myself.

I'm going to blame it all on getting high. Because I like to think I wouldn't be doing any of this in my right mind. Also, Sonny and Cher have more to do with it than I like to admit. Between her joint and her tits, I've lost all common sense.

Not only did I steal a shovel out of some poor sap's open garage, but I let Vivian drive me back to the cemetery and now I'm digging up her poor friend's grave. And it's raining. It's fuckin' raining again. No wait, X that out, now it's hailing. I guess the only good thing that's happened in the past two hours is that they left the tent up. I'm still soaking wet but at least I'm not being pounded by hail.

I've been digging for two hours.

"That's one hour for each tit," I say out loud.

And I'm down in a mucky hole over my head. Vivian smoked cigarettes and watched me dig, but took off about twenty minutes ago, leaving me with strict orders to keep digging.

I make a mental laundry list of all the illegal crap I've done in the past twenty-four hours: stole a car. Smoked some dope. Broke into a garage. Stole a shovel. Destroyed public property with a stolen shovel. Grave robbing.

I hit wood. Finally. I scrape a few inches of dirt off the casket with my boot and scramble back out of the hole. I set the shovel on the dirt pile and sit wearily on the edge of the grave.

"I found it!" Vivian hollers from out there in the dark somewhere.

"Found what?" I yell back.

"My shoe! My Choo shoe! My Choo shoe you threw!"

"What is this, a Dr. Seuss book," I grumble. "When I'm in jail it'll all be so worth it."

I wipe the sweat and rain out of my face and see her walking my way, dodging hail bullets. God, nothing can faze this woman.

"Done?" she asks sweetly.

"I could've used some help, you know."

"Well, if you had stolen *two* shovels maybe I could. But nooo, you're not thinking ahead. You just steal one," she scolds.

"Why do I have the eerie feeling you just made me dig my own grave?"

"You're kidding, right?" Vivian leans over the hole and peers down deep. "Actually, that's pretty good. You did a good job, Lee."

"Thanks, Viv, I really appreciate that."

"Think you can open the lid now?"

"Me? I'm not messing with a dead person. I did the digging, you do the opening."

"Oh, fer chrissakes, why do I have to do everything around here?" she actually has the nerve to say. "Dead person, my ass, I'll just pretend it's an Englishman and walk on his back."

She hops down into the grave and when she lands on top of the coffin she does a little extra bounce on her toes. I half-expect her to clap and yell, "We've got spirit, yes, we do, we've got spirit, how 'bout you?" But instead, she crawls off the coffin and into the space next to it. She bends, grabs the lid of the coffin and grunts and groans until her face turns red, but she still can't get it up.

"Use your legs, not your back," I encourage.

She takes a deep breath, grits her teeth and tries again. The lid groans and makes a weird sucking noise. I stick the lip of the shovel in under the edge of the lid and two groans and a couple of sucks later, *voila!* as Vivian would say. The lid is up and

I'm looking down at the whitest, deadest person I've ever seen. "Gross, man, that's just horrible to look at."

Vivian shakes her head sadly. "You're sooo right. That make-up is just awful. Poor thing. They'll never let her into heaven looking like that." She licks her thumb and corrects the dead woman's makeup, smearing the red stuff on her cheeks around in little circles.

"Viv, I don't think we have time for a makeover right now. I'm breaking about ten different laws up here."

She takes one final swipe at the dead woman's cheeks. "Do you recognize her now?" she asks.

"Nope," I answer.

"It's Tanya, silly."

"Tanya who?"

"Tanya Spencer? The basketball queen our senior year? She was a good friend of mine. She got really fat, but you know she just lost over a hundred pounds? Then she died. Figures, right? That's why I don't quit smoking. If I did, I'd probably just get hit by a bus the next day. She had her stomach stapled so she wouldn't eat so much, then she had an Alka-Seltzer and her stomach inflated, the staples flew off and she imploded. It killed her instantly. Sad story, really."

"Mmhmmm, okay. Now can you tell me why I dug up the former fat basketball queen?"

"Okay, check this out," she says, pulling up on the dead body's ankles, trying to raise its legs. The legs refuse to bend. "Rigor mortis, damn..." Vivian says.

Vivian puts her shoulder into the job and tries again.

Nothing.

"I need some help here," she says, looking up at me.

I shake my head. "We went over this already. No fuckin' way I'm messin' with a dead body."

Vivian glares at me a moment, then tries again. This time she braces one leg against the dirt wall, grabs the ankles and pulls with her whole body.

Snap!

Oh my God, I don't want to even think about where that snap came from.

Unfazed, Vivian lifts Tanya's legs and pulls two big leather bags out from under the body and her miles of taffeta. She heaves the bags up to me. I catch them and set them on the dirt pile.

"Open 'em up," Vivian dares.

I kneel and unsnap a bag. I open it and cannot believe what the hell I'm seeing: stacks of money, more money than I've ever seen or even ever dreamed of seeing in my lifetime.

"Good hiding place, huh? Nobody would ever think to look here."

"How much is here?" I ask, awestruck.

Vivian shrugs. "Half a mil give or take."

"How the hell did you get it in her casket?"

"They had a private viewing of the body yesterday," she answers like it's the most logical thing in the world.

"That's a little on the sick side, Vivian."

"It worked didn't it? And it's not like she minded," she reasons.

There is a certain logic there, I have to admit.

I open the other bag and, yep, it's full of bills, too. I grab a handful, stick them under my nose, close my eyes and take a deep whiff. Newly minted, crisp hundred dollar bills. "They should make car air fresheners that smell like this," I say, looking down at Vivian.

But Vivian isn't looking at me. She's looking at something behind me. Her eyes are open wide and her mouth is in the shape of a big O. I whip my neck around and—

"Freeze!" A flashlight beam hits me full in the face.

Shit fire. It's a Rent-A-Cop. The fat kid in school who plays with action figures and grew up but still lives with his parents type of Rent-A-Cop. The bad thing about Rent-A-Cops is they're wannabe policemen and they have a tendency to try too hard. The good thing about Rent-A-Cops is they couldn't pass the I.Q. test to be real cops. At least that's what I'm counting on when I whisper, "Help...Please, God, help me."

"What's goin' on?" he asks and takes a couple of tentative steps closer to me.

I chance a glance behind me and see that Vivian is crouched down, hiding, in the open grave. "You gotta help me," I whisper plead to R.A.C. I throw in a couple of fake sobs to make my act seem more realistic. “They killed my friend. They’re making me bury her. They’re going to kill me next.”

R.A.C. plays his light beam over the freshly dug grave. I edge a bit closer to the shovel, saying, “They’re making me dig my own grave.”

“Where they at?” R.A.C. whispers back.

Hook, line and sinker, this guy. Dumb as a rock.

I point into the darkness behind him. He spins on his heels and in one swift movement, I grab the shovel and land a solid whack against the back of his head.

The sound the shovel makes connecting with his skull makes my stomach lurch.

R.A.C. drops to his knees and stays that way for so long I think he’s going to get back up. But he doesn’t. He finally falls face forward into the mud.

I drop the shovel, look down into the grave and straight at Vivian. “I killed Rent-A-Cop in the graveyard with a shovel,” I say. “And I know I just said that like it’s the end of the game of Clue, but I wasn’t trying to be funny and I think I’m actually going to throw up.”

“Just breathe,” Vivian says, “and help me outta here.”

Vivian holds out her hand and I pull her out of the grave. She stands still beside me looking at the motionless body. “Is he breathing?” she asks.

“I dunno, I’m too afraid to look.”

Vivian runs over to him, squats down in the mud beside him and puts her fingers on the inside of his neck. “He’s alive,” she says. “You just gave him a helluva headache for when he wakes up.”

“Are you sure?” I ask.

She nods. “You going to be okay?”

I nod. “I really wanna leave, though.”

“Okay,” Vivian says, taking control of the situation. “Get the bags and go to the car. I’ll take care of stuff here.”

I do what she says because my brain has declared mutiny and refuses to work on its own. I toss the money bags in the back of the Pinto and sit in the passenger seat and practice taking deep breaths so I won't hyperventilate. I roll down the window and light a cigarette and try not to think about how easy that was for me. I could've killed that man just like that. Just that easy. Oh my God, I'm still thinking about it. I need to stop.

I think I just reached the point of no return. I'm in this as deep as Vivian now. Deeper maybe.

Two cigarettes later, Vivian gets in behind the wheel and starts up the car.

"What were you doing out there?" I ask.

"Wiping the fingerprints off the shovel and the casket."

"Where is he?"

"He's down in the hole giving Tanya a thrill," she says.

"You buried him?!" I scream. I don't know where the fuck that scream just came from, but it hangs in the air until Vivian screams back at me, "I didn't bury him! He's alive! I'm not going to bury a live person!"

"Oh. Good." I go back to concentrating on breathing again.

Vivian pulls her big-ass red bag into her lap, digs out the aspirin bottle, pries the lid off with her teeth and shakes some pills into her palm. She hands me two little blue pills. "Take these."

"What are they?"

"Feel good pills, just take them."

I don't even argue. I just throw them in my mouth, dry swallow, lay my head back on the seat and close my eyes.

I feel Vivian throw the car into D and take off.

Am I asleep or awake? My eyes are closed so I must be asleep. But this dream seems really real.

I open my eyes. Vivian is driving with one hand and smoking with the other. I turn and peer into the backseat. Two bags are sitting there as easy as you please. That part wasn't a dream.

Half a million dollars. Holy shit. If she gives me half of that then I'll have half of a half of a million dollars. My brain can't calculate right now, but I still know that's a lot of money.

What the hell will I do with that much money? I pull my journal and pen out of my jacket and make a list. At the top of the list I write Harley Heritage Softail.

Vivian is talking. Has she been talking this whole time? What are those pills she gave me? She's right about them, though, I feel really, really good.

Vivian's constant stream of words weave around thoughts of my future Harley: "One Thursday I went over to Prince Charles's mansion and I'm early and I find him wearing my favorite Victoria Secret lingerie and my lipstick and my heels. I hate it when men wear my clothes, don't you?"

Black or two-tone purple and cream? Black. You just can't go wrong with black.

"So I drop a couple of viagara in Prince Charles's scotch and handcuff him to the bed and after four hours his willie hurts and he's crying my mascara down his face. So I take pictures of him with his cell phone and send them to his entire address book."

Whitewall tires. I love that retro look.

"And I leave him there in my panties with a blue willie that won't wilt and I break into his safe because he's stupid enough to have his birthday as the combination, but even that took me a while to figure out because you know how we write the month, the day, then the year? They write the day first, then the month, then the year."

Maybe I can find a Softail with some ghost flames. Or even some orange flames shooting up from the front fender and along the tank.

"But once I cracked it, I took everything in the safe, and his wife had this stupid toy poodle that was always shitting on the carpet, so I took some of that poodle poo and locked it back up in the safe. I hopped a plane and here I am half a million richer for it."

Vivian pauses, so I jump in, "Is that the boyfriend who's chasing you? Prince Charles that you stole the money from?"

"Honey, I earned that money. Every cent of it." Vivian dismisses me with a wave of her hand. "And now you and I are a couple of rich bitches driving off into the sunset."

"Sunrise."

"What are you going to buy?" she asks. "Whatever you want, darlin', it's all yours, compliments of Prince Charles."

I whisper reverently, "A Softail. My dream bike. A Harley Heritage Softail."

"It's yours," she says, "it's all yours. As long as you promise to take me wherever I wanna go. Do you know where I can find Choo shoes in Oklahoma?"

That one makes me laugh. I am so laughing now. Great big bubbles of laughter. She begins laughing, too, and the Pinto weaves around the road.

"Drive!" I yell. "Don't forget to drive." Then I add as an afterthought, "Thelma."

"Nu-uh," she says, bringing the car back to the American side. "You're Thelma. I'm Louise."

"No, I wanna be Louise. You can be Thelma."

"That wouldn't make sense, Lee. I have to be Susan Sarandon," Vivian explains. "I always drive, number one. You're taller, number two. And, number three, I have bigger tits."

"Touché," I say. "So, where we going, Louise?"

"Any fuckin' where we want," Louise says, with a cackle. "Any fuckin' where we want." She lights a cigarette off her last one and asks, "What d'ya keep writing down over there?"

"It's my journal," I explain. "I've written in it ever since I was a kid."

"Am I in it?"

"Maybe."

"Can I read it?" she asks.

"You'll have to wait for the movie to come out," I answer. "Right now this would be the montage scene. You're buying Choos inside a fancy shoe store. Cut. I'm riding a new Harley. Cut. More Choos. Cut. I'm trying on some bitchin' leather chaps. Cut. You're buying thigh high leather Choos. Cut..."

She jumps in, "I'm getting liposuction. Cut. Botox injections. Cut. Modeling my new, huge pert tits. Cut."

"New tits? Since when do you need new tits?"

"Oh, honey..." she sighs. "These have been through the wringer. I'm ready to trade them in for a newer model. I'm thinking something French this time."

"I emphatically disagree."

"Then you can keep your own little titties. But mine are going to be sufuckingperb."

I try to look at the bright side. "Can I least help you pick them out?"

"Sure," she agrees, then whoops gleefully, pounding the steering wheel, "Mama's getting a fucking overhaul!"

"You swear too much," I say. "Louise didn't cuss as much as you."

"Why, I hardly swear at all," she says.

"I bet you can't go an entire five seconds without cussing," I dare her.

"Five seconds? No problem."

And just to prove me wrong, she does. An entire five seconds. I count the seconds down on my fingers, one Mississippi, two Mississippi, three Mississippi...

"Okay," I say, "but you didn't even talk. It doesn't count if you don't talk. I dare you to talk and *not* swear at the same time."

"Okay," she says.

Silence. She looks perplexed. Confused. She opens her mouth. Then shuts it again. By now I'm grinning from ear to ear. She looks like she's going to speak...then doesn't.

Finally, she opens her mouth and says, "Shitfuckpissyouwin!"

Oh God, I laugh so hard, I double over and fall onto the floorboard. I hold my stomach and laugh so hard tears stream down my face.

Vivian taps on the brakes, looking at me seriously. "You want I should pull over? You're not going to fuckin' piss your pants again, are you?"

Just when I thought I couldn't laugh any harder...

CHAPTER FIVE

Knock, knock.

"Who's there?" I mumble.

Knock, knock.

"Go away," I say a full octave lower than my normal voice, squeezing my eyes shut even tighter.

Knock, knock.

I curl into a smaller ball and wish the knocking to go the hell away.

Knock, knock, knock. Louder now. What the hell is that? A woodpecker?

I open my left eye just the tiniest bit. What I see makes no sense at all. I have my head on some kind of animal. I'm curled up, sleeping, with a tiger?

I sit upright and wince because my left arm is asleep. I rub the pinpricks and start putting the pieces of the past few hours together. I'm inside a car. The green Pinto. I was sleeping in the front seat with my head in Vivian's lap. That's not a tiger. It's Vivian's skirt.

I shake my head to chase away the aftereffects of the feel-good pills and look around. We fell asleep. At Sonic. They were closed when we got here so we parked and waited and—

Knock, knock, knock, knock.

A muffled voice says, "Excuse me?"

There's a girl standing outside the car with her hands cupped around her eyes, peering through the windshield at me. She raps on the glass with her knuckles.

Knock, knock, knock.

I roll down my window halfway and unglue my tongue from the roof of my mouth. "Wha'?" I ask.

"You can't just sleep here. The manager told me to tell you this is a restaurant, not a motel. The manager's a dick. I don't care if you sleep here, but you need to order something so he doesn't call the cops," she says.

I look her up and down while all that sinks in. She's blond with eyes that are too green to be human. Wait. She has one green eye and one blue eye.

"You have different colored eyes."

"Contacts," she says. "You gonna order?"

I look over at Vivian. She's asleep and snoring, reclined in the driver's seat as far back as it'll go, all stretched out and peaceful just like she's in a king-size bed. There's a little trail of blue slobber running out of the corner of her mouth. She must've thrown back some blue pills, too.

I look back to the cute carhop. "We'll have one of everything."

"Excuse me?" she asks.

"One of everything on the menu. I'm hungry."

"Ooookaaaayyyy," she says.

I roll the window back up and watch her skate away. Damn. Nice asses keep getting younger and younger.

I move Vivian's knee out of the way, turn the key in the ignition and snap on the radio. It only gets AM stations. I scan through several until I find the one I want. A man's voice rattles through the tinny speakers: "High of seventy-two with ten to fifteen mile an hour winds and a twenty percent chance of rain for your Thursday weather report. In local news, Tulsa police are looking into a grave robbery incident at Burr Oak Cemetery. The cemetery's security guard, Thomas Winant, interrupted the robbery and was assaulted with a shovel and thrown into the open grave. Mr. Winant is recovering from his head injury at St. Francis hospital and has described his assailant as a white male, six feet four inches in height and weighing two hundred pounds. Anybody with any information is urged to contact the Tulsa police department."

I turn the radio off. It's the first time I've ever been glad to be mistaken for a man. I can't fuckin' believe he said I was two hundred pounds, though. That kinda hurts.

"I left my Choo shoe in the grave," Vivian says.

She's awake now and sitting up.

"You left your Choo shoe there?" I ask a little panicked.

"It's okay," she says. "Right now they're looking for a big man who wears heels. They're probably rounding up every drag queen in town."

"They wear inline skates now. Used to be quads back when," I say.

Vivian and I sit on the hood of the car, surrounded by everything on the menu. It's like fast-food heaven if there really is a heaven and they actually serve fast food there.

I slurp hard on the last of my chocolate malt, shake the cup to find more, and slurp harder. "You gonna eat that fried pie?" I ask.

"You're like a bottomless pit," Vivian says, handing over the pie. "I don't know how you can put all that food away and stay so thin."

"I haven't eaten since IHOP," I say around a mouthful of pie.

"Fucking genetics. My body stores fat like there's going to be another potato famine," Vivian says, dipping one of her french fries into the dregs of my malt and then licking it off.

Our carhop with the mismatched eyes spins to a stop in front of us and hands me another chocolate malt on a tray. "Here you go, ma'am."

Ma'am? I'm a ma'am? Shit, when'd that happen?

Vivian hands the carhop two one hundred dollar bills. "I'm buying everybody here a sundae. Sundaes on the house. Can you do that?"

"Sure, if that's what you want."

"That's what I want, sundaes all around. And you can keep the change," she says generously.

"You sure?" the carhop asks, her mismatched eyes widening.

"Sure," Vivian answers. "Get yourself a sundae, too."

"No, thanks," the carhop answers, patting her perfectly flat belly, "I'm trying to lose a few l.b.'s before the homecoming dance." She grins and adds, "Go Chargers and all that, you know?"

Vivian perks up. "Homecoming? When is it?"

"Tomorrow night. Thanks for the tip, ma'am," she says, skating off.

Vivian and I sit in silence for a while. But it's not the good kind of silence, it's the kind filled with thick tension, the kind filled with dread, my dread, because I know Vivian well enough now to know exactly what she's thinking.

Vivian and I turn our heads at exactly the same time and look at each other. She smiles. I don't.

"We're going to homecoming, aren't we?" I ask in a tiny scared voice.

"You got it, babe. We are coming home!" Vivian exclaims, hopping energetically off the hood. She darts around the side of the car and hurriedly gets inside. "You ready?"

I turn to look at her through the windshield. "Ready for what?" I ask.

"Oh my God! We have so much to do! So little time, so much to do!" She honks the horn and I slowly slide off the hood, already knowing this won't be any ordinary homecoming.

"Beauty is not natural," Vivian argues, pulling me down the sidewalk by the sleeve of my jacket. "And anybody who says beauty is natural is ugly."

"You're naturally beautiful."

"Oh, honey, this ain't natural. You don't think I was born this way? This is the direct effects of lots of makeup, hair straightening, freckle remover and spandex."

"I don't have freckles," I say feebly.

Vivian pulls me through the double glass doors of The Luna Bella Spa. "You have tattooes," she says.

"So?"

"How is that any different than me putting on makeup?"

"My tats don't smear when I cry," I say.

"Listen," she orders, putting her hands on her hips. "We have a trunk full of money. We can sure as shit treat ourselves to a Day of Beauty," she says like the words are capitalized.

"But this place is too expensive," I whisper.

"You get what you pay for," she says with a tiny wink.

The fourteen-year-old boy who lives inside me looks at her tits and says, "Okay, you win."

Vivian turns and struts up to the receptionist, leaving me hanging out by the door. I watch her ass walk away and remember a bumper sticker I saw once: Be like a dog. If you can't eat it or play with it, then piss on it and walk away. I look back through the glass door and wonder what would happen if I really did just piss on the floor and walk out?

I'd blow my chances with Vivian, that's what would happen.

I move over to the nearest corner, hoping to be somewhat inconspicuous by hiding behind a tall plastic palm tree. The interior of this place is Pepto-Bismol pink trimmed in silver with touches of shiny chrome. Women are everywhere, sitting, standing and reclining. And they're all talking at once. It's a cacophony of chirps and giggles and whispers. There are women with their hair in painful looking rollers sitting under hair dryers; women wearing shower caps with thin strands of hair sticking out of little holes; women fake-smiling in mirrors; women patting, poking and prodding other women's faces. My eyes start to water from the battling aromas of lotion, hairspray and chemicals. In fact, if smells were music, this place would sound like Rimsky-Korsakav "Flight of the Bumble Bee" meets Sid Vicious singing "My Way."

I'm right smack-dab in the middle of Frank Capra's *Miracle Woman.*

And I'm drowning in estrogen.

I stick my hands in my pockets and offer a fake toothy smile to a gossipy little circle of hens who are staring at me like...well, like I don't belong here.

Vivian talks animatedly to a receptionist, using lots of hand gestures. They both look at me for a second and I smile back, but the receptionist frowns and jots something down in a notebook. I hope I never see what she just wrote because it'd probably scare the shit out of me.

The receptionist jots down a few more notes while Vivian nods and points at me, takes a wad of bills out of her cleavage and talks some more. What the hell? I turn away from them so they can't see how red I'm turning and I really shouldn't have done that because now I'm face-to-face with myself in a big mirror and for a split second I have one of those out-of-body experiences where I'm looking at myself with somebody else's eyes. The woman in the mirror looking back at me really needs some professional help. She looks like she just got back from that reality show *Survivor.* Then I realize that the reflection is me and I look away before I see me staring at me. Vivian is right. I'm a mess. That's the second where I decide to let these women have their way with me and any kind of makeover would be for the better.

The receptionist crooks her finger at me to approach. I slide my boots over to her and lean on the desk. She smiles sweetly and talks to me like I'm a four-year-old. "Sonja will be taking care of you. She's good with your type."

"What type?" I ask, then immediately regret asking.

"You know," the receptionist, Paula, (her pink name tag reads Paula) says. "The *au naturale* type." She waves the back of her hand up and down my body in a Vanna White gesture. "Sonja will love you."

I hope Sonja is not some big German woman with muscles and meaty hands who will pummel me half to death.

I just nod.

"Follow me," Paula says. She leads the way and I lag a little behind. I glance over my shoulder at Vivian who shoos me with a wave of her hand like I'm some fly she's trying to urge out the screen door.

Paula leads me down a short hallway and opens a door and I walk inside. She winks at me, saying, "Your friend said you've never had a facial before and to give you the works."

"The works?"

She smiles mysteriously and says, "Don't worry. Sonja is very good. You'll like her."

She shuts the door, leaving me alone in the small pink room. I try to make myself at home. Which means I take off my jacket and throw it over the back of the chair before I sit down. It's one of those hydraulic up/down chairs that eerily resembles something in a dentist's office. Not a good omen.

I fold my hands in my lap and look around. There's a sink and mirror and a countertop with all kinds of painful looking surgical implements that send a shiver down my spine. There are a few Georgia O'Keeffe prints on the walls. Am I the only person in the world who knows she just painted pussies and gave them flower names? I always get a little embarrassed looking at them in a public place.

I sniff the air. The absence of smell makes me nervous.

I feel like I'm waiting for something excruciating to befall me. I'm all alone in this little windowless room. I hate small spaces. They make me feel crowded and too big for my own body. I lay my head back and try to relax but I only end up searching the ceiling for any possible escape hatches.

The door opens and in walks Sonja. I know it's Sonja because her name tag says so. Sonja is dressed, or rather, barely dressed, in clothing that leaves nothing to the imagination. She has explosive tits (Donny and Marie) that she must've spent an hour coaxing into a red T-shirt that's a good two sizes too small. She has on a black leather skirt that she must've bought over in the children's section because it certainly doesn't cover a grown woman's ass. Long, wild-ass blond hair and pouty lips. Paula the Receptionist was right. I like Sonja.

Sonja locks the door behind her. I guess she recognizes the panic in my face and thinks I may be a flight risk.

I try not to openly gawk at her as she walks up to the side of my chair.

"Hi." I smile.

She doesn't say a word. Maybe she doesn't speak English. I'm thinking about trying out my high school French, but when she takes my face in both her hands, I can't remember a damn thing. I can say how are you in seven different languages, but right now I can't even remember how to say it in English. I am mesmerized by her green eyes. Green with little flecks of gold. And those damn lips. The image of those full lips sears itself into my brain.

Then Sonja does the most amazing thing. She leans over me, her hard nipples brushing across my surprised face. I close my eyes and just wallow in this moment. She must be reaching for the chair's lever, because suddenly I'm being lowered and reclined at the same time. I wonder how much one of these things cost. I sure wouldn't mind having one of my own.

I guess I moan or do something encouraging (okay, I admit it, I may have accidentally put my hand on her ass) because she throws one leg over and sits on me cowgirl style. She just sits there a moment, looking at me. I guess it's my move. I slip both my hands under her skirt and raise it up around her hips. She's not wearing any panties and she's a natural blonde.

Sonja raises up on her knees, stares straight into my eyes and has my belt and pants down around my thighs in no time flat. She strips off her shirt, pops a nipple in my mouth and rubs herself all over me.

Holy shit. This must be the works Paula was talking about.

Sonja takes my right hand and sticks my index finger in her mouth. She takes her time licking and sucking and cleaning each and every finger. When she's done, she guides my hand to exactly where she wants it the most. I realize she was planning this before she walked in the door because Sonja the Cowgirl has been ready for a while.

She grabs my tits like they're a saddlehorn and rides me like a broncobuster in a rodeo. It doesn't take her long before she's ready to come. I know this to be true because she tells me so. The whole thing has blindsided me in such a rush that I'm half surprised to find myself coming right along with her.

I shatter into about a thousand little pieces and barely have time to put the pieces back together before Sonja gets out of the saddle, inches her skirt back down and wrangles Donny and Marie back into her shirt. She leaves as quickly as she came. Pun intended.

Did that really just happen? Are all spas like this? Is Vivian doing the same thing right now?

I take my time pulling my pants up over my wobbly knees and washing my hands. I look in the mirror and think the same thing I always think when I first see my reflection: *Help! I'm trapped in a body that doesn't look anything like me.* I reverse directions and try on a smile for size. A smile looks fake as all get-out. What's wrong with me? I just got laid and most people would be happy, but all I feel is guilty. I wipe the smile off, sniff my hands and promise not to look in a mirror again that day.

I open the door and reenter the bright world of reality. As luck would have it, the first person I run into is Vivian. I feel like apologizing to her and I want to tell her it's not really cheating on someone if you were actually thinking about them the whole time. I clench my teeth so that what I'm thinking stays inside my head where it belongs.

Vivian takes one look at me and staggers backward half a step. "You look great!" she exclaims. "Your skin...you're absolutely glowing."

"Thanks..." I say, reining in my thoughts with a forced smile.

"Where's your girl?" Vivian asks. "I want her to do to me exactly what she did to you."

"No, you don't." I grab Vivian by the elbow and lead her down the hallway as far away as quickly as I can.

I've given in to the swift current of Vivian's glamor treatment and I float lazily down the river in my innertube trailing my fingers along in the water.

I jerk my fingers out of the cup of goo, Vivian's laugh jerking me out of my reverie. Vivian and I sit side by side in front of twin Vietnamese manicurists. The only way you can tell these little women apart is that one talks constantly and the other never opens her mouth.

I have the one who talks constantly. And right now she's examining my hands and nails and chirping in her strange little accent, "Big hand. Strong hand. Big like man."

"Thanks," I respond.

"Nail, bad. You no take care. Nail too short. Why short nail?"

I shrug. I don't really care to get into all that with a perfect stranger.

"This is the life, huh?" Vivian says dreamily. "This is the fuckin' life."

"Personally, I enjoyed the facial more," I reply dryly.

My manicurist attacks my nails with a file and a vengeance and I jerk my hand away out of sheer terror. "No, no," she scolds, "Nail ugly. Give hand. Me make pretty."

I give her my left hand, saving my best hand in case she damages the other, praying she doesn't have a chainsaw under her table.

Vivian continues in a lazy voice, "You know if they make a movie of our lives, I want Drew Barrymore to play me."

"I want Queen Latifah to play me."

Vivian gives me a strange look. "Queen Latifah? She's black."

"Oh, I'm sorry. I didn't realize we were dealing with reality here. Then I choose Hillary Swank."

"Okay..." she relents. "I guess she'd look okay in dreads."

Vivian's tits buzz. She digs her cell phone out of its hiding place with her free hand, glances at the caller ID, and bites her lower lip.

"What's wrong?" I ask. "Is it him? The Prince Charles guy?"

A lightbulb pops on over Vivian's head. She looks at her Vietnamese girl and asks, "Wanna make a quick two hundred bucks?"

The manicurist's eyes open wide at the prospect. Both sisters talk excitedly back and forth in Vietnamese, then Viv's girl asks, "Do what?"

"Answer this phone and talk dirty to him."

"Talk dirty?" the girl asks. Her twin talks to her in Vietnamese and they both giggle with their hands over their mouths.

"Real dirty," Vivian says. "Nasty. Sexy. Dirty," she emphasizes.

The girl smiles big and grabs the phone, answering, "Hello, big sexy man. Me talk dirty. Sexy nasty dirty."

I hear a garbled male voice on the other end.

The little manicurist giggles and continues, "Me suck big dick. Ten dollar, titty only. Twenty dollar, me suck dick all night long. You likey suck? Me number one sucker. Hundred dollar, me suck dick, sister put thumb up ass. You likey big boy?"

Dial tone on the other end.

The manicurist frowns, shuts the phone and hands it back to Vivian. "No likey thumb up ass."

That sends Vivian and I both into loud guffaws. The manicurists look at each other and chirp again in their own language. Vivian's girl holds out her palm, saying, "Me two hundred. Sister one hundred."

Vivian pulls the wad of hundreds out of her tits, peels off three hundred dollar bills and hands them to her, exclaiming, "Worth it. That was so fucking worth it."

I'm still laughing when my little manicurist exclaims. "Done! Give other hand."

I look at my done hand and flex it a few times. It doesn't look any worse than it did before and it appears to be in working order, so I hand over the other.

"Think we can we go get my Harley after this?" I plead.

"Sure," Vivian promises. "But first..." Then she says the two scariest words I've ever heard in my entire life. "...bikini wax."

If Vivian can do it, so can I, I keep repeating over and over in my head.

It's not helping at all.

I have allowed Vivian to lead me to a private back room in the spa and now I'm lying on a cold table bare-ass naked from the waist down. I've kept on my shirt and my leather jacket and boots in case I decide to flee.

There's a pink curtain running down the middle of the room, separating me and Vivian. She's over there just chatting away like she gets a Brazilian wax all the time. Maybe she does for all I know. Personally, I like my woman parts just fine. I don't see any need to fuss with them. I fig leaf my privates with both hands and pray for this to be over real soon.

"You'll love the feeling, Lee," Vivian says from behind the curtain. "Smooth and silky."

"I don't want to look like a seven-year-old," I grouse.

The door opens and Julia Child walks in. Not the real Julia Child, of course, but a big, older lady who's the spitting image of Julia Child. She has huge hands with hairy knuckles and a faint mustache on her upper lip. Ironic. She waxes people's junk, why can't she do her own mustache?

Her name tag reads Marquis de Sade.

Okay, not really, but I wouldn't be one bit surprised if it did.

"What're you wanting today, honey?" Julia Child begins. "Heart? Heart's are all the rage right now. Triangle? Boring. Landing strip?"

That's why they call it a bush, I guess. Because just like a bush you can trim it into cute little shapes.

"How 'bout a teddy bear?" I ask.

"Give her the full monty!" Vivian yells from the other side of the curtain.

"Full monty it is," Julia says. "Now move your hands, darlin', let me get a look at you."

"I'd rather not," I say.

Julia grabs my hands and throws them away. I grimace while

she gets her face right down next to it. She looks for a long time.

"Gonna need more wax!" she yells over her shoulder.

"Hah!" Vivian barks.

"Is this going to hurt?" I whisper.

"No worse than a good spanking," she answers with a wink.

Julia grabs a bottle of talcum powder with one hand and with her other hand she grabs my right ankle and yanks my leg up in the air. She shakes baby powder all over me. Then she grabs my other ankle and throws that leg up above my head and shakes some more. When she's done, she slaps me hard on the ass and grins like she just floured me and next she's going to throw me in a skillet of hot grease.

She grabs a huge pot of hot wax and spreads it all over with what looks like an ice cream stick. It might be a tongue depressor, but I can't let my mind go there right now.

Julia lets the wax cool for a moment, then looks at it closely. She gets her nose right down next to it and blows on the wax. I'm about to make a blow job joke until Julia grabs a corner of the wax and rips the funny right out of my head.

Holy shit! I bolt upright into a sitting position. I don't know if I scream or just gasp, but the pain is fucking intense. Tears spring to my eyes. I look down at myself. My God! I look like a plucked chicken.

I look up at Julia. She's holding the dried strip of wax up like it's a scalp and she's a triumphant Indian war chief.

I collapse back onto the table and take a deep, ragged breath. "Thank God, that's over with," I gasp shakily when I can finally talk again.

"Not quite, darlin'," Julia says. "Turn over."

"Turn over?"

"That's what I said, honey, flip over. You've paid for the Hollywood, so you're getting the Hollywood."

"What's a Hollywood?" I ask with the appropriate amount of alarm.

"I'm going to clean your basement," Julia says.

"Oh no..." I protest not quite fast enough. Julia grabs my hips and flips me over like I'm a crepe in a pan. And before I can say nether regions, she has my cheeks spread and wax slapped on my nether regions. A few seconds and one mighty tug later, I've gone from hair to bare.

There's a delayed reaction. I'm thinking that didn't hurt at all but it takes two or three seconds for the pain in my ass to register in my brain. I bite my hand and pound my forehead on the table to keep from screaming. I cannot believe women put themselves through this. I'd rather be waterboarded.

Julia slaps my ass again and says, "Remember no sex for forty-eight hours."

"No sex? But tomorrow's homecoming!"

Julia wags her finger in my face. "Licky licky, yes. Sexy sexy, no."

"Oh. Well. I can live with that," I say, rolling over onto my back.

But before I can even sit up, the door bangs open and a man is filling the doorway. He's dressed in a three-piece expensive-looking suit and penny loafers.

"No men allowed in here!" Julia scolds.

I know who he is in one glance. It's Prince Charles, the guy from IHOP, the woman-beater, the man who no like thumb up ass. He looks at my face. He looks at my now bare crotch. He says in his sissy-girl accent, "Where is she?"

"Run, Vivian!" I yell, jumping off the table and grabbing for my boxers and pants at the same time.

He steps in the door and makes a lunge for me, but Julia blocks him with her big body, shouting again, "You are not allowed in here, sir!"

He throws her against the wall. I make a quick decision that there'll be plenty of time for pants-putting-on later. I grab the pot of hot wax and toss it at him.

The wax splashes across his crotch, but I don't stick around for the grand finale. I rip open the curtain to Vivian's side.

She's gone.

I jump over the table and bolt out the open door and down the hallway with Prince Charles's screams chasing me out. I hit the lobby just in time to see Vivian hauling bare ass out the door. Good. I'm not the only one. I try to cover myself with my pants, slamming against the glass doors, spilling onto the sidewalk and exposing my whitest parts to everybody on the street.

I run through the middle of all the double takes and pointing fingers and make it into the passenger seat of the Pinto just as Vivian starts the car. She guns the engine, jerks the wheel to the left, trying to unparallel park, but ends up taking the taillight of the car in front of us halfway down the block.

After a couple of heart-thudding turns I look over at Vivian. She looks back at me.

She grins. "Don't I always show you a good time?"

"I've had better times with my pants off," I mumble, trying to get my damn boxers on over my boots.

Vivian slams the Pinto to a screeching stop in the middle of the street, damn near causing a four-car collision and throws it in park. She leans over the seat, sticking her bare ass in my face while she fishes a skirt out of the jumble of clothes on the back floorboard.

I want to bite her on the ass so bad. I don't know if it's lust, adrenaline or anger or if there's even a big difference between the three. But before I can act on my impulse, she pops back up, wiggles into a skirt and takes off again just like she does this every day.

Vivian drives, going nowhere as far as I can figure, and I have my feet up on the dashboard and my hand down the front of my jeans. Vivian was right. It is smooth and silky. And calming. I'm just starting to relax a little when Vivian says politely, "Can you please get your hand out of your pants?"

"I don't want to. It's soothing."

She looks at me sternly. "I can't focus on driving while you're over there masturbating."

"I am not masturbating. I'm just...feeling it. I can't help it. Like how when you were a kid and you lost a tooth. You just keep poking the hole with your tongue."

"You start poking the hole with your tongue and I'll wreck for sure."

I'm the first to laugh. Vivian joins in and just to be nice, I take my hand out of my pants. For now.

"I am BIG. It's the pictures that got small."

Norma Desmond's giant face looms in front of me. I sit up, take my hand out of my pants and click off the TV.

I reorient myself. I was watching TV and fell asleep. Gloria Swanson in *Sunset Boulevard* woke me up. We're at the Crowne Plaza hotel in downtown Tulsa. Vivian checked us in to the Presidential Suite (two bedrooms, sigh...), passed out some hundred dollar bills, then shut herself in her room with the bags of money.

She left me in my room and the rest of the suite. The place is huge. Anne Frank's entire family could live in just my bathroom.

I wonder what time it is. How long was I asleep? I look at the window. It's dark inside and out. And way too quiet.

I get up and walk silently on the plush carpet to Vivian's room. I press my ear against the door. I don't hear anything.

"Vivian?"

Nothing.

I open the door to her room and peek in. Sure enough, she's passed out on her bed, lying catty-corner, arms flung out and legs spread. The only way I know she's breathing is because she's snoring.

I sit on the edge of her bed and watch her sleep. With her makeup off and her hair every which way, she looks even more beautiful. I don't think she knows it, though. She can't know it or she wouldn't work so hard to cover it up with all those artificial cosmetics.

She's left an opened bag of one hundred calorie cupcakes near her feet. I munch on one while I watch her. I smile to myself because I know she's going to wake up and be all mad, 'Who the hell ate my cupcakes? Where are all my cupcakes?!'

I eat them anyway. Then I see a lone blue pill laying near her hand. I pop it into my mouth, too. I figure the worst thing that will happen is that I go back to sleep.

I lie on my stomach and turn on the TV. I turn it down low so I won't wake up Vivian and flip through the channels. A million channels in this hotel and I can't find anything worth watching.

I turn it off and open the mini bar. I take out all the little bottles of booze and line them up on the bed. I'm a sucker for miniature things.

I start with the browns. When I've drunk all the brown stuff, I start in on the clear. It doesn't seem like you're actually drinking that much when it comes in tiny bottles. I count them. Eight. Eight little bottles.

I lie on the bed beside Vivian and watch her eyes flicker back and forth under her eyelids. I wonder if her dreams are as vivid as mine. Dreams. I haven't had a good dream in a long time. When I was a little kid I always dreamed about flying. Zooming down low over clotheslines and rooftops, peeking in windows, the feel of no gravity and being able to go anywhere and everywhere. That incredible rush of freedom and infinite power. Now all I have is nightmares. Nightmares filled with darkness, a crushing weight that pins me to the floor, loud voices and shattering explosions. For a long time now I've approached nighttime with dread and foreboding.

Getting to sleep in prison isn't a cakewalk either. The screaming, talking, coughing, fighting and frenetic grasps at hurried lovemaking are the sounds I lived with and slept through for twelve years. Now it's the silence I find hard to deal with.

I hope Vivian is having a nice dream. A good dream. A fluffy, marshmallow dream.

When I was about three or maybe four years old, Mom used to sneak into my bedroom extra early in the morning while I was sleeping and stuff marshmallows down the back of my panties. I'd find them in the morning and show them to her. Mom told me I was a special, magical child whose dreams were real. That when I dreamed of flying high in the clouds, it was really true. And that's why when I woke up I had bits of clouds down my panties. I called them my fluffy dreams.

I stuff a handful of little cupcakes down the back of Vivian's panties. Maybe she'll have fluffy dreams.

Between the tiny booze and the tiny blue pill, I'm starting to relax and that's a good thing. I was numb before I met Vivian and I didn't even know it. She makes me feel. Sometimes she makes me feel happy, sometimes she makes me feel sad, lots of times she even makes me feel mad. But, at least she makes me feel. I like that.

Vivian makes me laugh. I like that, too. I've laughed more in the past couple of days than in my whole life. She surrounds me with a big bubble of laughter and like that old John Travolta movie, *The Boy in the Plastic Bubble*, nothing bad can get in.

I wonder what life would be like if Vivian and I did get together? I think the future with Vivian would be fun. Even the little things would be fun. I'd go off to work every morning and when I got home, Vivian would be in the kitchen making supper. I'd walk in and give her a kiss and say something goofy like "Mmmm...that smells good." And she'd say, "What smells good? The dinner or me?" And I'd laugh while I scrubbed all the oil and grease off my hands at the kitchen sink. Then Vivian would hand me a pickle jar and ask me to open it for her. And I'd open it even though I know she could probably open it herself, but it's just her way of telling me she loves me.

I think I'm in love with Vivian. I mean, I must be if my fantasy revolves around pickle jars and I have the dream when I'm wide awake. I better not think about love. I should just throw that thought away right now. I'd be better off just thinking about laughing with her. Or even sex with her. Much safer. And healthier in the long run.

Vivian has pretty feet. And ankles. I bet she hates her feet, but I think they're pretty. They look way better out of those high heels she likes to wear so much. Those shoes are sexy, yeah, but her feet are even sexier unconfined and free. I bet she'd like to have her toenails done. I could paint them for her. She'd probably sleep through the whole thing. I bet she'd like her feet then.

I grab her red bag and dump out all the girlie shit. I pull out five bottles of nail polish from the mountain of junk. Which color should I use? I can't make up my mind. I don't know if I should go with something pale and unassuming or something bright and bold. I contemplate the choices for a long time before realizing that I don't have to make a choice. I can use them all. I'll just paint each toenail a different color. It'll be like looking at a bouquet of beautiful balloons.

I open the first bottle. I'm going to take my time and paint each one like I'm a famous artist and the toenail is my canvas.

When she wakes up, she'll be so surprised and happy.

CHAPTER SIX

Vivian stands on the far side of the room with her back to me, looking out the open window. The lights are off and the room undulates in moonlit shadows. A light breeze teases the curtains back and forth. I stand absolutely still, admiring her. She's fresh out of the shower, wet hair, and wearing only a thin, short silky robe. She looks so tranquil and peaceful. I make a small noise in my throat so she'll know I'm there, but she doesn't turn around. Instead, she unties the belt and lets the breeze open her robe and caress her naked body.

I softly walk up behind her and press my body close to hers. If she doesn't want this to happen now is the time for her to say something. But she doesn't. She leans back against me and tilts her head back onto my shoulder.

I reach around her and lightly trace my fingers from one hip to the other. She relaxes even more. My hand moves upward and I caress under each breast. She moans deep from the back of her throat. Encouraged, my other hand—

She turns and whacks me upside the head with her shoe.

"What the hell?!" I yell, jerking awake. Suddenly and painfully awake now, I shout, "Where'd that shoe come from?!"

I shake the remnants of the dream from my head. I'm lying on the floor and Vivian sits cross-legged on her bed, fully dressed and looking way too innocent.

"Why the sam hell did you hit me?" I demand.

"I don't know what you're talking about," she says in a really stupid, innocent voice.

I pick up the shoe lying next to me and point the evidence at her. "You do too. You clobbered me in the head with this damn shoe."

She snatches the shoe from my hand. "Did not," she replies.

"Listen," I say. "I was having a great dream. I'm going to finish it now if you can refrain from hitting me." I lie back down and close my eyes.

"That was for Joey."

I open my eyes. "What?"

"That was for fucking Joey Hanes behind my back. Now we're even," she says simply.

"No we're not," I say, leaning up on one elbow and grinning. "Twice. I actually did him twice."

"What?!"

"Yeah, *twice*," I say, rubbing it in. "A couple of weeks later he saw me hitchhiking into town. He picked me up and we drove down to the river, smoked a joint and did it for hours. This time it was fantastic."

"You bitch!" she yells. She throws the shoe at me so fast, it hits me in the forehead before I can even duck.

"Dammit," I mutter, rubbing the dent in my forehead. "We're even, okay. Truce?"

"Maybe," she says. "If you can tell me what the hell happened last night."

"Nothing. Why?"

"Something must've happened. I woke up shitting cupcakes and my toenails are painted different colors," she says, sticking one of her feet in my face.

"Pretty."

"I don't remember doing it. I must've been real fucked up to paint them all a different color. That's just not like me."

"Well, it is unique. I kinda like it. Don't you?"

"I guess," she says, sitting down and examining her feet. "It is kinda pretty in a weird kinda way. But that doesn't explain the cupcakes in my panties."

I'm saved by a knock at the door.

Vivian looks at me.

I shrug.

The next knock is louder. More insistent.

I open my mouth to ask who's there, but Vivian shushes me with her finger. She tippy-toes out of the room and up to the main door, looks through the peephole and goes into panic mode. She hops up and down and motions wildly with her arms.

"What?" I ask.

She shushes me with her finger and mouths without sound, "Black dick."

"Black dick?" I say a tiny bit louder than her.

Pounding on the door.

Vivian shakes her head furiously and mouths again, "Black dick."

"Black dick?" I ask again, thoroughly confused.

A deep, husky voice calls out in that girlie accent, "Vivian! Open the door. I know you are in there and I am not pleased."

"Fer Chrissakes!" she sputters. "Pack quick! Pack quick!" And she runs back to her bedroom.

"I don't have anything to pack," I protest, slipping on my boots and jacket as quickly as possible. At least I have my fucking pants on this time.

I follow Vivian into her room. She has both bags of money in her arms and the red bag slung over one arm. She opens the sliding glass doors with her shoulder and runs out onto the balcony. She leans way over the rail, looking down somewhere below.

"We have to do it," she says. "It's the only way out."

"Maybe we can just talk to him. Let him have the money back or something."

"He will kill you," Vivian over-enunciates. "He will kill you *dead*. You understand?"

"I understand. Kill. Dead."

Vivian tosses the bags over the balcony rail.

"What're you doing?!" I yell.

I look over the railing. The bags are laying on the tiled floor of the balcony directly under us.

Vivian grabs my arm and looks at me earnestly. "You go next," she says.

"Like hell," I respond.

"Dead, Lee. But he'll torture you first."

"I'm scared of heights, Viv, there's no way—"

The front door crashes open.

"Vivian!" Prince Charles shouts.

Vivian and I both jump ass-first over the balcony. We hang by the top rail with both hands. Hanging in midair, Vivian and I look wide-eyed at each other. Then I look down to the ground, ten stories below, and almost shit cupcakes myself.

"Don't look down, Lee, just look at me. Do what I do," Vivian whispers.

A voice from within our suite calls out, "She's not in here! Check the loo!"

Using her legs, Vivian rocks back and forth, like how kids on a swingset do. She swings higher and longer and I follow her example.

"On the count of three," Vivian says. "One, two, three!"

We let go and somehow, someway, we end up on the balcony below with nothing but a few bruises for tomorrow.

Vivian hops up and throws one of the bags at me. Cradling the other bag, she opens the sliding glass door and we run into the bedroom. We both stop when we see a man and woman in flagrante in the middle of their bed. They both turn their heads and look at us over their shoulders.

"Never mind us...just playing through," I say.

Vivian and I dash out of the room, into the hotel's hallway, and into the nearest elevator.

We stand in silence for a moment, the sound of Beatles muzak and our own heavy breathing in our ears. I watch the elevator floor numbers tick downward. Without looking at Vivian, I utter, "Black dick."

She giggles. I look at her and giggle, too. We break into loud guffaws.

The elevator dings and its doors slide open. Stifling our laughter, we run through the hotel lobby and out the front doors.

We stop and scan the rows and rows of cars in the parking lot. I see a flash of green and point. We haul ass across the lot and jump in the car. Vivian finds the key between her boobs, sticks it in the ignition and peels out of the lot, leaving yards of burnt rubber in our wake.

I turn and look through the rear window. I see Prince Charles, staring after us. He clenches and unclenches his fists, watching us leave. Two goons appear beside him. Their skin is pale and sickly looking, but their bulging muscles imply a great deal of health.

Vivian drives without direction, never even touching the brakes. After about five minutes of weaving in and out of traffic, and getting lost in general, I chance a conversation, "Hey, Viv, I have a good idea. Kinda simple, but I think it might work. GIVE HIM BACK THE MONEY! That way maybe we won't both die!"

"Oh, he'll kill us anyway. He'll take the money and kill us too. The Mafia doesn't leave loose ends."

Mafia? Fucking British fucking Mafia? That's a little piece of information I could've found useful about twenty-four fucking hours ago.

"Fuck me," I say, slipping way down in the seat. "Fuck. Me."

Vivian drives like a normal person now and makes turn after turn like she knows where she's going. I keep my feet braced on the dash just in case she cuts loose again. She pulls a cigarette from out of her bra and flicks her fingers for me to light it for her. I push in the cigarette lighter on the dash. That's a good thing about these old cars, they came with cigarette lighters back when. I hold out two fingers to her in a peace sign and she gets another cigarette out for me. What's another cigarette going to hurt if I'm going to die soon anyway? When I stick it in my mouth I can smell her all over it. Another good reason to start smoking.

We share the lighter between us and both inhale deep, holding the smoke in our lungs for a long time like it's not just tobacco.

"Charlie saw this car. We're gonna have to dump it." Vivian exhales. "Find us another. Preferably a Mercedes. Black. Blend in, you know."

"You could always just get me a Harley. Like you promised. If I'm going to die, then I want to go out on a Harley."

"Don't get your panties in a wad. You're not going to die and you'll get your damn motorcycle." She slows and turns on the right blinker.

"You remember Mark from high school?" Vivian asks.

"Which Mark?"

"Mark Thompson, the cute baseball player. I went to the prom with him."

"What about him?"

"He is now the proud owner of a car dealership."

Vivian swerves into a used car parking lot, and sure enough there's a big gaudy sign looming over us that reads: Mark's Pre-Owned Vehicles.

"Start picking out your next car, darlin'. Mark's always had a thing for me ever since senior prom. He'll give me whatever I want."

"Nononononono, not here," I say. "Let's go somewhere else. Another lot."

"I just have to flirt with him some. Saw him a few years back and he kept hinting for a blow job. This is going to be so easy. Our new Mercedes will give itself to us." She turns off the engine and sticks the key back down her cleavage.

"Please," I plead, "can't we just go somewhere else?"

"Why? You know a better way to get a car?"

"Pay for it?"

"Why the hell would I pay good money for a car? I've never had to pay for a car in my life." She adds under her breath, "Not with money anyway."

"Go do what you have to do then. I'll sit here. I don't wanna see this guy."

"Why? What's between you and him?"

"Nothing."

Vivian turns sideways in the seat and stabs me with her stare. "Spit it out. What's the history?"

I shrug in what I consider to be a very innocent manner and stub out my cigarette in the ashtray. "No history. I just don't want to see him at this particular moment in time is all."

"You're such a god-awful liar." She pooches out her bottom lip and puts her hand on my knee. "You can tell me."

"I don't want to hurt your feelings," I say, picking up her hand and dropping it back into her own lap.

"You're not going to hurt my feelings. I promise. The past is the past is the past is the past. Tell me."

Vivian's like a dog with a bone, she's not going to ever give it up. I swallow a deep breath and say, "...Senior prom..."

"Senior prom...?" she urges.

"He left in the middle of prom. I didn't know he was there with you. And we snuck off together."

Vivian's jaw muscles tighten and flex. To the untrained observer, she's not a bad actress, but I can see the storm brewing behind her purple eyes.

"And?" she asks with just a little too much casualness.

"And..." I just spit it out and hope for the best. "...We broke into the basement of the First Baptist Church. And didn't come out till morning."

Uh-oh. This is going to be bad. She's way too quiet. Then the dam breaks. She pounds the steering wheel with her fists. "You fucked my prom date?! In a church!?!"

"You said you wouldn't get mad."

"I said I wouldn't get my feelings hurt! I didn't say shit about mad!"

I am totally expecting her to whale on me, but at least she

has the presence of mind to jump out of the car. She slams the door way too hard and the little Pinto rocks from the aftershock. She paces. Screams and paces and kicks the tires. "I can't fucking believe this! I'm the cheerleader! I'm the one everybody's supposed to want! Not you! They're supposed to want *me*!" She hits the hood with her fist and stomps around toward my side of the car.

I roll up my window and lock the door.

"First you fuck Joey! Now you fuck my prom date?!" she screams through the glass.

I roll down my window a crack. "If it helps any...we didn't... do *that*," I offer.

Vivian stops cold, squints one eye at me and asks breathlessly, "What exactly did you do?"

"He went down on me."

"Shit!" she screams, slapping her palms on my window. "You bitch!"

I roll the window back up just in time and cover my face in case she shatters the glass. I deserve that last one. That was definitely poking the snake, but I just can't seem to stop from poking it again. I inch the window back down one more time.

"Um...Viv. Calm down. It's not like it was very good anyway."

Her eyes turn icy cold and she freezes.

I continue, "I finally figured out he was just writing the alphabet with his tongue. I told him it'd work a lot better if he just stuck to 'o' or 'l'. I mean he must've been down there for half the night before—"

"You goddamn gloating bitch!" she screams.

I get the window back up and cover my face. I chance a peek through my fingers and see a man walking this way. Shit, that's Mark. That's cute little baseball champion Mark in a brown polyester three-piece suit and tie. He still walks like he's bouncing on the balls of his feet. Except for a little bit of a paunch starting and some gray around the edges, he looks pretty much the same.

Vivian follows my gaze and when she sees Mark, she does an abrupt about-face. Miraculously, she's all girlie and charming and dripping sex.

Mark starts in with his latest sales pitch, "Anything you'd like to drive today?" Then he recognizes Vivian and smiles even bigger. "Vivian! Long time no see. Damn girl, you look good!"

"You bet your sweet ass I look good," Vivian oozes. "You're looking pretty good yourself, Mark. You're not still mad at me, are you?"

She slips right into his personal space and runs her fingers up and down his tie. Mark's eyes stay glued to her bazooms.

"Not me," he says directly to her tits. "I never hold grudges."

"I was just telling Lee that you and I had a little unfinished business," Vivian says while toying with his belt buckle.

"Lee?" he asks, and his eyes flicker to me inside the car.

I wiggle my fingers at him and offer up a half-smile that I hope looks genuine.

"Well, I'll be damned. I haven't seen her since prom," he says.

Vivian yanks his tie like he's a dog on a leash. "I was hoping maybe we could work out a deal. For a Mercedes, maybe?"

"Yeah, a deal, sure. Why isn't she getting out of the car?" he asks.

"She's shy," Vivian says, tugging harder on his buckle.

"She's not shy that I remember."

Vivian gives up, puts her fists on her hips and says, "Christ... Lee, get out of the damn car."

I crawl out of the Pinto and hook my thumbs into my belt loops. "Hey ya, Mark."

"Whewww." He whistles under his breath. "I like the look, Lee, I like the new look."

"Well, you haven't seen me since...for a long time, you know."

"You still look good," he drools.

I don't get it. What it is with me and men? I do my damnedest to get them to go away. I wear their clothes, I'm a good head taller than most and I could kick the shit outta most, but that just seems to keep 'em coming.

"Not as good as Viv," I say, deflecting his attention.

Mark moves up close to me, too close, maybe just a dick's

length away. "I heard a rumor about you," he says. "They say you got sent up. Any truth to that?"

"Maybe." I take a small step back.

Vivian interrupts, "Let's talk deals, Mark."

"Hold on a minute, Viv. Maybe Lee here wants to deal a little. What d'ya think? You wanna deal? For old times sake?"

I give him a little push in the chest with one finger, "You're barking up the wrong tree, Mark."

"Am I now? I heard other rumors, too. They must be true."

"Where there's smoke, there's fire," I retort.

He looks at me. Then Vivian. Back and forth a couple of times. "Oh, I get it. I get it. Prison changed you, huh? You two are queer together."

I start to tell him no, but I catch Vivian out of the corner of my eye, giving me the slashing the throat signal.

"That's right, Mark. We're together," Vivian interjects, slinking up next to me and looping her arm around my waist. "Can you blame us?"

He rubs the palms of his hands together and says, excitedly, "Now, we're getting somewhere. I think maybe I do have a deal for the two of you."

Vivian's fingers are now playing with *my* belt buckle. I start to panic just a little bit. What the hell is happening here?

Vivian purrs, "What'd you have in mind?"

Mark wiggles his eyebrows at us. "How 'bout a show, huh? Starring the two of you. I'll just watch, I promise. Like a good boy."

I'm going to faint or something. This can't be happening.

"We love an audience," Vivian says. "But we want a nice car. A *really* nice car."

"Let's go to my office."

He leads the way, bouncing on the balls of his feet. Vivian starts to follow, but I grab her arm and yank her back. "What the hell are you doing?" I hiss.

"Giving him what he wants."

"We are not, I repeat NOT, going to have sex while that man watches."

Vivian laughs. "Not for real, silly. We'll act."

"How in the hell do you act like you're having sex?"

"Good God, you'd think you'd never done this before."

"I haven't!"

"Just follow my lead. And don't forget... You want a Harley, then you're going to do it *and* you're going to like it," she demands.

Like I've never heard that before.

Good God, I'm stuck in the middle of a porn movie set. This office is disgusting. Cobwebs, dust, clutter, dank and musty, and the smell of old testosterone.

Vivian works this scenario like the pro she is. She pushes Mark backward until he stumbles into a chair in the corner.

"Whoa there," he mutters. "Take it easy on me."

Vivian straddles his lap and rips his tie off with her teeth. She puts his hands behind the chair and ties them together with his own necktie. But he doesn't seem to mind at all because this puts her tits right in his face.

I can't believe I'm watching this. But it's like when somebody says, 'Ooh, this stinks. Smell it.' You know it's going to stink, but you always go ahead and smell it anyway. So, I just hold my breath and watch.

Vivian gets up and backs away from him. I can't help but notice the obvious bulge in his pants. It's like he's pointing a loaded gun right at me.

Vivian struts up to me and grabs my belt. In my mind, I know she's just acting, but my body doesn't quite know the difference. Damn, my jeans feel way too tight. She takes both my hands in hers and leads me behind the desk. She slides down into the swivel desk chair and wraps her legs around me. She leans forward, pressing her tits into my belly, puts a hand on each of my shoulders and pushes me down between her legs.

"Why do I have to do all the work?" I ask.

Now I'm stuck down here under the desk with its modesty board separating me from Mark's view and Vivian's crotch hovering right in front of my face. My first thought is *Thank God, she's wearing panties.* I don't know exactly what I'm supposed to do—I mean I know what I'm supposed to do in reality, but not what I'm supposed to do right now. So, I do the obvious—nothing.

And, that turns out to be the right thing to do, because Vivian's got it all under control. She twitches and moans and rolls her head, mumbling oh God's and right there like I like it, baby's and all kinds of shit I've never heard before.

Her acting looks fake as all get out to me, but it must be working because I hear Mark's pleasure moans joining in with hers. Vivian builds it a little and starts thumping on the desk with her fists and moving her hips. I feel a little intoxicated just from the vibe and kinda giggly, too.

This isn't the first time I've had a cheerleader's crotch right in my face. Jamie the Cheerleader used to tease me all the time our junior year. I sat near the back in English class. The jocks sat on the left side of the room and the cheerleaders (Vivian included) sat on the right side. All the pheromones they shot back and forth at each other made me gag.

Jamie would turn around backward and hike her legs up on Vivian's desk, showing off her tiny blue cheerleading panties. She'd catch me looking at her and spread her knees even further apart so I'd get a really good shot of her panties.

God, I hated her. I hated her so much I couldn't keep my eyes off her.

One night, I was walking down the dark street on my way to spend the night in Chopper's shop when Jamie pulled her car over and asked if I needed a ride. I climbed in and she acted like we're best friends and told me all about how she just let some jock feel her up but he can't ever get her off. She pulled her car into a dark alley and threw it in park, but left the engine running. She turned the radio up, slid her skirt up all the way to her waist, hooked her thumbs into the elastic of her sheer pink panties and slid them down her long legs. With her panties dangling off her left ankle, she threw her right leg up onto the seat and dared, "I bet you can get me off good." She licked two of her fingers, slipped them down her slit and massaged. She leaned back with her head against the driver's windshield and twitched her narrow hips against her slow-moving fingers. She looked at me lazily and whispered, "It's not going to lick itself." I dropped down on my knees into the floorboard and grabbed her hips in my hands. I pulled her toward me and used my nose to push her fingers away. She moaned with each flick of my tongue. Emboldened, I spread her wider with my thumbs and used only my tongue to caress more moans out of her. I went down on Jamie the Cheerleader for not just one mighty orgasm but two little ones right after it. I knew right then and there that God had given me a natural talent to please women and it was my duty from there on out to use that gift often and wisely.

The whole cheerleaders-are-a-bitch part of the story? Jamie pointedly ignored me the rest of the school year except when we were alone in the girls' room and she said, "Come on over tonight. I'll let you eat me out again."

Bitch.

My eyes have been glued to Vivian's crotch for a good five minutes. Her hips moving in little circles have hypnotized me. Finally, she builds her sex act to a giant crescendo and tops her faux climax with a series of ohmygod's and Jesus's.

Oh, wait a minute, false alarm. Damn, she's setting the stakes pretty high if she's going to top that outburst.

Then I see it! Oh my God, this is too good to be true! There's a black felt-tip pen on the floor under the chair. This is going to be so good!

I sneak the pen out from under the chair, pop off the cap and inch my way closer to Vivian. She's so wrapped up in her performance, she doesn't even notice what I'm up to. I push her knees out even wider to make room for my arm and draw a nice black arrow up the inside of her thigh, pointing straight at her crotch. Now she definitely notices me, but can't do a damn thing without stopping her performance. Then above the arrow I slowly and carefully write the words: *Abandon hope all ye who enter here.*

That's for whacking me with your shoe.

Vivian thumps me on the head with her fist. I edge back under the desk, suppressing my giggles. The next thing I know, her hand appears under the desk holding out a set of keys. I take the keys from her. What the hell am I supposed to do with these?

She kicks me toward the side like she's wanting me to get out from under the desk. But I don't get it because she's still up there doing her thing and she hasn't finished yet.

Oh! Now I get it.

I lie down on my belly and inch my way out from under the desk. I army-crawl through the open door behind her, hoping her acting is good enough that Mark won't notice anything else. Once I'm in the hallway I jump up and run out the back door.

I stop outside and look at the keys. Which car do they belong to? The tag just says Mercedes. I hit the unlock button and hear a beep. There it is. A shiny, new black Mercedes blinks its lights at me.

I sprint to the car and hop in. I squeal the tires all the way up to the back door, fling open the passenger door and seconds later Vivian runs out and dives into the seat. I take off again, aiming for the Pinto on the other side of the lot. I screech up alongside the Pinto, Vivian hops out, grabs the bags of money, jumps back in and I get us the hell out of Dodge, leaving only dust and smoke in the rearview mirror.

Vivian laughs hysterically. "That'll teach the fucker for dumping me at prom," she gasps.

She throws her leg up on the dashboard, raises her skirt and looks at my artwork on her thigh. She reads it silently, then raises one eyebrow at me.

"That's the inscription at the gates of hell," I explain.

She laughs, "I know Dante, shithead. Masters in English Lit, remember?"

"Well, it was between that and 'Caution: Slippery When Wet.'"

"You could've just written 'Open All Night.'"

We laugh and Vivian plants both of her feet up on the dash. She stretches out her leg and punches on the radio with her big toe. May God strike me dead if I'm lying—Janis Joplin's voice rasps through all five speakers, pleading with the Lord to buy her a Mercedes Benz.

Vivian and I grin from ear to ear and sing along.

CHAPTER SEVEN

"I am making it my personal mission to turn you into a girl," Vivian states, handing me three more dresses.

"Yeah, well, good luck with that." Especially if being a girl means wearing dresses, shopping for dresses or trying on dresses. The only thing I do like about dresses is their up-and-under easy access.

Vivian shoves me into a dressing room with an armload of lace and taffeta. She may make me try these damn things on; I may even wear one of them to homecoming tonight, but what she doesn't know is that I'm still going to wear my boxers. What she can't see won't hurt her.

I try on a god-awful purple thing with layers over layers over layers of pouf. I step out into the hallway and Vivian purses her lips and gestures for me to turn in circles.

"Lee Anne," Vivian lectures, "you need to stand up straight. Shoulders back. Tits out. And it would help if you weren't wearing those boots."

"I only take my boots off for one thing," I retort.

"To take a shower?" she asks flatly.

"Okay, *two* things."

"See how pretty you look?" she asks, pushing me in front of a full-length mirror and spinning me around.

I look at myself and wince out loud. "I look like the blueberry girl in Willie Wonka. Violet, you're turning violet," I joke.

Vivian doesn't laugh. She just shoves me back in the dressing room.

When I come out and stand in front of the mirror, I feel absofuckinglutely ridiculous. This dress is tight and gold and only has one long sleeve. Somebody forgot to sew on the left sleeve. There are several two feet long, white tassle-like things hanging off it from the waist. I hold up a tassle and shake it at Vivian, asking "What the hell're these?"

"If you have to ask..." she sighs, obviously exasperated with my beauty pageant naivete.

"I bet I know what they are," I state. "They're Shetland pony tails."

She shakes her head in disgust.

I continue, "You know how many Shetland ponies had to die to make this dress?"

Vivian is so not amused. She shoves me back toward the dressing room.

When I come out of the dressing room this time, I don't even bother to look in the mirror. "It's pink," I say.

"And tangerine," she adds.

"With pink flowers," I say.

"And orange crème highlights," Vivian adds again.

"With pink ribbons," I say.

"Okay, you win," she says with a definite edge to her voice. She throws her hands dramatically into the air above her head. "What the hell *do* you want?"

Wow. What *do* I want? Accepting the fact that I have to wear a dress...then what do I want to see when I look in the mirror?

"I want..." I begin, "I want a dress that will...make my boobs look bigger, make my hips smaller, make my ass higher, and will coordinate with my tats."

Vivian bites her upper lip and closes her eyes. She takes a deep breath and studies me for a long moment before asking, "What color?"

"Black."

"No," she says, "I'm wearing black."

"So?"

"We both can't wear black," she says.

"Why?"

"I don't have time to explain to you everything about beauty in the few precious moments we have left before homecoming. Choose another color," she says in my mother's voice.

"You don't have to explain *everything*," I say, "Just the part about why we both can't wear black."

"Take my fucking word for it!" she yells. "Choose another fucking color!"

"Okay, okay... Red, I guess," I whimper.

Vivian stalks over to a nearby rack, rips the first red dress she sees off a hanger and throws it at me. "Here's your fucking dress," she says and walks away.

I trail after her, rustling taffeta as I go. "Vivian!"

She turns to me and puts her hands on her hips. The hands on the hips thing is not a good sign. I have to think of something fast that will calm her down.

"I need your help," I pout. "Hair. Makeup. I can't do this myself." I add a whine into the mix just for good measure, "Pleeeease. I really need you."

She squints one eye at me. "Okay," she says, "but you have to do what I say. No arguing."

"I promise," I lie through my teeth. I clasp my hands together in front of me. "Just help me, please."

"All I need is running water," Vivian says. "And I don't even have to have that."

Vivian has us locked into the bathroom at a Kum & Go with piles of makeup and hair stuff. She has me sitting on the floor on top of the bags of money while she bends down over me and liberally applies another coat of paint to my face. The only reason I'm not complaining is because...well, because she's bending down over me.

"This may not be the best idea you've ever had," I say.

"Don't worry," she says and licks the tip of the eyeliner pencil. "When I'm done with you, you'll look fabulous."

I catch her by the wrist and say seriously, "I didn't mean that, Vivian. I meant going to homecoming while on the run from the Mafia may not be such a good idea."

"It's a great idea. Look up, quit blinking." She leans in close, drawing on my fake eyes. Her lips are only a mere couple of inches from mine. If she didn't have a sharp pointy stick aimed at my eyeball I could just—

She interrupts my fantasy. "Number one, he has no idea where we are or where we're going. Number two, we'll be in the middle of a crowd and what's he going to do in front of that many people? And number three..." She stops drawing on my face and steps back to examine her artwork.

"Number three?" I ask.

"Number three," she continues, "by this time tomorrow we'll be far away with two bags of money."

"Back to number one: How do you know he doesn't know where we're going?"

"Because I don't know where we're going, silly. And, as long as I don't know, he can't know."

There's knock on the door that makes us both jump. We look at each other wide-eyed.

"Is somebody in there?" a woman's voice asks from the other side.

We both let out a shaky breath at the same time. "Occupied," I say to the locked door. Vivian reaches into her red bag and shakes a blue pill out of the aspirin bottle with nervous hands.

"Me, too," I say, holding out my palm. "Or I'll never be able to get through this night sane."

She hands me a blue pill and we pop them into our mouths

and dry swallow. Next, she pulls a small tube out of her bag and takes off the cap. It's bright red, blood red, lipstick. "The *coup de grâce*," she says.

"Isn't that what you say right before you kill somebody?"

"Really? I thought it meant icing on the cake."

"No lipstick," I protest. "Especially if I'm going to eat cake."

She starts smearing it on my lips anyway. "You really have a pretty face, Lee."

"I feel a but coming on..."

"But...it's like you do everything possible to be unattractive—Now smack your lips together a couple of times—If I had your cheekbones and your full lips, there'd be no stopping me."

She likes my lips? She's obviously been paying more attention to me than I thought. "I don't like men looking at me," I say.

"Well, they're gonna look tonight," she says, turning me toward the grimy mirror. "Tell me what you think."

Wow. The only way I recognize myself is because I'm looking back at me. Vivian is a miracle worker. I actually look...kind of... good. She's piled all my dreads up on my head like I have a little octopus perched up there. It doesn't look half bad. But what's that smear on my cheek? I reach up to brush it away and Vivian grabs my hand.

"Don't touch your face, you'll fuck up all my hard work," she reprimands.

"There's a smear," I say.

Vivian uses her Kleenex to swipe at the mirror. Oh. It was a smear on the filthy mirror, not on me.

"And, how do I look?" Vivian asks, striking a pose in her slinky black dress.

She looks gorgeous. Good enough to eat. "You're..." I begin, leaning in close to her and summoning all my courage.

She places a finger in the middle of my chest and pushes me back. "Your lip liner is crooked," she says.

Damn.

"Quit chewing your lipstick off," she scolds and hands me the tube. "Here. Tuck it into your cleavage. That way you can freshen it up later."

"Yeah. Thanks, I'll be sure to do that," I say, trying not to sound too dejected and tossing the lipstick into her bag when she turns away.

She reaches over and pops the top off an economy size can of Alberto Vo5 hairspray, saying, "Close your eyes." I scrunch my eyes closed and listen to the hiss of aerosol for a long time. When I open them again, we're both smothered in a fog of sticky hairspray stink.

"Oh my God," I cough. "That shit burns all the way down my windpipe. Isn't that stuff highly flammable?"

"You'll be fine," she says. "Just don't smoke anywhere near your hair."

"How come when my nipples are hard I just look cold or scared, but when yours are hard you just look hot?" I ask.

"Because you're cold and scared," Vivian explains. "And because I'm hot."

"And you're humble, too," I add under my breath.

She guides the Mercedes into the high school parking lot and finds a slot right near the main entrance. She probably used to park here in the cool section all the time with the cheerleaders and jocks while I had to ride the bus with the rest of the losers.

I adjust the damn straps on my damn red dress while Vivian checks her makeup in the rearview mirror. I use the word "dress" lightly because it's hardly a dress at all. It has spaghetti straps and the flimsy fabric hangs just right above my nipples. It only comes to mid-thigh and has no back. At least it covers my boxers.

Vivian looks super hot in her black dress. Now I'm glad I didn't wear black because I'd just end up looking like her ugly shadow. The dress is way too tight on her, which is a good thing, and I don't think she's wearing any underwear whatsoever. Which is another good thing.

I've come up with about a million different reasons why I can't go to this homecoming shindig, but Vivian isn't buying any of it. "You know what would be fun?" I say, trying a different tack. "We could hire a couple of drag queens to pose as us and just spy on what happens."

"I don't like men who look better in heels than me," she replies without a trace of humor.

I try again, "Or we could just sit in the car and get high and eat cupcakes. Make fun of everyone going in."

She throws me an exasperated look and says, "I'm going in. You're going in. End of story."

"Are you sure we're allowed? Isn't it just for the students?"

"It's called homecoming, stupid," she says. "Alumni come home to visit during homecoming."

"Okay," I say, giving up and opening my door, "let's go get this over with."

"Good idea. You go first. I'll wait a couple of minutes then make my grand entrance."

I cannot believe my ears. All this makeover fantasy hoopla shit she's put me through and now she pulls this. "You're afraid to be seen with me. Why don't you just say that? Instead of this grand entrance shit?"

I sit back in the seat, close my door firmly and cross my arms over the gooseflesh on my over-exposed boobs. "Maybe I don't want to be seen with you either. Ever think of that?" I sulk.

"Better idea," she says, putting on more lipstick. "We go in together. I always look better with contrast." She opens her door and hops out like she's popping out of a cake at a bachelor party.

I decide right then and there that I don't like her anymore and I am definitely not going to have any fun tonight.

Oh my God, I'm not even all the way inside the front door before my nostrils are assaulted by the fumes of sweat, smelly feet and angst. My heart lurches inside my chest and the smells bring back a spinning kaleidoscope of unwanted memories: Mrs. Banana (I don't remember her real name, just that everyone called her Mrs. Banana) and her one good eye and one glass eye.

Just like a horse, both her eyes would move independently of each other. One eye would look straight at you while the other eye roamed the room. It always gave me an eerie feeling—like she could see me even when I was standing behind her. And Mark Thompson sat in front of me in psych class and tossed little balled up notes on my desk. I'd put them in my pocket and take them home and read them. His notes read like teen erotica complete with bad grammar about all the things he wanted to do to me in the dark. Little did he know I learned how to please a woman by pleasing myself after reading his nasty confessions.

I feel like I'm a teenager again, too tall and skinny, trying to crowd my too-long legs under those wooden desks, hunched over my English homework, diagramming sentences with slash marks that ripped through my paper, wearing some of Chopper's old work overalls for the third day in a row until I could sneak back into my house and grab some clean clothes. I overheard the quarterback of the football team, Mr. Popular, whisper to his friend, Mr. Cool, that he can't tell if I'm a boy or a girl. And pretty soon the whole class pointed and snickered at me.

Except for Vivian. Pretty, red-headed Vivian, sitting on the front row, turned and looked at my shamed face and rolled her eyes at the quarterback. That's all she did. Rolled her eyes and looked back to the front. But it was enough to get me through another day.

Vivian grabs me by the elbow and pulls me down the empty hallway, talking ninety to nothing, "Was that Sue Anne that just went inside? Christ, she's fat as a cow. Or pregnant. Maybe both, who knows?"

"Maybe she has a stomach tumor," I add.

"There's always hope," Vivian giggles. She stops and looks me up and down, long and hard. I wish for maybe the umpteenth time that I had a shawl or whatever to cover up my tats and tits. "You okay?" she asks. "You look like you've just seen a ghost."

"Go ahead without me, Viv, I'll catch up."

"I'm not going in there without you, you big goof," she says, giving me a look like I'm being ridiculous.

"You belong here, Vivian." I stammer, "Not...me."

"You belong here. You went to school here same as me."

"You know what I mean," I whisper to my feet.

"Uh. No. I. Don't." Viv says, looking down at my feet, too.

"Vivian...you were the popular one. You were the pretty one. Everybody loved you. Me...at best, I was a nobody..."

Good God, am I going to cry? I can't cry now. I bite my lower lip, hitch my boxers up a little higher and clear my throat. "I just can't go in there, okay?"

Vivian sighs. She plants her feet shoulder-width apart and puts her fists on her hips. She looks at me coldly. "You want to have it out right here? Okay...here's the God's honest truth. I moved here when I was in fourth grade. I had a wild orange afro and freckles over my entire body. I had Coke bottle glasses and elephant-size ears. I used to put bubblegum behind my ears to try to get them to stick and lay flat. Between my freckles, my glasses, my Dumbo ears and my home perm, I wasn't the prettiest girl around. Everybody made fun of me. But what did I do? Did I quit? Did I stand in a dark hallway and cry about it? No. I learned how to do the splits and backflips and I tamed my hair and became the best damn cheerleader in this school. I got even. And so did you. We both got out of this godforsaken town." She points dramatically to the gym doors. "And they didn't. They're still stuck here. And that's why you and I are better than all of them put together."

"I didn't get out," I mumble. "I just went to prison."

"So what?" she retorts. "I learned to spread my legs and get paid to do it. But we still got out and they didn't. So, like my football-coaching daddy always told me, 'Get up and walk it off.'"

I manage to peel my stare away from my feet and look at her. "You really have big ears?"

I reach out to move her hair and have a look, but she swats at my hand.

"You ever mention my ears again and I'll knock you on your ass," she says with true grit. And she looks like she means it too.

I force a small smile. She gives me a little smile back. "Okay," I say, "Let's go show 'em what a real football queen looks like."

Vivian steams ahead and I'm the caboose. She flings the

gym doors open and they both slam against the brick walls and I swear to God, just like Rita Hayworth, she makes a 1940's style grand entrance. She pauses at the top of the stairs with her arms outstretched just to give everyone the full effect of her dazzling beauty before descending into a bevy of male admirers.

I pause dramatically at the top of the steps too, but only because I don't think I can make it safely all the way down in high heels. I slip them off and kick them to the side. I'll come back and get them later.

I inch down the stairs barefooted and look around for Vivian. She's been swallowed by the hordes, so I sidle over to the closest wall and make myself inconspicuous. I've never been to a homecoming shindig before so I have no idea if this one is decorated abnormally or if all homecomings look like Martha Stewart threw up in the gym. Probably all of them.

There's crepe and balloons and confetti everywhere. Hard, pounding music that I don't recognize reverberates through my feet and pounds its way up to the top of my skull. I need a drink in a bad way. I wonder if anyone's spiked the punch yet?

Everybody's fat. And I don't mean the alumni like me that are scattered about the floor; I mean the students. They're fat and they're sweaty too. I guess putting those snack and pop machines in the halls wasn't such a good idea after all.

I catch a glimpse of Vivian over by the basketball goal. She's flirting and smiling in such a fake way, but nobody knows that but me. I guess she's happy. She's talking animatedly to two women who look like...oh my God, they *are*. They're The Pattys. The Pattys were two best friends in high school and nobody ever saw them apart. One was Patty Cooper and the other was Patty Porter and we all just called them The Pattys. They were like Siamese twins, doing absolutely everything together. Well, I don't know about *everything* but I wouldn't doubt it. Patty Porter was the skinny one who everyone called Port-a-Patty and Patty Cooper was the fat one who everyone called Fatty Pooper.

Vivian finishes talking to The Pattys and swings her way over to Beau Jackson. Beau was a kind of quiet little guy back when. He hits Vivian at about chest level and I can see what he likes about being so short. He used to have a big tight afro but now it's thinned down the middle and it looks more like a Ronald McDonald. Back in high school a story circulated about him on a senior boys camping trip. They said he got drunk and fucked a box of twinkies. That's why everyone started calling him Twinkie. I never quite understood that whole story. Did he actually put it inside a twinkie or did he just stick it inside the box of twinkies and do it to that? I'll have to remember to ask Vivian later.

Vivian and Beau start dancing together. It's a kind of upbeat song, but Beau grabs her and slow-dances. He lays his face right on her tits and wraps his arms around her waist and she's smiling down at him and I'd like to punch him right in the gut.

"Lee Anne?" asks a deep voice. This guy steps directly into my line of vision and...shit, it's Joey Hanes. What're the odds?

"Joey?" I ask tentatively.

"Yea, damn, woman, you look good," he says. His eyes stroll leisurely up and down my half-naked body and loiter on my headlights. I wish there was a way to turn them off.

"Yeah, you, too," I mumble. My cheeks burn hot. I hope he can't tell that for all the blush I already have on.

He grabs my hand and pulls me onto the dance floor. "One dance," he says, "for old-times sake." He wraps his arms around me, grabs my ass and grinds my pelvis into his and he's barely moving and, Christ, he has a banana in his pocket.

I glance over his shoulder (he's grown a lot taller since high school) and try to locate Vivian. There she is. I see her red hair bobbing above the sea of bodies. She's still dancing and talking with Beau.

"You know we could leave this place," Joey says. "We could pick up where we left off."

"Where we left off? Which part is that?" I ask. "The part where you threw up on me or the part where I tossed you out of your own car?"

"It's true, huh?"

"What truth is that, Joey?" I ask. I look toward Vivian for help. Maybe she can get me out of this mess, but I've lost her again.

He presses his banana harder into my belly and says, "Twinkie told me you were a lesbo now."

"Twinkie? How the hell would he know?"

"Everybody knows. But I don't believe it," he says, grinding into me a little harder.

Suddenly, a hand grabs my shoulder and spins me around. It's Vivian. I smile for a split second until she rears back and slaps the holy shit out of me.

"Ow!"

"You bitch!" Vivian screams.

Joey leers at Vivian and throws one arm back over my shoulder. "This your girlfriend?" he asks me. "You gals want a third?" he asks Vivian.

Vivian slaps the holy shit out of him next. He's no fool. He puts his hands in the air to block any future attacks and backs away.

Vivian turns back to me and screams above the music, "You're a lesbian?! I came to homecoming with a fucking lesbian?!"

I look around and offer an apologetic "I don't know what the hell she's talking about, the lady is crazy" smile to all the stares.

"Ssshhhhh..." I say to Vivian. I grab her hand and pull her off the dance floor and behind the bleachers to a semi-private space. "Don't just scream that shit, Viv. Not at homecoming. Not in Oklahoma. You want me to get killed by the Baptist Student Assembly?"

She looks at me stunned. "It's true? Everybody here knows you're a lesbian except *me*?"

"Well...yeah, it's true. Of course it's true. You knew that. For Chrissakes, Vivian, you *knew* that."

"How was I supposed to know that? You never told me!"

"C'mon, Viv, get real. I talk like a dyke, I walk like a dyke. I'm probably a dyke."

Does she ever look pissed. Those little muscles are working in her jaw and there's a big vein popping out in her forehead. I've never seen her this angry.

"You're mad at me?" I ask.

"I could fucking kill you," she grates and I don't think she's lying either.

I try to defuse the anger with a little humor. "Well, you don't have to go and scream it to everybody, okay? It's like the lesbian golden rule. You don't out somebody without their permission. That's rule number one. Rule number two is...you don't go down on a first date."

She's not laughing. I'm so nervous I keep talking, "It's written down in the lesbian rulebook." She's still staring at me like she wants to choke me to death, so I keep rambling, "Just two rules. Pretty easy to remember really."

She takes a deep breath and one step in closer to me. "Let me try to understand this," she says, ticking off points on her fingers. "You had sex with Joey. You had sex with Mark. You're a lesbian, but you didn't even try to have sex with *me*?"

Oh my God, I should've seen this one coming. She's not mad I'm gay, she's mad I haven't put a move on her. How can I be that stupid? All straight women want lesbians to want them.

"All lesbians want me," Vivian says, underscoring what I'm thinking. "We've slept in the same bed! You've seen me half-naked. You were under that desk pretending to go down on me, for fuck's sakes!" She does a "look at me" gesture up and down her body and adds, "And here I stand looking hotter than I've ever looked in my life and you don't even make a move on me. Why the hell don't *you* want me?"

Are those real tears in her eyes? I can't believe this. And I really can't believe what I do next, but I do it anyway before I think myself out of it. I grab Vivian by both her shoulders and pull her to me and right here in front of God and everybody I kiss her. I kiss her like I've been wanting to kiss her since the second I laid eyes on her.

The music stops. The crowd hushes. Everyone claps and cheers and I have the woman I'm desperately in love with in my arms.

Okay, not really. Everything is just like it was.

Vivian steps back. She looks a little startled, maybe even a little confused. Then Whack! She slaps me again.

"What the fuck was that one for?" I ask, rubbing my other cheek.

"I'm not a lesbian," she shoots.

I flinch like I got four bullets, one for each of her words, straight to the heart. It hurts and it pisses me off that it hurts.

"I didn't try anything with you because...because you're straight and if you told me no..." I shake my head, then say it anyway, "You don't know, Vivian...you just don't realize how much I love you."

And there it is. Just like that. I didn't even really know how much I meant it until I said it out loud. So I say it one more time, more for me than for her, "I love you."

Then I turn and walk away, leaving those words hanging in the distance between us.

I don't get it. I just don't get these damn straight women. They want you to want them, but then they shut you down. Damned if you do, damned if you don't. My mind is reeling and both sides of my face are stinging and I walk out of this damn place. I walk out the doors without looking back. My tears are so hot, they burn my face and my makeup is running and I just don't care who sees. I just don't care.

Fuck the shoes. I'm not going back after them.

Vivian has the car keys hidden somewhere down her magic tits and I'm stuck without a ride unless I want to walk but I'm not desperate enough to walk down the middle of town in this god-awful getup. I trudge across the parking lot, not even caring about the gravel biting my bare feet and throw open the door to the Mercedes. I sit in the passenger seat with my elbows on my knees and my head in my hands and my feet on the dash and I cry and hiccup and think about how fuckin' pitiful I am.

The driver's side door opens and I try to turn the waterworks off and come out of this with some semblance of pride, but my damn heart hurts too bad.

Vivian quietly clicks her door closed and scoots over next to me until our shoulders touch.

"It's all like some game to you, isn't it?" I finally blubber. "You want me to want you, but you don't want to want me. I'm supposed to fall in love with you, then you slap me and walk away feeling all good about yourself. Well, it's not a game to me, Vivian. It's my life. I have to live it."

She reaches down her cleavage and pulls out a tissue. She swipes at my tear tracks and smudges and then tucks it back away.

"I can't believe all this time you didn't know I was a lesbian. I thought you knew. How the hell could you not know?" I ask. "Even Sonja could tell just by looking at me."

"Who's Sonja?"

"Never mind."

"You've been a lesbian the whole time I've known you?" Vivian asks.

I look at her straight-on. "What d'ya mean?"

"I thought maybe you turned into a lesbian for me," she says matter-of-factly.

"Are you kidding me?"

"No."

"Your ego's that huge, Vivian? Your ego's so huge, you thought I actually *turned* into a lesbian just for you?"

"Well," she says, "I've had gay men go straight for me. What's the difference?"

"Really? Damn..."

"And who has the huge ego here? You expect me to turn into a lesbian just for you."

"No, I don't," I explain. "I don't expect that exactly."

"Then what do you expect exactly?"

"I just want you to love me. That's all."

"I do love you, you big goof."

"Physically, too."

Vivian shakes her head sadly. "I can't. I don't know how to do it and I probably wouldn't be any good at it. I don't want to do something I won't be good at."

"We could practice."

She laughs.

"I don't want you anyway," I reason. "You're too high maintenance and you make me wear weird girlie clothes."

"You know what your problem is?" she asks. When I don't answer she tells me anyway, "You have your loves confused."

"No, my problem is that I keep falling for straight women."

"Listen, Lee, if I were a lesbian, I'd be the best damn lesbian in the world. In the universe, that's how great I'd be at all the lesbian stuff that I don't even have the slightest idea what it is. I'd be the best lesbian with a capitol L and, honey, you'd be my first choice to be with. We would go off and do whatever lesbians do till the cows came home. But, believe you me, we're better off this way."

"*You're* better off maybe."

"No, darlin'. The sex would wear off eventually and then we'd be fighting and then we'd hate each other and then we'd be alone. But friends, like we are, real friends, this will last." She reaches over and wraps her fingers in mine. "Till death do us part."

She gently wipes away a few of my tears, hugs me to her chest and holds me tight.

I don't know if it's her words or the fact that she has my face sandwiched between her tits, but I'm starting to feel a little bit better.

"You're sure?" I ask, raising my face to hers. "You're sure you can't love me the way I love you?"

She looks into my eyes for a long time before she answers, "Lee, if it'll make you feel better...on my eightieth birthday...if we're both unattached and alive...we'll do it then."

"Eighty? I don't think I want to do it with an eighty-year-old woman."

"We'll turn out the lights," she laughs. "We'll turn out the lights and take our dentures out and turn our hearing aids down. And it'll be the best sex we ever had."

Well, at least I have something to look forward to.

Suddenly, Vivian wraps a hand around the back of my head and shoves my face in her lap, ordering, "Get down."

"You changed your mind?" I mumble into her crotch.

"Ssshhhh," she warns, lying down flat over my body. "They're here. They just pulled in."

I spit her dress out of my mouth and ask, "Prince Charles?"

"Him and two other guys." She raises up and peeks over the dashboard. "I don't think they saw us."

I peek over the dash with her. Prince Charles and the same two goons I saw earlier are getting out of their BMW and heading for the school.

"Goddammit. I'm tired of this shit." I twist around, reach into the backseat and grab my boots and pants.

"What're you doing?" she asks, alarmed.

I slip on my boots and stick my hands in the pockets of my jeans until I find my knife. "Buying some time," I answer.

I pop open my door and drop to the ground. I push the door almost closed and duck walk to the front bumper. I raise up a little and peek over the hood of the car parked next to us. As soon as P.C. and his goons open the school doors and walk inside, I scramble to their BMW.

I flip open my knife and stab a back tire. As soon as I pull my knife out, I hear a satisfying hiss. I do the next tire. And the next. And the next.

No way they're getting four new tires this time of night. And good luck finding tires early on a Saturday morning.

I run back to the Mercedes and throw myself inside. Vivian guides our way out of the parking lot without turning on the headlights.

"Where to now?" I ask.

"The one place he knows I'll never go. Home."

CHAPTER EIGHT

I am calling this part of our adventure, *A Glimpse into the Life of a Cheerleader.* I have to admit, I'm excited to see the way Vivian grew up. Exactly what it is that makes her what she is. If I were to tag it myself, I'd put all my money on a *Leave it to Beaver*-type of childhood. June wears pearls and bakes pies. Ward works and always has time for his kids. The Beav, Vivian, approaches everything with a lopsided grin and a sense of well-being that every problem can be solved in thirty minutes. I guess that would make me Eddie Haskell. Goofy, bumbling, always into trouble, Eddie, that's me.

Vivian maneuvers the car to the side of the street in front of her childhood home, and I am treated to a vision much like I expected. The only thing missing is the white picket fence. Do they still make white picket fences, I wonder? Next to the rented house I grew up in, Vivian's home is perfect.

"This place is perfect," I tell her with genuine awe in my tone. "I would've stayed here and never left."

"Perfect on the outside," she says. "Just like my mother. Appearances are everything. Thank God for my daddy. C'mon, let's go see what old folks do at night."

"Sleep probably," I say. "Like normal folks."

"Nothing's normal about these folks. My mother never stops talking and Daddy's going deaf. The result is that my mother screams constantly."

Vivian gets the front door key out from under the welcome mat, unlocks the door and leads me inside.

Stepping into the living room is like one of those dreams/nightmares where you suddenly find yourself thrust on a stage and you're in the middle of a live performance but you have absolutely no idea what play it is or what character you are or what your lines are. And you're naked.

Little tiny lights beam down at us. I look to find the source of the light. Track lighting is everywhere—and I do mean everywhere. Little spotlights are shining down and illuminating dolls. Dozens upon dozens of dolls. My God, is that...?

"Marie Osmond. My mom loves Marie Osmond," Vivian says simply like it's the most natural thing in the world.

I find myself both attracted and repelled by a large four feet tall Marie Osmond doll. It's eerily life-like. Especially the large, white teeth.

"She must have hundreds of Maries," I whisper.

"It's her life's work," she whispers back without a touch of sarcasm.

Dear God, what I have gotten myself into?

Vivian opens a cabinet, snags something from inside it, tippy-toes through the living room and disappears down a hallway. I trail after her, acutely aware of hundreds of little brown eyes following me out of the room.

Vivian's room is not a bedroom, not by my standards and certainly not by any other standards. It's a shrine. A shrine to Princess Vivian. The walls of the room are painted a deep, dark purple. Blue ribbons and certificates and trophies entirely cover one whole wall. In the far corner sits a large canopied bed. Purple, of course. There's about a billion princess pillows and stuffed animals on it. A white vanity table with a little wicker stool sits in another corner. And there's even her own bathroom and a huge walk-in closet. Princess all the way.

I say the first thing that comes to mind. "You should've painted the room purple."

"I hate purple," she says.

"That was a joke. Your room *is* purple."

"I know," she explains. "My mom hates purple, too. I did it just to piss her off."

Vivian holds out both of her hands and shows me what she's been hiding behind her back. It's two porcelain dolls.

"Is that Elvis? Two Elvis dolls?"

"Elvi," she corrects. "Just like cacti. And peni. Elvi. They're decanters. Full of whiskey. It's a game Dad and I play. I drink all the whiskey out of the Elvi. He fills them back up. Neither one of us tells Mom and we both pretend it never happened."

She bites on one Elvi head and pops the cork. She spits the head onto her bed and chugs deep. "You can have fat Elvi," she says, handing me a grinning Elvis decanter in a white jumpsuit.

Two Elvi later and I am bombed. Literally smashed. I sit under the purple bedspread which we have fashioned into a makeshift tent between the vanity table and the bed. It's like we're camping. Except we're inside. And we're drunk on Elvi. And we've taken some of her mom's Xanax that Vivian found in the medicine cabinet. And the tent is a bedspread and not a real tent. I guess maybe it's not much like camping after all.

Vivian raided the kitchen earlier and came back with an armload of cupcakes and a jar of peanut butter. I'm eating the peanut butter with my fingers and thinking about how long it's been since I've had anything taste this good. I feel like laughing. Not because anything is particularly funny, but just because I can.

"So what do they call English muffins in England?" I ask around a glob of peanut butter. "Are they just muffins or what?"

Vivian stuffs another cupcake in her mouth and swallows it whole. She sucks on her front teeth before answering. "Scones."

"And why don't British people have an accent when they sing?"

She shrugs and pops another cupcake in her mouth.

I ask another. "Why do they call cigarettes faggots?"

"They think it's weird that we call faggots faggots."

"Are we supposed to call them cigarettes?"

Vivian laughs like that's the funniest thing she's ever heard. I grab a cupcake and eat it in tiny bites like a squirrel.

"I'm glad I'm not a faggot," I say through my squirrel teeth.

"I'm just glad I'm not a man," Vivian says.

"Yeah, if I was a man and had a penis..." I pause to swallow the mushy chocolate.

Vivian interrupts, "Most men do have a penis."

"But if I had a penis, I'd be very proud of it. I'd stick it in every hole I could find. I'd be touching it all the time. They'd have to lock me up," I say.

"I would fuck anything and everything that moved," Vivian agrees. "We'd be in prison right now sharing a cell."

I laugh. "Well, just don't bend over around me."

"You're such a faggot," she says.

I burst into loud guffaws. We laugh together, doubled over, and when we finally come up we're both wiping away tears.

"I just love drugs, don't you?" she asks.

"I like the taste of baby aspirin."

"Pain pills are my favorite. Especially little blue ones. Gotta love those blue pills."

"I haven't done too many drugs. Tried cocaine once. Never again."

"Why?"

"I ended up in bed with a professional body builder."

"Man or woman?" she asks.

"I'm still not sure," I answer. "But at the end of three days, I swore right then and there if I could ever walk again, I'd walk out the door and never do it again.

"You know what I wanna do to you?" Vivian asks, peering at me wide-eyed and childlike.

"No," I say straight-faced, "but I know what I *want* you to do to me."

She slaps me playfully on the arm. "Stop it."

"Nope, can't do that. If I can agree to your so-called straight tendencies and agree to never touch you, the least you can do is acquiesce to my verbal flirtations."

"Say that again. In plain English," she counters.

"I said...show me your tits."

"Okay. Why not, everyone else has seen them," she agrees. "But only if you let me do to you what I want to do."

"Hmmm..." I weigh the possibilities in each hand like a scale. "Done. Do with me what you will."

This wasn't exactly what I was expecting. Here I stand in the middle of Vivian's fantasy bedroom, fully dressed in her old cheerleading uniform. She has on an identical uniform and looks happier than I've ever seen her. She has on the home games uniform and made me put on the away games uniform. "My mother would be so proud," I say.

"I can still do the splits," she brags.

"Yeah, well, I could never do the splits. So I'm sure as hell not gonna try them now."

She tosses an extra set of pom-poms at me, saying, "Follow me."

I've done some things I regret in my life but somehow I think this is going to be at the top of the list. I lethargically follow Vivian's pom-pom motions.

"C'mon!" she shouts. "Where's your spirit?"

"My spirit has been smothered by humiliation." To prove my point, I plop down on the bed and cover my face with my arm.

"Get up," she says, throwing a pillow at me. "You can do this. It's simple."

"I don't wanna," I mumble into my arm.

"Listen, if I can teach stupid Sue Anne, I can teach you. On your feet."

"Okay, okay," I sigh and get back up.

"Just clap your thighs when I do. Watch." Vivian makes her arms rigid and slaps the outside of her thighs, saying, "Ready. Okay."

I give it a try. "Ready. Okay."

"Do it like you mean it," she instructs. "With me."

"Ready. Okay," we say, slapping our thighs.

"Again," she drills. "Do it *with* me."

Again. "Ready. Okay."

Vivian sighs. "By *with* me, I meant at the same time as me. Not after me. Not before me. Try it again."

I really try this time. I give it my all. "Ready. Okay."

By the look of her disgusted face, I guess I didn't do so good.

She grabs my pom-poms from me. "You don't deserve these," she says, tossing them into the corner.

"Cheerleading's harder than I thought," I say in a half-hearted effort to cheer her up.

She perks up again. "Wanna play Barbies?"

"You wouldn't like how I play Barbies," I answer. "I shave their heads. Bury them in the backyard up to their necks and pour syrup on them."

"We can do that later," she says and tosses me an old used Barbie. She grabs another Barbie, one much prettier than mine, I notice, but decline to comment.

Vivian sits on the floor Indian-style and pats the space across from her. I sit where she wants, but don't have the slightest idea what to do. "I've never done this before," I admit.

"Just follow my lead and do what comes naturally."

She holds her Barbie up in the air by its legs and speaks for the doll, "What do you want to do tonight, Midge?"

"I can see your lips moving," I retort.

Vivian glares at me and through clenched teeth snarls, "Play along or I won't show you my tits."

Feeling oh-so-stupid, I hold my doll up in the air by its legs and pretend she's speaking in a little high voice, "Can you believe it's been fifteen years since high school, Barbie? Seems like only yesterday when we were cheerleaders. I wonder if I can still do the splits?"

Barbie deadpans, "Looks like you've had a few *banana* splits."

"Yeah. Now I'd probably be at the bottom of the pyramid."

"You would be the pyramid."

"You're so hateful," Midge says. "And I know why. It's because you can't bend your arms. If you could bend your arms and pleasure yourself once in awhile then you wouldn't be so hateful all the time."

"No, my problem is that Ken has no genitalia. That would make any girl grumpy," Barbie reasons.

Midge responds, "We should complain to Mattel. Grab a pen, Barbie, write this down. 'Dear Mattel, as our creator, you must know that I have lived for thirty-two years without a belly button, nipples or any girlie parts. Could you please reconsider your stance on this very important issue?'"

"Also," Barbie writes, "I would prefer to be paired with the manly and bearded G.I. Joe doll as Ken is a eunuch."

"And instead of pink high heels," Midge interjects, "can I have some flip-flops? Water retention and bunions are killing me."

"And a pink feathered merkin," Barbie adds. Vivian looks at me and says in an aside, "What the hell, the squeaky wheel gets the grease, right?"

"And P.S.," Barbie continues, "can you make my arms bendable? I'm awfully cranky. Sincerely, Midge and Barbie."

"P.S.S," I add, "while you're at it, can you give my best friend Skipper bigger tits?"

Vivian whops me in the arm with her Barbie, laughing.

"Now show me your tits," Midge says to Barbie.

Barbie strips off her blouse and sexy dances in front of Midge.

"You're a dirty girl, Barbie. A dirty, dirty girl," Midge says.

Hours go by in minutes and seconds tick on for days. That's the miracle of whiskey and Xanax. By now we're both back under the tent. I'm in just an old T-shirt of Vivian's and my boxers and she wears some cute little baby-doll pajamas. How long we've been under here I have no idea, but it feels like centuries. In a good kinda way. We're both really sleepy, but like little kids we want to stay awake just one more minute.

"So what do you do, anyway?" Vivian asks, sleepily, "just live off all the women who throw themselves at you?"

"I've never had a woman throw herself at me. I've had them throw shit at me."

"C'mon...all the women stare at you. Everywhere we go. You think I haven't noticed?"

"Everyone stares at freaks," I respond. "It's human nature."

"Self-deprecation is not a lovely quality," says Vivian. "What do you do for money?"

"You mean before you threw yourself at me and started paying my way?"

"Exactly."

"I buy old motorcycles. Fix 'em up. Sell 'em."

"There a lot of money in that?" she asks.

"Not much. I really want to start my own motorcycle repair shop, though."

She perks up. "Really?"

"Yeah, I think I'd be pretty good at it."

"Does it hurt to get a tattoo?" she asks, tracing one finger lightly over my sleeve.

"Not really. A little. You want one? I could make a tattoo gun, I know how. I could give you a butterfly or something."

"I think not," she yawns. "But if you ever learn to do breast implants let me know." Then she closes her eyes and promptly falls asleep.

I watch her still face for a moment before I whisper, "Are you asleep?"

She doesn't answer, so I guess she is.

"If you don't wake up, I'm going to peek at your tits," I whisper lightly.

"Leave my tits alone. Tell me a bedtime story so I can go to sleep."

"Okay...a bedtime story. This is the story of our adventure. Once upon a time, in the not-so-distant future, there is a pandemic flu that wipes out most of mankind. Only the lowliest, the scourge of the planet are left. Which means me, of course. I steal a Harley and ride across the scorched earth. I sleep in Walmarts at night. I live on pork rinds and Oreos. I answer to no one. I only change my clothes once a week and I find great comfort in my own smell. My hair dreads naturally. I never shave my armpits or my legs ever again. And when I find you trying to walk across the desert in your fancy Choos, I give you a ride. We wear surgical masks as we ride through the desert sandstorm. We eat canned beans and laugh at our own farts. We raid pharmacies and count ourselves as lucky to still be alive days later. I defend your womanhood from the lowly scavengers by using aerosol hairspray and a Bic lighter. I paint my surgical mask to show flames coming out of my mouth. I am known to all as FireBreather. And one bright moon-filled night, you awaken from your drug-induced slumber. You walk out to the Walmart parking lot and find me in a compromising position with Queen Latifah. She's taking me from behind by brute force and I don't look like I'm enjoying it. You pull a bow and arrow out of your big, red bag and harpoon Queen in her fleshy buttocks. She screams like a little girl and limps away. I am most grateful for your defense of my womanhood. To show my undying adoration, I self-tattoo a picture of you with only one breast, aiming your bow and arrow. On my left calf. Forever after you are known as Amazonia. You are highly feared by all. FireBreather and Amazonia rule the earth. Such as it may be. There is no money on this new earth. The only currency we have is your womanly flower which we use to barter for gasoline. And I like to ride my bike a lot, so get ready."

Vivian sighs, "Oh, I just adore happily ever after." Then she's off to sleep for good.

I crawl out of the tent and find my ugly Midge doll. I strip her down naked and carefully dress her in Ken's jeans and turquoise wife-beater. Somehow this small act comforts me. I crawl back inside the tent and lay down beside Vivian with Midge clasped tightly in my fist.

I pose aloud the question that's been bugging me lately, "If I never have sex again, am I still a lesbian?" With this question echoing in my soggy brain, I nestle up next to Vivian and fall into a deep, deep sleep.

I wake up to a nightmare. Vivian's face is hanging upside down just inches from my own. Why is her hair suddenly orange? Her upside down mouth moves—she's yelling and talking non-stop—oh my God. That's not Vivian, it's her mother. Her mother has pulled up a tent flap and is looking in at us. I just manage to catch the last bit of what Mom is saying: "—Are you pregnant?!"

Vivian props herself up on both elbows and shouts back to her mother, "I'm not pregnant and stop yelling! I'm not deaf either!"

But that doesn't faze Mom. "Well, then you better stop stuffing your face with Daddy's cupcakes because you look pregnant! And what in God's good name is with your hair? Did you cut it that way on purpose?! Get ready, I'm going to take you to my beautician! She can fix that mess! She does wonders with overprocessed hair! I've been wanting you to meet her!"

Mom rips the bedspread off us and whips it back on the bed, shouting the whole while, "She's the prettiest little thing! Though Lord knows she wasn't always so little! She's lost a whole bunch of weight, but she always did have such a pretty face! Her name is Cindi and she married a Negra man and has three kids! Those Negras don't seem to mind a big tookus on a woman, but she lost it anyway, thank the good Lord!"

Mom smooths out the wrinkles on the bedspread and stands back with her hands on her narrow hips to admire her handiwork. "Those kids of hers are all such a pretty color!"

She looks over at me still lying on the floor and wrinkles her nose in disgust. She whispers loudly to Vivian like I'm not even in the room, "What have I told you about bringing strange men into this house?"

Vivian giggles and shouts back, "He's not that strange, Mom!"

Mom spins on her pointy high-heeled shoes, shouting through the doorway, "R.J! She's back!! And she brought home a tattooed sailor this time!"

Mom exits the bedroom with a bounce and a flourish, taking most of the oxygen with her.

Vivian and I stare at each other, unblinking, for a solid minute.

"She'll calm down after her morning pills kick in," Vivian states.

I fetch my jeans and boots and jacket out of the car while Vivian takes a shower. I go through her closet and find a really cool old Chargers T-shirt. I jump in the shower after her and scrub all the makeup off my face and let my dreads down. I've never felt so good to be just myself.

By the time Vivian and I make our appearance in the kitchen, Dottie (Vivian told me her mom's name is Dottie) is flipping the pancakes off the griddle. Vivian's dad, R.J., is pouring a gallon of syrup over his stack of pancakes.

R.J. is a pretty good-looking man. Kinda skinny, but in a good wiry kinda way. Strong chin and bright blue eyes. His hair's all gray, but he has lots of it. And the man's not afraid to eat.

Vivian beelines straight up to him and plants a kiss on his cheek. He doesn't say anything, but his eyes light up.

Dottie points her spatula at Vivian like it's a weapon (and maybe it is for all I know). "Aren't you even going to introduce us to your young man?" she asks.

Vivian laughs, cups her hand around her mother's ear and whispers. Dottie's eyes open wide and she looks me up and down.

"Well..." Dottie starts, "does your *lady* friend want some pancakes?!"

"Yes, ma'am, please," I say, taking the chair across from Vivian.

I feel the urgent need to fill the conversation void so I steer to friendly territory. "I see where Marie Osmond has another fan. Besides me, I mean."

Vivian throws me a look like I've lost my mind, but Dottie brightens and gives me a huge smile. "Oh, do you like Marie also?" she asks.

"Who doesn't," I say. "You know her career has spanned forty years now. That right there is a testament to her God-given talent," I lie profusely, "...if you ask me, that is."

And that's all it takes. Dottie is off and running. "Marie has eight children, you know! And she still finds time to run her doll business, write books and even do shows in Las Vegas with Donny, that adorable brother of hers! She's lost a lot of weight, too! She's on a commercial for that diet lady! Jenny Craig? No, I think it's Nutrisystem! She says she's lost forty-one pounds! But I think they're lying! It looks to me just like they fluffed her hair higher and had her stand at an angle!" She leans down and whispers, "Poor thing. Her son killed himself, you know."

Vivian and her dad and I grin at each other over our pancakes.

I volunteer to wash the breakfast dishes like a good Eddie Haskell and as I dry and stack, I listen to Vivian and Dottie yelling at each other in the back part of the house. "You're not supposed to take three ibuprofen all at the same time, Vivian! The directions say to just take one tablet every four hours!"

"I'm taking a whole day's worth!" Vivian shouts back. "Besides, those are suggestions, not directions. The more pills you take, the happier you feel!"

"You take this lightly and you die!" Dottie shouts again.

"Well, I wish someone would put me out of my fucking misery!"

A door slams from somewhere deep within the bowels of the house.

Then, thank God, I hear the siren call of an engine in distress.

I walk out to the backyard and see R.J. sitting on a brand-new riding lawnmower. He's red in the face and sweating in the hot sun. He's giving 'er hell, turning the key and pumping the gas, but the engine only catches hold for a few seconds before petering out. He's tried to turn it over so many times the battery's damn near dead. I watch him for a moment in silence. I know better than to tell a man anything about engines.

He catches sight of me and one side of his mouth turns up in a self-conscious smile. "Must've flooded it," he says.

"No, sir," I say. "Sounds like you got some condensation in the fuel line. Happens a lot round here with all the humidity in the air."

"You think?" he asks, his tone neutral.

I take his response as an invitation to proceed, so I do. I locate the gas tank and follow the fuel line to the in-line filter. I unclip the filter, drain it, and wave it around in the air, drying it out. After a while I blow on it just to make sure.

R.J. interrupts my blowing by asking, "How long were you in for?"

I shrug like I'd been expecting the question. "Twelve years. How'd you know?"

"I didn't for sure. Till you just told me."

I smile. I think I'm going to like this man.

"Does Vivian know?" he asks.

"Sure. She knows," I say. "I told her all about it."

I pop the filter back on the fuel line and clip it.

"I mean does she know that you got feelings for her?" he asks.

That one sets me back a minute. I look him in the eye. Vivian's got his eyes. It's like he's looking straight into my head and seeing what's there. "That obvious, huh?" I answer.

"She have those kinda feelings for you?"

"No, sir, she doesn't."

"There's been a man calling here for her. Has a foreign accent. Like that Benny Hill character. You know anything about it?"

I look down at my shoes for the answer, but when I don't find it I say, "I might know something."

He pooches out his bottom lip, deep in thought (just like Vivian does), climbs back on the mower and looks out over the yard like he's surveying it.

"You'll have to excuse my wife for yelling all the time," he says. "After thirty years I started ignoring her. I guess she got it in her head that I was going deaf. Now she screams and I pretend not to hear. It's just the way it is."

It reminds me of the old Hell's Angels adage, 'It is what it is.' Sometimes that just explains it all.

R.J. doesn't seem to need a response from me, so I don't give one. He pumps the gas pedal, pulls out the choke and turns the key. The mower coughs a couple of times, starts up with a loud growl then idles to a purr. He gives me a big thumbs-up and shouts over the engine, "Be careful!"

Somehow I know exactly what he's talking about.

He takes off on the mower, spitting cut grass out on the driveway, leaving me nodding after him.

I amble back inside the house. It's deathly quiet. Vivian isn't in the kitchen. She's not in the Marie O. living room. Or if she is, she's standing so still she blends in. She's not in the bathroom. I open the door to her bedroom, but it looks the same as when we left it. She's not in her bathroom either. I hear the lawnmower cut off outside. I'm thinking I might have to go have a second look at it when Dottie looms in the doorway.

"What're you doing to her?" she asks.

I look over my shoulder thinking maybe she's talking to someone behind me. Nope, nobody there.

"With who?" I ask, softly.

"You know who," she says. "She's all hepped up on pills and God only knows what else."

Dottie's slurring a little herself. Guess those morning pills are working their magic. She continues, her eyes glazed over, "She looks like homemade soap. She used to be so pretty. Now she's dressing like a you-know-what and doing drugs. What're you doing to her?"

"I'm not doing anything," I answer. "I found her that way."

"I know what you are. You're one of those..." she pauses for emphasis, then hisses the word, "...liberaltines."

"You say that like it's a bad thing."

I make a move to leave the room, but, oh my God, she sways over in front of the doorway blocking the exit. I glance around the room, looking for another way out. There's the window, but I don't know if I want to do anything that drastic.

"A sexual deviant is what you are. Doing all kinds of nastiness with my daughter. You've brainwashed her with your ugly, unnatural ways."

"You got me pegged, Dot." A nervous giggle rises to the surface, but I swallow it back down. I can't laugh right now. This woman is so close to the edge, that would send her right on over.

"I've read about people like you. Miss or Mister or whatever you call yourself. I've seen entire TV movies about your type. Picking up unsus...unsuspectant...unsuspecting young girls and forcing them to do strange spelunking things," she says.

"I think you're getting me mixed up with a National Geographic show."

Dottie drops to her knees and clasps her hands in front of her face, saying, "I'm going to pray for you. Pray with me."

"I don't think we'll be praying for the same thing," I say before I open the window and crawl out.

I drop to the ground and hear Vivian scream, "Get your motherfucking hands offa me!"

I haul ass in the direction of the scream, but as I round the house I slam on the brakes. There's Prince Charles and his two goons. P.C. has Vivian backed up over the grille of his black BMW. The two goons hold her dad back. Each one has R.J. by an arm and he's fighting them like a madman, but he's no match for these heavyweights.

Vivian lays back on the Beamer's hood and kicks her spikey heels at P.C., letting loose with the longest stream of obscenities I've ever heard. I can't hear what he's saying over her screaming, but he still has control over his composure. Of course, he's British and they always seem composed.

I hide behind the corner of the house. I run through all

my options. I don't have a gun. They probably do. They got us outmanpowered, so mano a mano won't work. I could call the cops, but what would I tell them? That these nice British men just want the money we stole from them? We're in the middle of a residential street and it won't be long before a neighbor calls the cops. I don't have much time.

Then I remember Elvis.

I climb back through the window and am relieved to see that Dottie has finished praying, left the room and moved on to another corner of her Republican, Xanax-soaked mind. I go straight for the cabinet in the living room, throw open the door and pull out fat Elvis. I hope Vivian wasn't exaggerating about the game her and R.J. play. I uncork Elvis's head and find, sure enough, R.J. has already filled him back up.

Next I dash into the kitchen and grab the newspaper from the top of the table. I rip off the top sheet (leaving the sports section behind in case R.J. hasn't had time to read that yet) and wad it up. I take a giant swig from Elvis, thinking what the hell's it going to hurt, and stuff the newspaper as far down Elvis's throat as I can. I pat my pocket. Yep, I got my trusty pocketknife and my Bic lighter with me.

Ready to roll. I run out the front door and sneak Davy Crockett-style to the Mercedes we left on the street the night before. I climb in and peek over the dash. Yep, Viv is still kicking like a hellcat and R.J.'s still straining against the goons. It's taking both of them to hold a seventy-year-old man and they're the ones sweating. Good for him.

I start the car, stick Elvis between my legs and the Bic in my mouth. Okay, you stupid British, red-coat wearing sumbitches, here comes the cavalry. Drawing on all my TV Roller Derby viewing, I gun the car straight toward the Beamer.

R.J. and the goons see me coming first. The goons drop R.J.'s arms and dive in opposite directions. R.J. backpeddles as fast as he can, which is pretty darn fast. P.C. catches sight of me, his eyes widen in terror, and he looks like he might just piss his pants. So much for composure.

Vivian rolls over on the hood, recognizes me and smiles the biggest smile I've ever seen. She hops up on top of the Beamer and, my God, I think, she's going to start cheering right here. I bear down on them fast and at the last possible second, pull out my best Roller Derby move. I jerk the wheel hard to my right, send the car spinning clockwise and hip-check the back of the Beamer.

Unfazed, Vivian jumps from the hood of the Beamer to the trunk of the Mercedes and before you can even say Revolutionary War she's in the passenger seat. I step out of the car, light the newspaper serving as Elvis's head, look P.C. directly in the eye and yell, "You English may have a Queen, but we've got the King!"

I wind up and pitch Elvis into the front seat of the Beamer. He shatters and a couple of mad flames jump.

I throw myself back into the Mercedes, stomp on the gas and we are so gone. We're already three blocks away when—BOOM!

Viv sits on her knees and stares out the back window. She mutters with awe, "Holy shit..." She turns to face me as I pull out onto the highway, merging with the traffic. "That was amazing, Lee, truly fucking amazing. I didn't know you had it in you."

I shrug like it was nothing. "Your mom called me a liberaltine. It pissed me off."

CHAPTER NINE

"It's not like I knew a Mercedes would just break down like that," I mumble to Vivian's back side.

Vivian and I are walking down some deserted country road and I have no idea if we're walking toward town or away from it. Thank God for a full moon or I wouldn't be able to even see the road under my boots. Vivian struggles to balance in her high heels and that leaves me to carry the two bags of money and her giant red bag that has all her essentials for life in it. I feel like some kind of damn packhorse. Sweat rolls down my back forming a little river down my buttcrack.

"You told me you were a mechanic," she answers without turning around.

"Not on cars. Especially German cars. Hell, they're not even supposed to break down in the first place. Mercedes is like the

Maytag of cars. And even if I could fix it where am I going to get the parts? Out in the middle of the country? You're the one who thought we should get off the main roads. Like we're Bonnie and Clyde or some such shit."

I set a bag down and unstick the back of my shirt from my skin.

"Pick it back up," Vivian orders with her back still to me. I heft it back up (not because she told me to) and wonder not for the first time how little pieces of paper could weigh so goddamn much. Is this what rich people feel like, money is a burden? I think I was a lot happier when I only had ten dollars in my pocket.

Vivian stops in her tracks and points off to our left. "Look. It's a midget farm."

I follow her finger and see what she means. There's an old ramshackle farmhouse set back from the road and it's surrounded by a dozen or more little plaster people with pointy hats, peeking over the tall weeds.

"Gnomes," I say, "not midgets. Those're decorative yard art."

Vivian picks her way through the yard and up to where most of the gnomes are gathered.

"I feel so tall," she remarks.

"Have you been taking some of your pills when I wasn't looking?"

"Just a couple of blue ones," she says reassuringly.

"I'm going to knock on the door. Maybe they have a phone or something."

"Be careful," she warns, "I saw this once in a movie and it didn't turn out so good."

"What movie was it?"

"I don't remember the name of it but there was this really pretty woman who could sing and these seven little men held her hostage."

"*Snow White*," I say. "It's a cartoon movie."

"It's still scary."

She perches her butt on top of an old camper shell sitting in the middle of the yard and takes off her heels. Rubbing her feet, she looks up at me and asks, "Can you look in the red bag and hand me some of my La Prairie age management balance lotion?"

"You're kidding," is all I say.

"No, it's really good on feet. It says for the face, but it works wonders on your feet too."

"Do you think right now is really the best time to be rubbing lotion on your feet?" I ask way too loudly.

"When should I do it?!" Vivian shouts back. "When my feet look *really* old? Then it's a little late, don't you think?"

I have my mouth open to yell back, but at that precise moment the porch light blazes on. I jerk my head to look and freeze with my mouth still wide open. Silhouetted against the harsh light is the strangest looking human-like creature I've ever seen. She's maybe four feet tall with a ginormous head and lopsided shoulders. I look a little closer and realize it's not that she's so short, it's that she's missing her legs from the knees down and is balancing precariously on her stumps. The next thing I notice is that she's got a double-barrel 12 gauge shotgun aimed right at me.

"Wrong movie," I whisper to Viv out of the side of my mouth. "This is more like *Deliverance*."

Vivian bounces to her bare feet, exclaiming, "Sandy? Is that you?"

Sandy swings the shotgun toward Vivian. "Who are you?" she snarls. "Did Bongo send you?"

"It's me! Vivian Baxter! From high school?"

Sandy's tough-gal exterior cracks a little. "The cheerleader Vivian Baxter?"

"Yes! Remember we sat next to each other in home ec? We made a chocolate cake together and we cheated and used canned icing from Walmart."

"I remember." Sandy laughs a little, then swings the gun back at me. "Who's that you got with you?"

"It's Lee Anne. From high school. Remember her?"

"Swallowed the guppy?" Sandy asks.

"Goldfish," I correct softly.

"That's her." Vivian laughs.

Sandy pulls her gun up into a tighter grip and asks, "What the hell happened to your hair?"

"I...um...I dreaded it," I explain.

"On purpose?" she asks.

"Yeah..."

"Looks like a cat sucked on it." Sandy laughs.

I don't think it's particularly funny, but I figure the best thing to do in this situation is to laugh along with her.

Appeased, Sandy sets the shotgun down inside the door and flips on the inside lights. "I'd invite you all in but the cats don't like people. Let me get my legs on and I'll come out to you."

She disappears back inside the house and as soon as she shuts the door, I shut my mouth and look at Vivian. "She's going to get her legs on."

"Thank God," Vivian says. "I was sure I was getting taller this time."

I'm still a little afraid she's going to pop back out with the shotgun, so I keep my feet planted where they are, lean a little to my left and peer through her front window. It looks like a pretty ordinary house from what I can see. Except for...is that a Christmas tree hanging upside down from her living room ceiling?

"Viv, I think she's got an upside down Christmas tree hanging from her ceiling fan."

"So the cats won't get in it," she says matter-of-factly.

"Oh." As an afterthought I add, "But it's nowhere near Christmastime."

Exasperated with my stupidity, Vivian says, "How the hell is she going to take it down when she doesn't even have legs?"

"Oh."

Vivian handles all this like it's a normal turn of events. Like seeing a half-legless woman aim a gun at her is just within the realm of usual. Me, myself, I'm a little weirded out. Like I just walked into a horror movie and even though there's scary music coming from the dark basement, I go down the steps anyway.

I hear Sandy before I see her. Eek, eek, eek, eek, her metal prosthetic legs squeak with each step. She eeks out onto the porch, holds up a bottle of Wild Turkey and announces, "Git your butts on up here. I haven't had company in so long, I'm gonna make this a party."

I follow Vivian on up to the porch and situate myself on the steps while Vivian sits on the swing next to Sandy. We all take turns taking long pulls off the whiskey bottle and relax to the cricket music.

"Our car broke down several miles back," I offer even though she hasn't ever asked.

"I figured," Sandy says. "That's all that ever comes out this way. Lost or broken-down people. I'd offer you a phone if I had one."

"I don't know who I'd call anyway," I say.

Sandy continues, "I'd offer you a bed but the cats have taken over everything inside. You're more than welcome to sleep in the camper shell, though."

I'd rather die than sleep in a camper shell that's just lying on the cold hard ground, but I tell her thank you anyway.

"Nice peaceful place you got here," I venture.

Sandy takes another drink and replies, "Yep. Got a couple hundred acres. My son, Bongo, lives next door on the other side of that there windbreak. Good thing you found my place before you found his."

Vivian asks the same question I'm thinking, "Why'd you name him Bongo?"

"On account of his head shape. He's not quite all there. Prolly 'cause I gave birth to him during my first psychotic break. He fancies himself an international spy or something like that. Says he works undercover for the CIA. He's not a bad sort, just a little off. He sure helps me out, though. Ever since the threshing accident." Sandy raises her fake legs up for us to see, just in case we had missed them the first time.

"I can fix that squeak for you," I offer.

She smiles real big, "That'd be nice. All this noise drives the cats crazy. They're always trying to pounce on me just to catch the mouse."

I jump up off the steps and grab Viv's lotion from the top of the camper shell where she left it. Just to be extra safe I push all the bags inside the shell. I sit back down by Sandy's metal legs and dab the lotion in every joint.

"So what happened after high school?" Vivian asks. "I heard you and Larry Dale got married."

Sandy nods. "Had a baby first. Then got hitched. Then got divorced. Boom boom boom. All in three years time. Don't feel sorry for me, though. Divorcing Larry Dale was the best thing I ever did. Don't know why I married him in the first place. He caught me in one of my low spells and popped the question so I said yes."

"Yeah, I know what you mean," Vivian agrees. "I married my first husband out of stupidity. My second and third was just plain ol' low self-esteem."

"Three?" I gulp. "You been married three times?"

Vivian ignores me.

"You had low self-esteem? You were always the prettiest girl in school. If not in the whole county," Sandy says.

"I didn't know that then. I was always trying to live up to my mother's expectations. To her I was always too fat. Or too stupid. Or too whatever. I think she always viewed me as competition for my daddy's attention."

I interject. "Where's he at now? Larry Dale, I mean."

"Six feet under. He was tearing down a big brick silo with a rented backhoe. Stupid little man. Silo fell one way 'stead of the other and he got himself crushed. I always knew something like that would happen to him. He walked through life like he was walking through a minefield, just waiting for one to go off. I think that's the main reason I divorced him. He was like that ol' cow out in the corner of the pasture. You don't wanna get too attached 'cause you know he's just gonna get et."

I screw the lid back on the lotion jar. "Test them out," I say.

Sandy works her legs back and forth and not a squeak comes from them. "I'll be damned," she says by way of a thank-you. She offers me the whiskey bottle and says, "I hope I'm not being too nosy, but I heard that you was sent to prison."

I take a long swig before I nod.

"I bet you saw some things in there you'd rather forget."

I don't know how to respond. Vivian studies my face, looking for a clue and I'm suddenly thankful for the darkness. "Most of the stuff I want to forget..." I begin, "happened out here. Not in there."

"What was prison like if you don't mind me asking?"

I think for a moment before answering. "You get used to it pretty quick. There's some good things. You always know what you're going to wear. You always know what you're going to do. What you're going to eat. You get to read a lot. I learned how to make eyeliner out of cigarette ashes and Christmas decorations out of sanitary napkins."

"Martha Stewart should do a program about that. Useful things. Not how to fold napkins into duck shapes," says Sandy.

"Maybe she could do a whole show about a thousand and one uses for face lotion," I joke.

That cracks them both up and I rest easier knowing the conversation is going in another direction. Vivian takes the lotion out of my hand and without asking begins to rub it on Sandy's leg stumps. She seems agreeable enough to the pampering.

"I can't help but admire your shoes, Vivian. Are those Jimmy Choos?" Sandy asks.

"Why, yes they are. Thank you for noticing."

"I pay pretty close attention to shoes," Sandy explains. "Never gave them a thought until I couldn't have them no more."

"I've always been addicted to shoes," Vivian explains. "I'll take a good pair of shoes over love any day. You don't have to feed them, they don't go out and fuck around on you, and they don't leave the toilet seat up."

"I like that philosophy." Sandy laughs.

"What's that over there?" I ask Sandy. "Over there by the big satellite dish. It's looks like a motorcycle under that tarp."

"It is."

"It's broke down?" I ask.

Sandy shakes her head. "No, the damn thing runs just fine. Loud as hell, though. That's the only thing Larry Dale left me when he went. A damn two-wheeled thing I can't never drive. Maybe he thought that was funny, I dunno."

"You ever thought about selling it?" I ask.

Sandy peers at me through the shadows, then asks, "Why? You want it?"

"I'd pay you the going price for it."

"It's not worth much to me," she says. "And I hate looking at it."

"I'll give you my shoes for it," Vivian pipes up.

Sandy laughs long and hard, swinging her metal legs up in the arm with each guffaw. "Now why on earth would I need shoes?" she chortles.

Vivian looks at her seriously for a long moment before saying, "Every woman needs a little hope, don't you think?"

"Hope for what?" Sandy chortles. "For my legs to grow back? Like my mama always said, 'Hope in one hand and shit in the other. See which gets full the quickest.'"

Vivian shakes her head and says quietly, "I'd rather be holding a handful of dreams than a handful of shit."

"I know what Viv means," I tell Sandy. "In prison I had a magazine picture of a countryside, just green grass covered hills and a road cutting through. I taped it by my cot and stared at it all the time. And dreamed. It got me through."

That makes Sandy stop and think. The bottle makes a full circle and when it comes back to her, she raises it in the air to Vivian and says, "It's a done deal. I'd rather look at those shoes than that damn motorcycle any day."

And we sit like that until well after the whiskey's gone. Just chatting and inhaling the sweet Oklahoma night air. It's like we're in the eye of the tornado, calm and peaceful, with all kinds of crazy shit whirling around us.

A couple of hours later Viv and I are drunk and sleeping it off on the hard ground inside the camper shell with nothing but an empty bottle of whiskey and an empty jar of lotion, using the bags of money as pillows.

I wake up at some point in the middle of the night, still half-drunk, all spooned up behind Vivian. I've been sleeping with my right arm wrapped around her and my tittie-dominant hand cupping one of her tits. I guess she's really drunk too, because she doesn't seem to know or care. I start to carefully remove my hand when I see a big white face peering at us through the camper shell window.

I freeze. For half a second, I think it's Prince Charles or one of his goons. Then I see the head shape. It's Bongo.

A mouthful of big white teeth grin at me through the darkness and I hear the face say, "You ain't gotta worry. I'm a secret agent. Them three British spies chasing you won't give you no more trouble." Then as quick as he appeared, he's gone.

I spend the rest of the night awake, blinking in the darkness, clutching Viv's tit for security. I don't fall asleep until dawn.

I've been up and about for maybe an hour checking out my new motorcycle. It looks to be in perfect working order once I brush off the cobwebs and kitty paw prints. It's a beautiful Harley. Scarlet Red and chrome with aferings and floorboards. I figure this bike cost a good twenty grand brand new. Even the tires still have all the tread on them. All that's left to do is get it on the road and blow the pipes out real good. I sit on it, testing out the balance and the shocks and daydream about the open road.

Vivian finally wakes up and crawls on her belly out of the shell. She stumbles her way over to the windbreak and crouches down in some tall weeds to pee. She squats in between a couple of gnomes and reaches out and turns their little faces away from her so she can pee in privacy.

"Question," Viv says, still bent down. "Do all girlie parts look the same?"

The stuff that comes out of her mouth never ceases to amaze me. "Good morning to you, too."

"Do they?" she asks again.

"I dunno," I say, half-embarrassed. "I'm no expert."

"Well, I've only seen my own. How many have you seen?"

"Viv, seriously, it's early."

She pushes, "How many?"

"Too many."

"Do they all look the same?"

She's not going to give up, so I play along. "Does all male genitalia look the same to you?" I throw back.

"God, no," she answers. "English men aren't even circumcised."

"Gross."

She hitches up her panties and takes her time scratching her butt. "Answer me this. Do Chinese women have slanted ones?"

I roll my eyes. I don't know why exactly but this conversation is starting to piss me off. I answer her in my exasperated voice, "Yes, Vivian, Chinese women have slanted ones. And white women have white ones. And black women have black ones. And Jewish women have cold ones."

She high-steps her way through the weeds and over toward me. "What about Indians?"

"Indian dot or Indian feather?"

"Indian feather."

Once I get a good look at her I know exactly what it is that's pissing me off and it has nothing to do with this topic of conversation. It has to do with her tits. Which right now are halfway spilling out of her bra and she doesn't even care if I see. Or maybe she does care. Maybe she's planned it that way and wants me to see them. Maybe she wasn't too drunk or asleep last night and she was fully aware I was latched on to her tits. She either really wants me, or she's teasing me just for kicks, or she's oblivious. And if that's the case, I'm tired of acting like I'm oblivious to her being oblivious.

"I asked you a question. What about Indian ones."

"Don't know and don't care," I reply sharply.

She turns her back to me and buttons up her shirt. "What's wrong with Indians?" she asks.

"What's right with them?"

When she turns back around her shirt is buttoned up higher than I've ever seen it before and she has a tone in her voice when she asks, "What'd they ever do to you?"

I don't understand where this line of questioning is coming from and I certainly don't understand where it's going. All I know is I'm hungry and cranky and hungover and she just buttoned her shirt up on me. "Free medical care. That's what they did to me. They get free fuckin' medical care and I don't get squat because I'm white or my grandma wasn't on their rolls. And they get free land and free houses built on them. Or if they rent a house they get most of their rent paid for. And they hire each other to work in the casinos but not white people. And butter and cheese. All the free fuckin' butter and cheese they can eat. All because five generations ago some white people gave them firewater and smallpox and made their soft little feet walk barefoot in the snow which means three generations later they get free cheese and don't have to pay taxes on cigarettes. And most of them don't even look like an Indian's supposed to look. But the thing that pisses me off the most is the cheese."

She sticks out her bottom lip and glares at me long and hard. "I'm Indian," she says flatly.

Oh, fucking great. This is exactly what I hate about women. They lure you into a trap and then snap your foot off. "That figures," I say.

"Well, then," she says and actually buttons the very last button on her shirt, "I guess that decides it then."

"Decides what?" I sigh.

She lobs a grenade right at me. "I was going to fuck you. But not now."

The bomb hits me right in the gut and explodes. "You were not," I say breathlessly.

She walks back to the camper shell and snaps and buckles the two bags. "No, I totally was. But not now. No, ma'am, not now, not *ever*."

She bends over and points her ass in my general direction, and just to spite her I refuse to look at it for longer than five seconds.

"I don't believe you," I say. "You're just being a bitch."

Vivian glances at me, then throws the red bag over her shoulder and picks up the two money bags. She sighs loudly, "Doesn't matter really. It was just going to be a pity fuck anyway."

"You pity me?" I yell. "The little red-headed Indian Princess pities *me*?"

"Not anymore I don't, you white supremacist bitch!" she hurls. And with that she turns and walks toward the road swinging the bags along with her.

I follow her a good ways. I don't know if I'm going to try and stop her or if I'm going to wish her good riddance. Maybe I just want to see how far she can get barefooted.

"Don't even think about following me," she says without so much as a backward glance.

"Where you going?" I yell. "Is there a free cheese line somewhere?"

She turns on her heel and glares at me. "Yep. And you ain't getting none of this cheese. Oh! One last thing before I never talk to you again..." She rummages around in her bra, pulls out a key and throws it at me. "Here's the key to your *free* motorcycle that an Indian Princess got for you."

I snatch the key out of the air before it smacks me in the face. Vivian turns back around and marches toward town. I watch her go until she's completely crested the little hill and gone from view. There's no way in hell I'm going after her.

An hour later I'm going after her on the bike. I catch sight of her about five miles down the road. I wince just thinking about her walking so far on this dirt road with her soft lotioned feet. I pull around her, then ease the Harley over to the side.

"Need a ride?" I ask, sheepishly.

"Nope," she answers without looking at me.

She walks a wide arc around me. I guess she's not going to make this easy. I get off the bike and run to catch up to her. "You gonna walk all the way to town?"

"Yep."

"But it's like ten more miles, Viv."

She flashes her eyes at me, then says, "My ancestors walked one thousand miles, I think I can handle ten."

"Oh for chrissakes, Vivian, just get on the bike and let me ride you into town."

"Nope."

"Okay," I breathe. "I'm sorry."

"What?"

I say it a little louder. "I'm sorry."

"What?"

"You heard me."

"Yeah, I heard you," she says. "I just want you to say it again."

"I'm sorry. I am really, truly sorry. Now will you please get on the bike and let me ride you into town?"

Vivian spins around and walks back to the bike, dropping the bags for me. She stands to the side the whole time, her arms crossed over her chest, while I stuff and bungee the bags to the bike. I hop on and pat the passenger seat.

"Your turn," I say.

Vivian swings a leg over and plants herself backward on the seat. She throws her bare legs over the saddlebags and crosses her arms over her chest.

"Viv," I sigh, "you can't ride backward."

"Sure, I can," she spits. "I'm still mad at you."

Oh, my God, these women are going to fucking kill me.

We must make a pretty weird picture driving down the busy streets of Tulsa. Vivian all puffed up and pouting on the back of my new bike, arms crossed, bottom lip stuck out defiantly, perched backward. I put my blinders on and ignore all the honks and stares and act like we do this every day.

I pull up behind a school bus at a stoplight and the little kids point and laugh and press their gooey faces up against the back glass. I choke down an urge to flip them off and just smile instead.

I don't have the slightest idea where we're going and Vivian's not in a talking mood, so this being Oklahoma and whenever you don't have anywhere to go or anything to do or you want to socialize but haven't been invited anywhere in particular or you're just passing time or bored with porch-sitting, I head to where everybody else in Oklahoma goes: WalMart.

I park the bike around the side by the employee parking lot next to Hell Camino. Yes, Hell Camino is still there just like Vivian said she'd be. She looks no worse for her neglect. I take my time walking around her, looking her over real good just to make sure she's okay while Vivian un-pretzels herself from the back of the bike, which she discovers isn't so easy when you're on backwards. She un-bungees the bags and starts immediately to work on reapplying her lipstick.

I'm down on my hands and knees, fishing the spare key out from under the front bumper when I see a pair of men's penny loafers approaching out of my peripheral vision. Two thoughts immediately flash across my brain: I think it's weird when men wear penny loafers and Prince Charles wears penny loafers. Then the third and most important thought hits me: "Oh shit! Run!"

I jump up and see that Vivian had the same thought a few seconds before me and is already running for the front doors of WalMart with all the bags, so I chase after her. The electronic doors slide open on the exit side and a legion of Pentecostal women with long skirts and high hair crowd through. Vivian and I knock them out of the way, using our shoulders and elbows and whatever else and manage to squeeze through all that high hair and carts. We run into the nearest aisle, which happens to be plus-size clothing for women.

Vivian dives into a circular clothes rack with all the bags. I can't even see her once she's buried in there. So, I drop to the floor and squeeze in beside her.

"Shit, he's got us," Vivian gasps.

"Ssshhh," I say, peering through all the OU T-shirts surrounding us.

Three pair of large penny loafers, the kinds with tassels, stop right in front of us, pointing their toes in three different directions.

"They can't be far," I hear Prince Charles's penny loafers say.

"We'll never find them in here, Boss," the largest penny loafers say.

Prince Charles's penny loafers order, "Go back to the car. In case they double back." One pair of penny loafers leaves. "You take the grocery section. I'll look over here." The second pair of penny loafers walk away. That leaves the shiniest pair still in front of us. I watch P.C.'s penny loafers turn in a complete circle before walking quickly in the other direction.

I pull two OUT-shirts off the rack and hand one to Vivian. "Put this on," I whisper.

"You have to be kidding," she whispers back. "It clashes with my hair."

"Fuck your hair!" I whisper harshly.

"Okay, okay," she mumbles, squirming into the shirt.

I get down on my elbows, peek under the rack of shirts and look both ways. I don't see any penny loafers. "Grab a bag and follow me," I whisper.

I bolt out from the rack with Vivian right behind me. I grab her by the hand and dash straight for the dressing rooms. I throw open the first door, shove her inside and close and lock the door behind us. I lean against the door, steadying my breathing.

"What're you thinking?" Vivian asks.

"I'm thinking he's going to kill us if he finds us."

"So, we're just going to hide in here?"

"Listen, I've had fantasies ever since I was a little kid about being able to live in a WalMart without anybody ever knowing," I explain.

"That's nice, Lee, real nice. Have you also had fantasies about dying a horrible, cruel death in a WalMart?"

"I've got it all planned out, Viv. Just do what I say." I lace the fingers of both hands together and hold my palms out to her. "Upsy-daisy," I say.

"Upsy-daisy where exactly?" she asks in a you're-too-stupid-for-words tone.

"The ceiling. Those panels just move aside. Get up there and sit your ass on a joist. I'll toss the bags up to you and be right behind."

Vivian's eyes widen, but to my surprise she doesn't argue. She steps into my hands, places her hands on top of my head and bounces up to my shoulders in one graceful movement.

"Good job," I say through gritted teeth.

"Of course," she says, "cheerleader, remember?"

"Hurry!" I urge. "Move the panel and get up there!"

Vivian lifts up on the panel with one palm and easily slips it out of the metal groove and moves it aside. She grabs a wooden beam and starts to struggle upward. I grab both her feet and push up with everything I've got. Vivian's apparently got more upper body strength than you'd think, because she swings up and through the hole in record time. I toss a money bag and her red bag up to her. I open the third bag and stick a wad of hundreds in my pocket before tossing it up also.

Vivian peers back down at me through the hole. "How are you getting up here?" she asks.

"I'm not. Just put the panel back. If I'm not back in an hour, you're on your own."

"NO!" Vivian whisper shouts.

"I'll be back, I promise. Just do it!"

Vivian slowly slides the panel back into place and I can't help but wonder if I'll ever see her again. God, I sure hope I don't die in WalMart. Target maybe, WalMart, please no.

I open the dressing room door a crack and look. Nobody. I ease out and walk toward the back of the store like I know where I'm going. I grab an OU ball cap off a rack and stick my dreads up under it. Next aisle I grab a pair of sunglasses and put those on too. Now I look like all the other customers—a deranged, rabid OU fan.

I weave my way through exiting customers, head for the back of the store and enter the first door I see that's marked Employees Only. Sure enough, it's an employee break room. I line up behind several other women at the time clock. When it's my turn, I grab any old punch card and stick it in the machine. It time-stamps the card and I look at the name printed at the top. Johnny Runningbear. Sorry, Johnny, you're going to be a little short this week. I put his card back in the slot tray just as the two women open the back door and leave.

A good-looking, tall Indian kid opens the door and walks in. He rips off his blue smock and tosses it on a table.

"Hey," I say to him, suddenly flashing on an idea.

He just looks at me.

I pull eight hundred dollar bills out of my pocket and fan them out like I'm holding a royal flush. "Want to earn a quick eight hundred bucks?" I ask.

He looks me over skeptically. Can't say I blame him. I pull my car key out of my other pocket and hold it up in the air.

"Alls you gotta do is drive my car to the other side of town and ditch it there."

He makes a show of thinking it over, but I can see his fingers twitching to take the money.

"Why?" he asks.

I tell him the only lie I can think of knowing he'll buy it anyway because he wants the money too damn bad. "My boyfriend's after me. You take my car, he'll follow you. And I can get away from him."

"I dunno," he says, playing hard to get.

"If you're too scared, I'll find somebody else." I shrug, tucking the money away in my pocket.

"What kind of car is it?" he asks.

That's when I know I have him. I hold the money and key back out and they disappear into his pocket before I even finish saying, "It's in the employee parking lot. 'Seventy-six black El Camino. V8, a hundred and eighty horses."

"Sweet," he says, grinning for the first time and heading for the exit.

"Don't fuck it up," I say to his back.

"Whatever," he mumbles, already out the door.

Welcome to my goose chase, P.C. Have fun catching that kid.

I grab the blue smock the kid threw down and pull it on over my OU T-shirt. I glance down at my name tag and read it upside down: Johnny Runningbear. Damn, Johnny, you and me. Must be destiny.

I grab a flashlight and a box cutter from the table and stick them in my smock pockets.

A couple of men employees walk in and head for the time clock without glancing at me. My luck is holding. I grab the swinging door before it closes and walk back out into the main part of the store. I haven't gone ten feet before a busy little bald man wearing a white shirt and tie bustles up to me. He looks at my name tag and orders, "Johnny, get over to aisle five with a mop and bucket. Some kid puked in the candy aisle. Clean it up before you punch out."

I nod a yes sir and head left.

"Johnny!"

I turn back to the little manager man. He gestures emphatically in the other direction and orders, "Get the mop and bucket!"

I nod about ten times and head in the direction he pointed. As soon as he's out of sight, I make a right turn and end up facing the restrooms. I opt for the men's room (I am Johnny, after all) and walk inside. I kick open all the stall doors. All empty.

I climb up on a sink, reach up to a panel and scoot it aside. Using the top of the bathroom stall door as foot leverage, I work my way up and into the darkness. I move the panel back in place and offer a little prayer of thanks to whoever is up there listening.

I hear a couple of men come in and pee somewhere down there below me. They pee for a really long time. How can men do that? They must have really huge bladders. I bet they only pee like twice a day. Hearing them pee makes me want to pee so I try to think about anything else except peeing.

P.C. is probably chasing after Johnny now. The employees should be all out of here in an hour or so. So, there's nothing left to do but wait. I turn on the flashlight and have a look around. Nothing much to see. Just some duct work and electrical junction boxes. Mouse droppings. I get my journal and pen out of my jacket pocket and play catch up. I don't wear a watch but after twelve years behind bars I know exactly what an hour feels like.

When time's up, I pull out the panel and exit the same way I entered. Sort of. After hanging out of the ceiling and trying about a dozen times to get some momentum going by swinging my legs, I finally drop to the ground, narrowly missing a potentially disastrous collision with the sink. Good thing I was never a cheerleader.

I leave my true blue smock on just in case and head back toward the women's dressing rooms. The door is hanging wide open on the dressing room we were in. I look up. The panel is moved out of place.

Vivian's gone already. I look around the women's clothing section but don't see hide nor hair of her.

Where could she be? If I were Vivian, all alone in an empty WalMart, where would I go?

Uh-oh.

I run for the pharmacy.

The pharmacy door is locked. It's a steel door with one hell of a deadbolt on it too. I run to the glass window and peer inside. There she is, all right. Looking like a kid in a fuckin' candy store. She has a look of absolute glee on her face as she empties containers of pills into her red bag. The money bags are on the floor and she scoots them down the aisle with her foot as she looks at the shelves of pills.

I knock loudly on the double pane glass window. Vivian looks up at me surprised. Then she smiles and waves.

I motion for her to unlock the window. She saunters over with her red bag on her shoulder, unlocks the window from her side and slides it open.

"You scared me for a sec," she says.

"How'd you get in there?" I ask.

"Just crawled on over through the ceiling," she answers.

Of course she did. "What do you think you're doing?" I ask. "Getting every pill in the place?"

"Not every pill." She looks in her bag, naming what she's collected so far, "Klonopin, Ultram, Skelaxin, Flexeril and Tramadol. That's all so far. I haven't gotten to the stimulant aisle yet."

"Viv," I start, "you can't take all these pills."

"I'm not going to take them all at once, you big goof."

"No, I mean you can't take them out of the store."

"Sure, I can. That's why I carry a big bag."

"How about just a handful? Grab a couple and leave the rest. How about that?"

"I'm just taking a few of each one."

"Vivian...I think you might have a problem here. A little pill problem."

She sighs like she's heard it a million times before. "There's no problem. As long as I have pills, there's no problem."

She waves me off and continues with her shopping, picking up containers and reading the labels. At least she's checking to see what they are first. That's something, I guess.

"When's the last time you were sober? Completely dry?" I ask.

"The day before I lost my virginity," she says without hesitation.

"Don't you think it's time to slow down a little?"

"You don't want to see me sober," she says. "I'm boring as hell. I don't do anything but crochet afghans and cross-stitch toaster cozies."

I give up. I don't think I can run an intervention right now when we're in the middle of a pharmacy. Kinda like taking an alcoholic to a bar and trying to get her not to drink. I'll have to save this conversation for another day.

"We're stuck here tonight, Viv. The place is locked up solid and if we try to leave we'll set off alarms like crazy. I'm going over to the camping section to set up a tent for the night. Come by there when you're done."

"Okay," she says absentmindedly, preoccupied with her shopping.

I'm halfway across the store when the intercom crackles on. Vivian's voice booms over the system, "Lee? Be sure to get stuff to make s'mores."

I sneeze a couple of times.

New jeans, new T-shirt, new boxers, new sportsbra, and new socks, all compliments of WalMart. I'm a brand-new person. I even dabbed a tester of men's cologne behind my ears. I thought I'd like it, but now I just smell like a man and cologne has always made me sneeze.

"Bless you," Vivian says.

I survey my handiwork from the hammock. I did a pretty good job of setting up a nice campsite. I cheated a little by blowing up an air mattress and grabbing some pillows and blankets, but I really don't want to have to sleep on the hard linoleum if I don't have to. The tent is one of those fancy ones that sleeps a whole family. I couldn't drive the pegs into the ground (obviously) so I held the ends down with free weights from the sports section.

And, yes, I got the s'mores fixin's which we cooked over the open flame of a gas grill. That made Vivian happy. She's eaten about twenty of them already. Now that I stop and think about it, I've never seen her eat anything but sweets.

"You ever eat anything but dessert?"

"Nope. Why would you eat anything else when sugar is readily available?" she reasons.

"But you never eat your pie."

"I don't like pie," Vivian answers.

"You always order it."

Vivian shrugs. "I just like to know it's there if I ever do want it."

There's a red flag in there somewhere but I'm too fucked up to put it all together right now. "How many of those blue pills did I take?"

"Just enough," she says.

"At least I'm not crocheting an afghan," I sigh. "I can't believe the stuff you talk me into."

"I don't talk you into anything you don't already want to do."

"You're probably right."

Vivian stands and stretches her arms high above her head. "So what do people do in WalMart at night for fun?" she asks.

"We could have sex," I say, figuring what the hell maybe someday she'll give in and that's what her stretching like that in front of me does to my thoughts.

"No, thank you," she says politely, then adds, "I don't get the whole lesbian thing. It's so confusing."

I hang one leg off the hammock and put my boot on the floor, rocking myself back and forth. "Sometimes I don't understand it either."

"I don't understand the sex part. How it all works."

"There's more to being a lesbian than just sex," I say.

"Like what?"

"I can have sex with a man...I mean, I have had sex with men, a long time ago, and sometimes it was okay. But I just can't imagine living with a man. Having to talk to him all the time. Sharing my bed with him. Sharing a bathroom with him. All that hair. Chest hair grosses me out."

Vivian crawls into the hammock and lays her head down by my boots. I pull her feet across my belly and massage them.

"What do lesbians do in bed?" she asks.

"Everything."

"Except there's no penis."

"No real penis. You can buy a penis if you really want one," I say.

"Do you have one?" she asks.

"Ginger got it in the divorce."

"So you're sans penis right now."

"Yep," I say. "And I don't think WalMart sells them either."

"Don't get mad at me," Vivian states, "but, I don't think two women having sex is really sex."

"Why?"

"It's more like heavy petting. It's like back when you were parking out at the spooklight with a boy and you let them feel you up. That's not sex."

"Some people think it is."

"It's not sex."

"Well, in that case, do you wanna *not* have sex with me?"

"No, thank you."

I grab her other foot and massage it. "Okay, then. You wanna have sex with me?"

"No, thank you."

"I'm getting a little confused now."

"See? I told you it was confusing."

"Having sex with a woman is something every woman should experience. It's way better than sex with a man," I say with a tad of hope in my voice. "'Cause a woman knows how a woman works, you know. It's about pleasing the other woman and not just getting yourself off."

"This is going to sound crass," Vivian says, "but sometimes I just want a man. I just want to be fucked."

"I can fuck."

She pats my knee like a beloved pet. "I'm sure you can, honey, I'm sure you can."

"I bet if you didn't know I was a woman...like if we were on *The Dating Game* and I was sitting behind the wall with two other men...and you couldn't see me...based on just my answers to your questions, you'd pick me. You would chose me above the guys."

She laughs. "Okay, Bachelor number one...What is your favorite food?"

"Toast," I answer without hesitating.

"Toast? Why?"

"Because toast is the best vehicle for butter. I love butter."

"Hmmm...okay," she thinks out loud. "So, if you and I were on a date in a restaurant, what would you order?"

"I'd order a plate of butter, smear it all over your body, everywhere, and then roll you in sugar," I say.

"Good answer," she laughs.

I sit up and swing both legs over the side of the hammock.

"Where you going?" she asks.

"The dairy section."

Vivian swats me on the arm and laughs. "Finish my feet, goofball."

I lay back and Vivian rests both her feet across me again. She resumes the game with another question. "Bachelor number one...Tell me something about yourself. What do you like to do?"

"Well...I like to poke dead things with a stick. I believe in aliens and ghosts and Bigfoot. And G-spots. I'm also a professional Roller Derby player."

"Ooh, how exciting! What's your Roller Derby name?"

"Lezzie Borden. Sometimes Phyllis Killer. Or Shelly Splinters."

"You've spent some time thinking about this," Vivian laughs.

"Yes, I have."

Vivian yawns big. "Do you really believe in aliens?" she asks sleepily.

"I *am* an alien," I confess. "I just wear this human body costume while I'm here visiting earth. My inside doesn't match my outside at all. I'm here in this costume to collect earth specimens to take back to my home planet."

"What kind of specimens do you collect?"

"I'm glad you asked," I say. "Orgasms. I collect female orgasms. I collect all that massive energy and put it in one big jar. So far I've collected about five times the energy of an atom bomb."

"What're you going to do with all that?"

"Dominate the universe."

"Of course," she says, closing her eyes and drifting off to sleep with a smile on her face.

I watch her sleep for a moment. She's beautiful. I wish there were some way I could show her just how beautiful she is to me.

"You're the best friend I've ever had," she mumbles.

"I love you too," I say softly.

I can't sleep. I settle down and write in my journal for a long while, then walk aimlessly around the store, snacking on cold chicken nuggets, and end up in the book department. Since there's nobody around to stop me, I do something I've always wanted to do. I pull all the Bibles off the shelf and restack them in the fiction section.

I almost drop Vivian. Damn, she's heavier than she looks. She's like dead-lifting three big dog food bags. I stuff her head first into a cart on top of our bags. Her legs hang out over the sides and kind of flop around when I push, but there's not much I can do about that. I roll her as gently as possible toward the front doors when I see one of those things the clerks walk around with. One of those sticker guns or whatever you call them. This is a big blue gun already loaded with a big roll of yellow happy face stickers.

I can't resist. I grab the gun and sticker Viv from head to toe. I put a yellow happy face sticker on every square inch of visible skin I see. I play nice, though, and don't put any on her face. I put on stickers until the gun runs empty. That'll teach her to pass out on me.

I hide in the aisles with my loaded cart until the doors to Wally World slide open. I waltz right on out the front doors, wheeling Viv and her happy faces. The little old Greeter even calls after me, "Have a good day!"

CHAPTER TEN

I sit on the bench just inside the doors of WalMart with a cart full of Vivian in front of me and no idea what I should do next. I haven't thought this through very far. I know I can't take my new Harley. Once P.C. discovers the kid in Hell Camino, he'll be looking for the bike.

I keep one eye on the lookout and the other eye on Viv to make sure she stays breathing. A dead body in a cart right now would really complicate things. Plus, I don't know how I'd explain the happy face stickers.

Vivian looks pretty dead, but she keeps on breathing. She even snorts a little once in awhile.

I finally come up with an idea. Maria, in prison, told me about it. It's how she always got around town. Of course, she got caught a lot and ended up behind bars. That's not what made her a lifer, though. She's got life because of her hot Latina temper. She told me her lover wasn't paying enough attention to her during a three-way so she accidentally killed her. I never asked how you accidentally kill somebody with your bare hands.

What the hell, I decide to give Maria's transportation scheme a try. I'm in it so deep now, one more little crime's not going to hurt.

A little old lady walks by me with a cart full of groceries. She pushes through the exit and out into the parking lot. I follow behind her a ways, pushing Vivian in my own cart.

The lady stops her cart at the trunk of a big white Lincoln Continental and beeps the alarm off. I push past her car to the other side and pull my cart up next to a Honda Civic. I try to look busy, like I lost my keys in my pocket.

The lady opens her driver's side door and puts her keys and purse in the seat. So far Maria is right about the stupidity of people. She unlatches the trunk, walks behind its open lid and begins to pile her groceries in.

That's my cue.

I open the passenger door to the Lincoln and as quickly as I can, I lift Vivian out of the cart and toss her in headfirst. I throw all the bags in on top of her and quietly shut the door. I run to the driver's side and scramble inside. I check the rearview mirror, but the old lady is hidden behind the trunk lid and is busy with her groceries.

I stick the key in the ignition and fire up the engine. I look over my left shoulder and see that the little old lady is frozen with a what-the-fuck? look on her face.

I lay on the horn and the lady jumps to the side.

I throw the car into reverse and peel out of the parking space, slamming into her cart and crunching some of her groceries under the tires. Whoops.

By now the lady is flailing her arms and hopping up and down and yelling. I power down the passenger window and toss her purse out.

"Sorry!" I shout and peel out of the lot.

We're not five minutes down the road before Vivian wakes up and is none too happy to find herself sitting on her head with her feet on the ceiling. She moans and groans a lot, but manages to get herself into a sitting position. She looks out the car window a couple of long, tense minutes and finally says, "What the fuck? Every time I go to sleep around you, I wake up in a different world."

"I couldn't get you to wake up," I explain. "And we had to get out of Wally World before P.C. came in after us."

She looks down at her body and blinks a few times.

"I know, I know. You got really fucked up on pills last night and before I knew it you were putting those stickers all over yourself. I couldn't make you stop."

I concentrate on the road, but feel Vivian staring hard at my profile.

"I will get even," she whispers. "Don't think that I won't." She peels the stickers off one at a time and resticks them to the dash.

"I don't know what you're talking about," I say in total innocence. "I also just stole this car and don't know where we're going. Any ideas?"

"Miss Jackson's," she orders. "I need some new clothes."

"We were just at WalMart!" I complain.

"Oh, my God!" she gasps, horrified. "You don't really think I'm going to wear WalMart clothes?!"

The highest priced, fanciest women's clothing store that Tulsa has to offer is Miss Jackson's. Or as I prefer to call it: the seventh circle of hell.

Vivian is in her element. She's like UberWoman with shopping superpowers. Chameleon-like in her appearance, German in her appetite for expensive clothes, dangerous and deadly with her tongue, she's able to find sales where none existed before.

I stand guard on the sidewalk outside the front doors,

smoking, reading some of my *Zen* paperback and hoping the cops don't find the stolen car before we can get to wherever we're going next.

"It's not called cheap, it's called reasonable," I argue.

"We have two bags of money. We don't have to be reasonable. Reasonable is for poor people," Vivian reasons.

She hands a hundred dollar bill to the bellhop after he drops the umpteen dozen Miss Jackson's bags inside the front door.

As soon as the bellhop (do they still call them bellhops?) closes the door behind him, Vivian smiles and says, "Money's no good unless you spend it."

We're in a different suite at the Crowne Plaza. The Presidential Suite was taken so Vivian had to settle for another. This one only has one bathroom, which is sandwiched in between two bedrooms. (The two bedrooms thing is rapidly becoming a sore spot with me.)

Vivian throws open the door to the first bedroom and says, "This one's yours."

She throws open the door to the second bedroom, the one with the view of the city, and says, "Put my bags in here."

I dump all the sacks of clothes at the foot of her bed and scooch the money bags under the bed with the toe of my boot.

"I don't think coming back here is the best idea you've ever had," I complain. "This Prince Charles guy is probably scoping the place out."

"Wrong," she counters. "Coming back here would be stupid and he knows I'm not stupid, so he won't look here."

"But if he knows you're not stupid, then he knows that you know he won't look for you here, so he's going to look for you here first."

"What?" she asks.

"I'm just saying that if I were him and I was looking for you, this is the first place I'd look."

"But he's too stupid to figure all that out," she says.

"He can't be too stupid. He's found us everywhere we go."

She doesn't say anything. I point at the back of her knee. "You missed one."

She reaches down and pulls the sticker off, wads it into a tiny ball and flicks it at me like a booger.

"So what're we going to do now?" I ask, plopping down on her bed.

"I'm going to shower and change," she says.

"You don't have to change for me. I like you the way you are."

"Off my bed," she orders.

"You still mad about the stickers?"

"Would you please remove your ass from my bed?" she asks, ever-so-politely with a light British accent.

I don't move. "Can I take a shower with you?"

"Nope."

"Can we just make out some?" I ask.

"I'm straight."

"So? I've made out with lotsa straight women. That didn't mean they were gay."

She opens drawers and piles her new clothes in. "No, thank you," she answers politely.

"You can close your eyes and pretend I'm a man."

"How very Yentl," she says.

"I can just watch you masturbate."

She orders, "Get out of my room."

"Or you could watch me masturbate."

Vivian marches to her door and holds it open, gesturing for me to exit.

"Okay," I say, dragging my feet out the door. "But if you change your mind..."

"...you'll be the first to know," she says, shutting the door behind me.

I go into my own room and slam my door. I sit on the bed and bounce. I hear the shower turn on in the bathroom. I lie on the bed with my hands behind my head and stare at the ceiling.

I can't believe I'm actually thinking that somehow someway someday Vivian is going to let me love her or love me back. I weigh my chances and know the odds aren't good. So why do I keep on keeping on? I guess I don't really have anything better to do. It's not like I left something better behind.

I must've fallen asleep because a man's voice jerks me awake. I sit up and will the grog to leave my brain. Maybe I just heard the TV or something.

I get up and open the door to the bathroom. It's steamy and there's two towels lying on the floor next to a pile of clothes that Vivian was wearing. She's finished with her shower.

I hear his voice again.

I press my ear against the door leading to Vivian's bedroom. I can't hear anything. I'm thinking about using one of those wrapped glasses by the sink—like how they do in movies—press it up against the door and stick your ear over it—then I hear the voice again and recognize a definite British accent.

Shit. I look around the bathroom for a weapon. My choice is wet towels or a drinking glass. Shit. I ease the door open and put one eye up to the crack.

I can't believe what I'm seeing. Vivian is full monty-showing naked. She's one of those women who look even better out of her clothes than in them. (Well, according to me, that's true for all women.) But then that thought disappears as soon as I see Prince Charles. He's wearing slacks, shirt and a tie. Vivian slithers up to him and rubs herself against him. She kisses his neck and works his belt at the same time.

He downs the glass of champagne he's holding.

Vivian growls, "Baby, you don't know how much I missed this."

His pants drop around his ankles. Tidy whities. He tosses the empty champagne glass to the floor. Vivian sits on the edge of the bed, wraps her legs around his and pulls him down on top of her.

The bedroom door opens and one of the goons pokes his head in. As soon as he sees P.C. laying on top of Vivian, he says, "Beg your pardon."

P.C. looks over his shoulder and commands, "Wait in the car."

The goon shuts the door. I hear him out in the living room talking to somebody, probably his twin goon. The front door opens and closes.

P.C. goes back to Vivian and smothers his face between her tits. And the part that hurts the worst is that she looks like she's enjoying it.

I can't bear to see anymore.

I shut the door.

I numbly walk into my bedroom. I turn in a couple of slow circles before I grab hold of the first emotion that runs by and I jump on its back and ride it hard.

I hate her. I hate every fucking thing about her. I hate her red hair. I hate her perfect tits. I hate her laugh. I hate how she makes me feel. Most of all, I hate her for making me fall in love with her. I even hate her for making me hate her.

I go back to the bathroom and quietly undress and put on every stitch of Vivian's discarded animal-themed clothes.

Two can play this game.

Fifteen minutes later I'm in the hotel bar. I wound my dreads on top of my head trying for the octopus thing again, but ended up looking like Medusa. I've got on Viv's panties, her short skirt, her matching shirt and those damn shoes she loves so much. I don't know where to scratch first. And I'm quickly developing a newfound respect for women who can actually walk in high heels. I hope I don't have to get anywhere quickly.

I try to look nonchalant and sexy at the same time as I plant my ass onto the first barstool I see. I peer through the ambiance and scout out a target. I get one in my sights and pull the trigger.

"Buy me a drink?" I coo to the man next to me.

He looks me up and down, takes a big gulp of his drink and scoots down three places.

This isn't as easy as it looks.

I'm well into my third (or fourth, who the hell's counting) drink and looking desperate when I hear a lip-smacking voice near my ear say, "Can I buy you drink, pretty lady?"

I almost look around for the pretty lady before I realize he's talking to me. "Sure, baby," I answer, "I could do with another."

He sits next to me and I see exactly what I expected to see: a middle-aged man with too much hair on his chest and not enough on his head. He's a little soft in the middle but not too bad for a man who sits at a desk all day every day. His eyes are a little unfocused which explains why he chose me. He's wearing his uniform of suit and tie with snakeskin boots and ten-gallon hat, and I'm guessing he wants to take a story back to his office in whatever town he's from. I glance down at his wedding ring and have a pang of remorse.

I gulp down the drink and dive straight in before I can change my mind. "What're you doing tonight?" I ask.

"Nothin', sugar," he says.

"You are now. You're doing me," I slur. (It worked on Joey Hanes in high school, I just hope it works now.)

"Sure, sure...okay," he stumbles.

Once we're both standing, I realize I'm a good head taller than him.

"You're a tall drink of water," he drawls.

That's when the panic sets in. I swallow hard and squeak a question to myself, "You doin' this or not?"

"Lead the way, little lady," he says.

He small talks all the way up in the elevator, but the only voice I can hear is that little Jiminy Cricket in my head that keeps telling me this is a really bad idea.

I ignore all the voices coming at me and put my card key into the slot.

I take off the heels once I'm inside the door and my toes cry from relief. I put my index finger over my lips in the universal quiet gesture and he does it back to me with a drunken "ssshhhhh."

We tippy-toe to my room and I turn on the lamp on the nightstand. He shuts the door quietly behind him. I toss my shoes into a corner of the room. Fueled by Jack, I strip down naked in about three seconds. I turn to face him.

He whistles low and between his teeth.

"I have to tell you something," I say. "I'm a lesbian."

"I'm from Houston," he replies.

Buckass naked and all too aware of the jiggle in my boobs, I do my best slither up to him. I imitate what I saw Vivian do and bury my face in the cowboy's neck while I try to get his belt undone. He has on some powerful cologne and before I can stop myself, I sneeze into his shoulder. I think I must be allergic to men.

"Bless you, sugar," he says.

He gently pushes me down onto the bed and unfastens his belt all by himself. His drawers drop and fall around his boots. He's already standing at attention and I give myself a mental pat on the back for at least being able to accomplish that much.

He takes off his shirt and tie, but leaves his hat and boots on. But at least he's polite about it because he actually tips his hat at me before he crawls between my legs. He squirms around a little bit and I feel as if he's going to crush my ribcage. When I try to wriggle out from under him, he mistakes this for excitement and shoves it right in without warning. He starts doing his thing and I just lie there allowing it and berating myself for ever thinking this would help with anything.

I punch him a couple of times on the back and he stops.

"You almost done?"

"I could do this all night long," he says in a slow Texas drawl.

"Oh, fer Chrissakes," I mumble. I push him off and get on my knees and elbows with my ass in the air. "Do it this way, so I don't have to look at you," I offer. "You've got five minutes."

"My wife won't do that," he says in true awe.

"I'd like to meet her someday. Four minutes thirty seconds and counting down."

He climbs on like the cowboy he is and begins again.

That's when Vivian walks in all dressed in her new Miss Jackson sexy-ass-dress-with-matching-new-heels-ensemble. Her seeing this this doesn't feel anything like how I planned it. It was supposed to make me feel good and her feel bad, but somehow all I feel is mortified. I bury my face in my hands. Maybe she can't see me if I can't see her. I peek between my fingers to see if it's working.

"Wellwellwell..." she smirks, crossing her arms and thrusting out one hip, "Where's a camera when you need one?"

Houston tips his hat at her and grunts, "Ma'am." He goes back to business and after a couple more thrusts, he's blessedly done.

Nonplussed, Vivian scoops up his clothes from the floor and tosses them at him. "Okay, cowboy, you done broke that wild pony, time to leave."

I hide under the bed covers while Vivian coaxes him out the door one pantleg at a time. I hear the door in the other room shut and her footsteps coming back toward me. She whips the covers back. "Lee, we gotta get out of here."

"I saw you fucking Prince Charles," I say.

"And I saw you fucking a fat cowboy. We got to get outta here before he wakes up."

"Before who wakes up?"

"Prince fucking Charles, that's who!" she whisper-shouts and walks into the bathroom, expecting me to follow. I wrap the sheet around me and tag after her. She quietly opens the door to her bedroom and motions for me to look.

I peek around the door.

What the hell?

"What the hell'm I looking for?" I ask.

She throws open the door, revealing what I already saw: Nothing. Nothing but a messed up bed and an empty room.

"Where the fuck did he go?" she shouts, running into the room. I pick up the end of my sheet and follow her in. She points to the empty bed, "He was right here. I popped some pills into his champagne... Boom, he's out cold..."

"You're sure?" I ask in a tiny voice.

"Of course, I'm sure!" she screams at me. "He was naked and passed out right here on the bed!"

"Well, you don't have to yell at me! I didn't sneak in here and take his damn body!"

"I'm not yelling at you!" she yells at me.

"I'm obviously the only person in here, so if you're not yelling at me, then who the fuck are you yelling at?"

"You're the one who's fucking doing all the yelling!" she yells.

"And you're the one who's doing all the fucking!"

"Me?!" she screams. "Then what were you doing in there with the cowboy if you weren't fucking?!"

"I didn't enjoy it!" I scream at the top of my lungs. I suddenly realize that what I'm yelling about isn't really what I'm yelling about. I take a deep breath and let it out slow. "It doesn't count if I didn't like it," I say slow and calm.

Vivian nods and says softly, "Yeah, I know what you mean." She takes a deep breath of her own, then throws her hands up in the air. "Well, where the hell is he?" she asks.

"Looking for me?" a voice slurs behind us. We both spin around.

Prince Charles leans in the doorway, naked and drugged and holding a gun. His eyes sluggishly take us in and he raises the gun, pointing it right at Vivian.

Hold on a minute. That's not a gun. It's an empty champagne bottle. He laughs and almost falls to the floor before catching hold of the door handle and straightening up again. "Vivian..." he laughs, stumbling a few feet forward. "Tsk, tsk, tsk. Shame on you, dearie."

"Charlie, I'm so glad you're not gone," she says, slinking his way. "I thought you'd left me."

"Don't!" he points the champagne bottle at her chest. "Move! Don't move."

Vivian freezes. He squints one eye, aiming the bottle at her like some kind of English Wyatt Earp. "Bang!" he slurs. "You're dead."

He raises his imaginary gun to his lips and blows a short puff of air on the bottle neck. And that's the last thing he does before he falls over, smashing face-first on the carpet.

I must stare at him for a full five seconds before asking, "You think he's dead?"

Prince Charles's butt twitches a couple of times, then he lets out a loud snort and snore.

"Nope," Vivian answers. "Just sleeping. But I think he's going to be really pissed off when he wakes up."

CHAPTER ELEVEN

We go from the lap of luxury to a rent-by-the-hour motel named Dick's Halfway Inn. I let Vivian register us at the front desk, which may have been a mistake because she signs us in as Fred and Ethel Mertz.

We're back to one room and one queen-size bed and I try not to think about the sheets. The carpet is so matted and gross I don't think about that either.

I jump in the shower and scrub like Karen Silkwood while Vivian runs next door for a bottle of something brown and cheap and strong. When I come out of the bathroom in my boxers and wifebeater, she pours me a lethal dose of the liquor and helps herself to several pills. We lie on the bed for a long time, staring at the ceiling without talking.

Finally, Vivian aims the remote at the TV, turns it on and

there's nothing but horizontal stripes flipping by on every channel. I get up and land the TV a couple of solid kicks. The picture flips and holds and stays there. I lie back down again. I must've found the animal channel because some documentary about prairie dogs is on. Vivian sets the TV to mute just as one little fuzzy dog climbs on the back of another and starts rutting away.

"Remind you of anything?" Vivian snorts.

"Fuck you."

"You changing teams or what?" She snickers.

My residual anger leaks out. "It was a mistake!" I take a big drink and choke out a miserable, "It was a mistake. You ever make mistakes?" I swipe away a couple of hot tears and look away from her searching eyes.

"C'mon, Lee. It was just one time. One guy. Nothing to cry about."

"That's not why I'm crying. You saw it and...I dunno."

Vivian reaches over and pats me on the knee. "Darlin', I don't care."

"That's why I'm crying! 'Cause you don't care!" I throw her hand back at her and finish off the glass in one big gulp. Vivian gets off the bed, grabs the bottle and pours me another. She sticks the bottle between my legs and lays back down with her hands behind her head, staring at the TV. The prairie dogs are still going at it.

"Sorry," I mumble, finally breaking the heavy silence.

"Do we really need to have this talk again?" she asks without looking at me.

"No."

Through the paper-thin walls, I hear the bed springs next door creak. The headboard bangs against the wall separating our beds. I watch the prairie dogs hump but the soundtrack is coming from next door. It's like humping in surround sound. And it really does seem like those cute little prairie dogs are the ones saying, "Do it, Daddy, do it, do it, Daddy, do it!" Or maybe I've just had too much to drink tonight.

"Maybe we need to break up," Vivian says.

"We're not going steady."

The banging headboard gets louder. Vivian looks at the shaking wall then back to me. "I just think I'm not so good for you. You go out and pick up a man when you clearly didn't want to. Then you blame it on me. You lesbians are so weird. And I mean that in the nicest way."

"I don't want to break up," I say. "I don't know what I'd do if I didn't have you."

Viv sits up cross-legged and looks at me long and hard. "You're tired and drunk. My pills are kicking in. Neither one of us is going anywhere tonight."

Now the headboard next door bangs the wall so hard our bed bounces. Vivian turns to the wall and pounds it with her fists, screaming, "Hurry up and come, already! What the fuck is taking so long!"

I giggle a little. She giggles back. The headboard stops.

"Thank you, Gawd," she drawls.

I reach out and take her hand in mine. I trace the lines in her palm with my fingertip. "I just want to know something, Vivian."

"What?"

"At the funeral...why'd you leave with me? Outta all those people there, why'd you ask me to take you away?"

She pooches out her lower lip, thinking hard. "I recognized you."

"From high school?"

"No," she says, quickly. "Not that kind of recognize. I mean I did, but that's not what I mean. I just saw something familiar in you."

"Like what?" I ask.

"I've always felt like an outcast. Like I never quite fit in. And that's what you looked like too. Like you were on the outside looking in."

I nod.

"We just fit," she says.

I nod again.

"Why'd you take me away? You didn't have to, so why did you?" she asks.

Because I just saw you and immediately I knew you were the one.

But I just think that because I know I can't say it out loud to her. So, instead, I shrug and say, "I liked your pom-poms."

"You're such a man sometimes," she laughs.

"I know."

I take a deep drink straight from the bottle and feel the burn work itself down to my toes.

"Vivian?"

"Yeah?"

"Where we going?"

"Wherever the road takes us," she says simply.

She looks to the TV and I follow her gaze. The female prairie dog is now giving bloody birth and shooting the pups out one at a time. I grab the remote and turn it off.

Vivian and I lie in total darkness and quiet for a long time. I listen to her breathing and am soothed by the rhythm. I'm drifting off to sleep when Vivian leans up on one elbow, facing me. She traces her finger across the scar on my forearm.

"Why were you in prison?" she asks gently.

"Where'd that come from?"

"Why haven't you ever told me? You think I'm going to freak out or something?"

"Maybe."

"Well, I won't."

"I don't like to talk about it."

I get all gooseflеshy from her fingertips and she senses this and rubs some warmth back into my arm.

"Murder?" she asks.

I pull my arm away. "I don't like to talk about it."

"I heard it was murder."

I sigh. "Depraved-mind second degree murder to be exact."

"Your father?"

"Stepfather."

She wraps her hand back around my forearm and caresses the scar. "He raping you? That how you get this scar?"

"Why're you asking if you already know?"

"I want to hear it from you, not from everybody else. I wish you'd trust me enough to tell me."

I'm quiet for a long time. She listens to my quiet and waits patiently for me to say something. So I close my eyes and try to find the words. "I got the scar when I was fifteen. I guess I'd had enough and I tried to fight back. It's my fault, really. I mean, I knew better than to fight. My mom left not long after that. He was doing the same thing to her, beating her and shit. I guess she thought I was okay, I dunno. She never put her bottle down long enough to see me. So, she just packed up one day and never came back."

Vivian snuggles up next to me and pulls me close. I open my eyes and look at her for a second. She wipes away the wet under my eyes with her thumb, and I continue, "He didn't do it all the time, you know. There'd be a couple of months go by...then he'd wake me up, drunk and sweaty... My senior year I hardly ever went back to the house anymore. There was this biker guy I knew when I was a kid. Chopper. He was actually married to my mom for like a year maybe. That's his pocketknife I have. With the red Maltese cross? I stole it off his nightstand the day Mom made him leave."

I laugh a little. I don't know why, it's just easier than crying.

"Chopper was cool. I worked in his shop when I was a kid, just cleaning up and stuff. So, I went there. I started living in his shop at night. He didn't know. I slept there and ate stuff out of his fridge. Then I'd go to school in the morning before he came in. But I had to go home sometimes. Get clothes and do laundry. I'd sneak in when the bastard was asleep and go through his pockets and shit and get whatever money he had in them. One time...he woke up. He grabbed me by the throat. Threw me down. He took his time. I didn't fight back...just...let it happen, you know. When he was done, I got up to leave. He went back to bed, was actually snoring and shit. I'm almost out the door and I dunno, I snapped or something. I looked at my body and it wasn't mine. I looked in the mirror and it wasn't even me looking back. The person looking back was horrible. She was beyond angry, had this crazy look about her. This other person, this girl... I watched her go to the closet and get the shotgun off the top shelf. She cracked it open to make sure it was loaded. She clicked the safety off. She walked calmly down the hall to his bedroom. She pushed open the door with the butt of the gun. She braced her feet and raised the shotgun and held it tight against her shoulder. She woke him up by saying, "You should've kept your dick in your pants." He sat up and she fired. It threw him back against the headboard and she spread her feet wider and aimed and shot again. She watched the blood spread across his chest and...actually marveled at how pretty it was. Then she laid the gun down on the foot of the bed and walked to the kitchen and picked up the phone and called the police. She said, 'I just shot the bastard. You don't have to hurry. He'll still be dead when you get here.' She hung up and went outside and sat on the porch steps and waited for the cops."

Vivian pulls me to her chest with my face in the crook of her neck and holds me tight.

"You're the only person I've ever told," I say softly.

"Thank you," she whispers. "Thank you for telling me."

I fall asleep with her arms wrapped around me and the sound of her heartbeat in my ears.

CHAPTER TWELVE

According to Vivian, the only way to get rid of a hangover is hair of the dog. Or in her words, "If you just stay drunk, you don't get hangovers." Which explains why we are in Boomer Sooner Sports Bar drinking one Bloody Mary after another. I think the bartender recognizes my hangover and is kind enough to help out by giving me more Mary than Bloody.

Boomer Sooner is like heaven for OU fans. The whole place is decorated in red and white, with OU memorabilia covering every square inch. There's a huge wall-sized TV set up in a corner of the bar and all the patrons watch the football game and scream obscenities at the coach and the other team. Personally, I think football would be a hell of a lot more interesting if they'd just take off all those pads and beat on each other.

Viv and I sit at a corner table, leaning back in our chairs with our feet propped up on the bags of money. I chow down on a dish of peanuts and pretzel sticks while Vivian licks on a celery stick. I'm a little embarrassed about my emotional incontinence of last night and, thank God, Vivian hasn't brought it up again. But at least she wasn't a scrooge with her tits and she let me hold onto one all night long.

"I'm allergic to nuts," Vivian states.

"I'm allergic to seafood."

"I had clams once. Not the seafood kind either," she states.

I raise an eyebrow and question, "Don't you mean crabs?"

"It was some kind of crustacean," Vivian says with a shrug. "Do you think they serve food here? I'm hungry. You think they have pie? Lemon or chocolate or something like that."

"This is a bar, Viv. You don't order pie in a bar. Just like you don't go into a Chinese restaurant and order a hamburger. Besides you won't eat it anyway."

"Don't tell me what I won't eat," Vivian says and takes a bite of her celery stick.

"We are talking about food, right?"

"Right," she chews.

I finish off the peanuts and scoot the bowl to the far side of the table. "I wish we'd known each other in high school."

"We did know each other," Vivian objects.

"Yeah, but we never talked. Did we? I don't remember us ever talking."

"I don't think you talked much," Vivian says.

"Not to you, I didn't. You were too popular to talk to somebody like me."

"I wasn't popular," Vivian says.

"Bullshit. Cheerleader. Football Queen."

"No boys ever asked me out. I never had one date in high school. I didn't even go to junior prom. Nobody asked me. I had to ask Mark Thompson to take me to senior prom. His girlfriend was a sophomore and couldn't go. I didn't even ask him myself. My daddy called his daddy and they set it up. I wasn't popular. Not by a long shot."

"I didn't know that or I would've asked you to the prom."

"Oh, that would've changed things. That would've made me real popular."

"You know I just did that night with Mark in order to get closer to you."

"Hmmm..." she says, squinting one eye at me. "How'd that work out for you?"

"Not too good," I admit. "If I could go back in time, I'd talk to you. I'd march right up to you and say, 'C'mon, let's go find some trouble.' Your dad would have to bail us out of jail."

"We can get into trouble now," she says. "We can make up for lost time."

I lean toward her and whisper, "Uuuhhhh...I think we *are* in trouble, Viv. We've got the English Mafia equivalent chasing our asses, I think that's trouble enough."

"Heeeyyyyy," the entire bar groans in unison. I look over and see that the football game on the TV has been interrupted and replaced by a newscaster who solemnly looks at the camera, announcing, "This is a Channel Six breaking news special report. Tulsa police are searching for two women who broke into an area WalMart. WalMart management just released this security camera video after discovering a large quantity of painkillers was stolen from the pharmacy."

I squeeze Vivian's arm and she grabs my hand, squeezing back. We both hold our breath as the huge screen fills with a black-and-white grainy film of Vivian in the red OU T-shirt crawling through the pharmacy window. Cut to me putting up the tent. Cut to Vivian eating a s'more. Cut to us both lying in the hammock in front of the tent. Cut to me carrying a stack of Bibles. Cut to me putting stickers on a passed-out Vivian in the cart.

Vivian leans over and whispers in my ear, "Aha. You did put those stickers on me."

The newscaster's voice continues over the footage, "The two suspects raided the pharmacy, camped inside the store, using a gas grill and erecting a camping tent. If anyone recognizes the suspects, they are urged to contact the anonymous toll-free line shown at the bottom of your screen."

The screen goes back to the newscaster's fake-smiling face,

saying "This has been a Channel Six special report. Now back to the football game."

Everyone in the bar slowly turns in their chairs and looks at us.

I give them all a tiny smile and wave weakly. Nobody waves back.

Vivian quickly stands and says, "Who wants a free drink?"

After a small pause, a big, bearded man in coveralls slowly raises his hand in the air.

Vivian asks, "Have you ever seen those two women on the TV?"

"What two women?" He grins.

"Bartender! I'm buying this man a drink!" Vivian shouts, pointing to her new friend.

"I've never seen them either," says another man.

A woman pipes up, "Me neither!"

"Two more drinks, bartender!" Vivian adds.

Then the whole bar chimes in with their own version of not knowing the alleged WalMart campers.

"Drinks for everybody!" Vivian laughs. "I'm buying!"

Everyone claps and cheers and shouts their orders at the bartender.

Vivian turns to me and raises her drink. I raise mine with her and she toasts, "Me and you, Lee. Back to back with our guns drawn and the bad guys circling us. Let's go out in a blaze."

"Okay, Louise," I laugh and clink her glass against mine.

"Okay, Thelma," she says, clinking back.

Vivian turns to the bartender and yells, "I changed my mind! Make it an open bar! Everybody drink as much as you want!"

The whole bar whoops and hollers and shouts some thank-you's. The bartender yells back to Vivian, "You sure of that?"

"I've never been surer of anything in my life. I want to celebrate. Today's my birthday."

I jerk back in utter surprise. "Today? Today is your birthday?"

"Yep," she says. "And I want to have the best goddamn birthday ever!"

"Happy birthday, Vivian Baxter! Happy birthday!" I raise my

glass and toast her. "Here's to you and your happy birthday!"

"Happy fucking birthday!" shouts a guy from across the room.

Everyone in the bar stands to face Vivian and raises their glasses with us. I take this as my cue to lead them in song. "Happy fucking birthday to you..."

We stumble down the street, leaning on each other for support, carrying our money bags between us. I'm wearing her high heels and she's wearing my boots, and I have no recollection of how that happened. I'm a happy drunk and so is Vivian. It must be after five o'clock because the streets are filled with rushing people and we stop and stand in the middle of the sidewalk like an island unto ourselves. We stand stock-still and people rush past us and around us and it feels like we're the ones moving not them. Everyone looks so sad and I don't understand why. I want everyone to be happy. I want all these sad five o'clock workweek faces to be as happy as we are.

"Happy birthday," I call out to a businessman who glances at me warily out of the corner of his eye.

"Happy birthday," I say to a woman dragging her kid on one of those doggie leash things. She ignores me.

"Happy fucking birthday!" I shout to a teenager on a skateboard breezing past us.

"Happy fucking birthday to you!" shouts the teenager back, flipping me the bird.

That makes me feel so good I shout it to the world in general, "Happy fucking birthday, world!"

"Happy fucking birthday world!" echoes Vivian, falling into me and almost knocking me to my ass.

People turn their heads and look at us nervously as they cut a large swath around us. I kick off those damn high heels and jump up into the bed of a parked truck and drop the bag. I stretch my arms out far and wide and shout, "Happy fucking birthday, world!"

Vivian's right behind me and she throws her bag into the

truck bed and jumps in with me. Barely able to stand upright, with her arms swinging wildly, she shouts, "Today is my birthday! And I wanna say happy motherfucking birthday to everybody who ever fucked with me these past thirty-three years! HAPPY MOTHERFUCKING BIRTHDAY!"

That stops a few people in their tracks and they look at us, each other and back to us. Viv laughs like a drunken maniac and continues, "Happy birthday to you Mother Dearest! Happy fucking birthday to you and thanks for the birthing hips and anorexia! Happy birthday from your never-good-enough-for-you daughter!"

Now people definitely stop and listen. A crowd forms and Vivian motions that it's my turn, so I clear my throat and shout and punch the air, "Happy fucking birthday, Ginger! Thanks for fucking everybody and their dog and their brother and the horse they rode in on behind my back! Happy fucking birthday to you!"

Viv jumps up and down a couple of times, spins around in a circle, then shouts, "Happy fucking birthday, Roger! Thanks for fucking that whore and giving me a bad case of the clams! Now I can't ever eat seafood without thinking of you, you asshole! Happy fucking birthday!" Vivian looks at her audience gathered on the street and says in an aside, "Whew! That felt fuckin' great!"

Most of the people laugh with her and so I grab Vivian's hand and hold it high up in the air between us and jump in with, "Happy Birthday, you French-speaking bitch who's lived in America for twenty years but still puts the adjective after the noun. And who tells me she's really straight and packs up and leaves in the middle of the night! Birthday Happy, you bitch fucking!"

The crowd has grown to about fifty or more people and they all laugh and hoot their approval. Vivian shushes them with a wave of her arms and shouts out, "Happy birthday, Mrs. Patterson! You seventh-grade history teacher with the amputated hand who used to clobber me in the head with your stump that looked like an Englishman's dick! Let's give her a big hand, everybody!" Vivian applauds and the crowd laughs and claps with her.

Then lo and behold, one middle-aged houswifey-looking woman steps up beside the truck, turns to the crowd, cups her hands around her mouth and shouts, "Happy Birthday, Daryll! Happy fucking birthday and thanks for the sperm! You, you, you, sperm-donor no-count father husband loser! Happy fucking birthday!"

Housewife gleefully turns to Vivian and they slap palms in a high five.

A big burly man jumps into the front of the circle next and adds his own, "Happy fucking birthday, Judge! Happy Birthday for giving my wife all my money and my kids and the house and totally fucking up my life, Happy fucking birthday!"

He barely high-fives me before he's pushed out of the way by the next woman who shouts, "Happy f-word birthday, you, you, you Mr. Dickwad! Happy birthday for ten years of awful sex where I never had a you-know-what! Happy f-word birthday to you!"

Right on her heels is a mousy little woman with the voice box of an elephant, "Happy fucking birthday to you with the brain the size of a planet who thinks it's A-Okay to run away from your wife and kids and go waste your life with some young slut! Happy fucking birthday and I hope you rot in hell!"

There's thunderous and cathartic applause. People all over the street smile and laugh and shout out their own birthday wishes. I catch bits here and there: "Happy fucking birthday! Side Show Freak! Manic-Depressive Asshole! Constipated colon! Dingleberry! Happy fucking birthday!"

Vivian laughs and slaps her leg and I punch the air with my fists, egging people on and—"Happy birthday, Vivian dear!"

I look toward the familiar accent and holy shit almighty! It's Prince Charles!

I grab Vivian and point.

She follows my finger, still laughing, then suddenly not laughing. I look for an escape, but the crowd is so thick, we're trapped.

Vivian screams at the crowd and points at P.C., "That's him! That's him!"

I put my fingers in my mouth and whistle as loud as I can.

The crowd quiets and jerks their attention back to us.

Vivian screams and points again, "That's him! That's the motherfucker who left me for a younger woman and now I have to raise three kids by myself and he hasn't paid alimony in four fucking years!"

"Asshole!" shouts a little lady. She swings her purse hard and slaps P.C. upside the head with it. He covers his face with his arms and back away from the mad, purse-slinging lady.

"He used to beat me too!" Vivian throws in for good measure. "Take the fucker down!"

The crowd converges on P.C. like a pack of wolves, howling obscenities. He's sucked under a tidal wave of angry faces. I grab Vivian, we each grab a bag of money and we leap over the side of the truck, running fast and hard.

Ten blocks later and, shit almighty, I can't run anymore, my lungs are going to collapse. I grab Vivian's hand and yank her into the dark alcove of a brick building. It smells like piss back in here. This isn't exactly what you'd call the nice part of town. Hookers, male and female, and stinky homeless people walk the streets and they're all throwing us looks like we're the weird ones. I'd yell a few choice words at them if I could catch my breath.

"How the hell," I gasp, "does that motherfucker," I gasp, "keep finding us every time?"

Vivian's tits BZZZZ and she takes the phone out of her tit safe.

We overlap each other as we have the same thought at the same time: "That's it! He's tracking us through your phone!" "We have to get rid of the phone!"

Shit, I could kick myself for being so damn stupid. I jerk the phone out of Vivian's hand, grab a couple of hundreds out of a bag and march out onto the sidewalk. I saunter up to the first hooker I see which happens to be a six and half foot tall black transvestite.

I wave the money under her eyes.

"Nu-uh, girl," she says, pointing a long red fingernail in my face. "I don't do none of that kinky girl-on-girl shit."

"All's you have to do is hold on to this phone. When the guy shows up for it, give it to him." I wink. "And tell him his blow job is paid for."

The transvestite grabs the bills and the phone and shoves them down between her tits.

Damn. Is that a girl thing or what?

CHAPTER THIRTEEN

"Sorry I lost your high heels again," I say. "I just took off running and forgot to get them first." I'm pretty sure I'm stone-cold sober now because one mother of a hangover is starting at the back of my skull.

Vivian's not talking. She's not even looking at me.

I take another stab. "This is my first cab ride."

Vivian just stares out the passenger window, still ignoring me.

"It's not very nice inside. And it kinda smells like old sex back here," I say.

Vivian doesn't move. Her silence scares me. If I could read her mind right now, I wouldn't.

I sigh deeply and tick off on my fingers. "We started with Ginger's Fatboy, then Hell Camino, green Pinto, Mercedes,

Lincoln Continental...can't forget my new Street Glide, which I hope is still at WalMart. And now a cab. Did I forget any?"

The cabbie (who surprises me by being white and wearing a cowboy hat and speaking plain English) steers the taxi down a narrow road. I look out my grimy window at all the passing gravestones. Right over there is where I met Vivian. The pole tent's gone now, but there's some yellow crime scene tape draped around the grave.

I don't give up on trying to lighten the mood. "When I was a kid I used to cross my fingers every time we drove by a graveyard. You ever used to do that?"

"Why did you tell him to bring us here?" Vivian asks with her nose still pointed away from me.

"I dunno," I say softly.

"Why are we in a cemetery?" she asks, looking directly at me.

I hold my breath for a few seconds, and when I let it go my words come tumbling out with it. "My mom's here. I've never been here. I just want to see her, can't explain why, I just do."

Vivian holds her breath for a long time, then nods.

The cabbie pulls over to the side of the road and Vivian orders him, "Wait on us here." She gets out, but for some reason I just can't will myself to open my door. I hear her bare feet crunching all the way around the back and then her face appears at my window. She gives me a what's-wrong-get-out-of-the-car look.

I shake my head at her.

She opens the door. "What's wrong? Get out."

"Maybe this wasn't such a good idea."

"I'll be with you, okay? We'll go together."

I nod numbly and let Vivian take my hand and pull me out of the backseat. She leads the way and I follow.

"Which one?" she asks, looking around at all the markers.

"I dunno," I reply. "I've never been here."

Vivian starts to say something, changes her mind and says instead, "I'll find her. What's her name?"

"Margaret Hammond."

Vivian marches off with a mission. I walk in the other direction, halfway hoping we don't find her.

It's Vivian who finds her first and she holds my hand all the way over to the grave. I don't know what to do now that I'm here. I'm not going to talk out loud or anything stupid like that. So, I just shuffle my boots in the grass.

"You don't have to tell me if you don't want, but how'd she die?" Vivian asks.

"Killed herself," I say without inflection. "That was the second time she left me."

Vivian's quiet. I mean seriously, what can she say.

"Let's go," I say, turning for the road, "I don't know why I came."

Vivian says, "Try to see it from her side. You know, maybe she just thought you'd be better off without her. Or maybe...you know for a lot of people life hurts too bad. Maybe she just hurt too bad all the time... Maybe she was just tired. You know, just plain sick and fucking tired."

"I'm ready to go, Viv."

"Stay here for a minute. Just for a minute. You came all this way, so it must mean something to you. I'll wait in the cab."

I watch her her walk away before I turn back to the grave. I know I should feel something, but I just don't know where that something is. It's buried down deeper than she is.

The last time I saw my mother in the flesh was when she showed up for my sentencing.

I hadn't seen hide nor hair of her for over a year, then she had the fuckin' nerve to show for my sentencing. She sat right behind me making a big show for the judge and jury with her tears and hand-wringing. I stiffened my shoulders toward her and refused to give her the satisfaction of even a glance.

The chamber's door swung open and the bailiff made everyone get up and the judge came in with a flourish of black robes and with one pound of the gavel I'm sentenced to Mabel Bassett prison for the next fifteen years.

Depraved mind. They said I had a depraved mind. It took all that time in the courtroom to rule that I had a depraved mind.

Hell, I could've told them that.

Mom screamed like she was being tortured. She rushed out of her seat and threw herself against me, pulling on my baggy jail clothes.

"Lee Anne! I'm so sorry, I'm so sorry," she sobbed pitifully. "Please forgive me, baby, please."

A guard pulled her off. I thought of a billion nasty things I could've said to her, but I didn't. Instead, I gave her my back and allowed the guard to handcuff me and push me toward the exit.

I'm shoved in the back of a police car and a couple of female cops drove me to Mabel Bassett. The cops talked about nail polish and their husbands and how they don't get any and what they're going to do Friday night. All I thought about was that I'd never have the chance to paint my fingernails or have a husband (didn't want one anyway, thank you) or do anything on a Friday night for about fifteen years.

Fifteen years. When I finally got out, I'd be an old woman. An old woman whose life has already passed.

It was all a blur. The cops signed me in. A guard made me strip down naked and then she scrubbed me in the shower with a stiff brush and some god-awful lye smelling soap. She stuck gloved fingers up every orifice without so much as a thank you.

The guard was a big woman, but not muscle, mostly flab. She seemed to actually enjoy the way she took up too much space by crowding me out of my own. She was none too gentle with the cavity search either, like she wanted me to know she was the one in control and my body wasn't my own anymore.

She didn't even let me dry off good before she threw my prison issue clothes at me and said, "Get dressed." The gray pants were too big in the waist and too short in the legs (so that's where the term 'jailin' came from), a baggy gray shirt and some kind of slipper/shoes. I was barely dressed before the guard said, "Warden wants to see you."

She led me down a series of gray halls to a big gray door. What the hell did they have against color? It was like I was in an old black-and-white movie.

The guard rapped on the metal door and a voice ordered,

"Come in!" The guard swung the door open, put her big hand on the small of my back and pushed me inside.

Behind a metal desk in front of a computer sat a square-shaped woman with a military-style haircut and no-nonsense shoes. She wore all gray too. "I'm your warden," she said, looking at me over her glasses perched on the tip of her nose. "Warden Johnston. Sit down, Ms. Hammond."

I sat down in the metal folding chair she offered. She studied me a minute before taking her glasses off. In direct conflict with the rest of her body, she had really soft eyes. I decided to concentrate on her eyes.

"I received a phone call, Ms. Hammond. Your mother passed away."

"I just saw her," I uttered, as if that meant it wasn't true.

"Yes," she said. "She passed away...just this afternoon."

"How?" I asked.

"Suicide." I guess she wasn't one of those women who believed in sugarcoating the truth to make it easier to swallow. I didn't breathe for a full minute or more and actually thought maybe I might pass out. When I realized it was because I was holding my breath, I let that one out and sucked in another.

"Okay," I mumbled, because I couldn't think of anything else to say and because the warden was studying me for a response.

"You can go to the funeral if you like," Warden Johnston said. "We can arrange for you to attend the funeral with a police escort."

"No, thank you."

She put her glasses back on and looked at her computer monitor. "You'll let me know if you change your mind?" she asked.

"I won't."

She nodded, then addressed the guard without looking at her, "Put her in with Teddy."

"You sure?" the guard asked.

Warden Johnston shot her a reproachful look and that's all that was needed to shut the guard's mouth.

That was my cue to leave, so I stood and the guard guided me toward the door. Then I thought of something and before I chickened out, I turned and asked, "Warden, ma'am? You think I could get some paper and a pencil or something?"

"You have somebody to write?" she asked.

"Just for myself," I answered.

She studied me a moment. "Two sheets of paper and one pencil for an hour a day," she ordered the guard.

"That's it?" I asked.

The warden moved her gaze to me without blinking and said, "Write quickly and tersely. You'll thank me later."

The guard ushered me back out the door. I felt Warden Johnston watching me over her glasses all the way out.

I was led outside and across a basketball court then into the maximum security building. A big guard pod was in the center with four wings shooting off the pod. Each wing held around eighty prisoners, two to a cell. That meant there was at least three hundred and twenty women behind bars. We were all murderers or attempted murderers. We were the reason people didn't sleep at night.

The guard opened the cell door for me and I stepped in. The door clanged shut and locked behind me.

The cell was maybe eight feet long and eight feet across. There were two little cots against the concrete block walls across from each other. There was a sink. A toilet with no tank. The toilet sat right out in the open. I knew right then and there that I'd never shit again.

My cellmate, Teddy, was lying on her bunk and she raised up on one elbow and glared at me.

I reflexively looked away from her stare.

Teddy was huge. She was big and black. And by big and black, I meant she was the biggest, blackest woman I'd ever seen. She took up so much room in that tiny box, I didn't know how I was ever going to fit in there.

I stared at my own feet a few moments, then I moved to the empty cot across from Teddy's and sat on the edge. What was I supposed to do? Just sit there and wait for Teddy to beat me or rape me or both?

She was the first to speak. "Rules: stay on your own side. I stay on mine. Don't fuck with me. I don't fuck with you."

I raised my gaze to hers and nodded the tiniest bit.

"And don't fuckin' look at me," she said. "Don't never fuckin' look at me."

I looked away and nodded again.

That first night after lights out, I cried into my pillow. No tears, just dry, racking sobs.

"Shut the fuck up," Teddy snarled. "You ain't the onliest one who's ever gone to jail."

I stuffed the pillow in my mouth to drown out my noise.

I turn away from my mother's grave and don't even realize I'm crying until I feel the snot dripping out of my nose. I snuffle it back up and wipe my wet cheeks with the back of my hand.

Shit. Now I have the hiccups.

I head back to the cab. I hate to admit it, but I actually feel a little bit better. Maybe I should have a catharsis more often. It's kind of like washing your insides then hanging them out to dry.

The cab's not where it was.

Where the hell?

I turn in a slow circle.

Where the hell?

She didn't, did she?

Did Vivian really just leave me out here in the middle of a cemetery? I don't want to think that. I really don't want to think that she just left me hanging out here in the middle of a bunch of dead bodies. But that's exactly what she just did.

There's a definite pattern developing here. She met me in a cemetery. She left me in the same cemetery. Vivian would understand and appreciate the full circleness of that, if that's a word. What she doesn't understand is that I'm not that easy to get rid of. Or maybe that's what she's counting on.

I walk down the middle of the gravel road toward the main highway. Damn hiccups. I stare at my boots and think. I kick a big rock, walk up to it and kick it again. I kick and walk and think. Vivian's last words scare me. Like she understood why somebody would kill themselves. Surely, she wouldn't. But she did say she was sorry for dragging me into this. She has been hinting about us "breaking up."

I kick and walk and think so hard I walk right into the back of a big, black hearse and fall face forward over the trunk. A short, fat man dressed in a black suit with a cowboy string tie throws opens the driver's door and jumps out. "What the hell're you doing?" he yells.

"Think you can give me ride into town?" I ask, wiping away my palm prints from the car with my jacket sleeve.

He sniffs hard and looks me over harder. "Yeah, okay," he finally decides. "I was just headed back anyway."

"I don't have any money, though," I add.

"Me neither," he says. "Hop in."

I open the passenger door and climb in. There's no way in hell I'm going to look behind me. Just in case there's a coffin with a dead body in it back there.

Where could she be? I close my eyes and think. Full circle. Vivian's going to keep going in circles. She wants me to find her. I have to believe that she wants me to find her.

"Redman Motor Lodge, please," I direct.

I give the driver a thanks for his trouble and climb out of the backseat. As he drives away, I look around the lot. There's maybe a dozen beat-up, seen-better-days cars. The shabby motel looks even shabbier in broad daylight. The concrete teepee is lonely and more ridiculous than the first time I saw it.

I walk into the motel office and ding the little bell at the front desk. It smells like burnt cheese in here. And if I'm not mistaken there's the tangy odor of pot underlying the food smell.

A skinny kid with bad acne and greasy long hair hanging over his bony shoulders comes out of the back, munching on some kind of gross-looking meat sandwich.

"Room?" he asks. "Thirty bucks a night. Cash."

"No," I answer. "I need to know if a friend of mine just checked in."

The kid does something with his lips that may or may not be a smile. "Can't tell you that, 'gainst the rules," he says around his sandwich.

I put my elbows on the counter and lean over until I feel my tits grazing against the dirty veneer. I roll my eyes slowly over him and say, "I'll give you a blow job if you tell me."

He backs up a step. I see myself through his eyes: Dreads, dirty, tats, a full foot taller than him. No wonder he looks scared. He probably thinks I'm going to bite his dick off.

"Lady," he says, "I'll give you the info if you promise *not* to give me a blow job."

"Deal," I say, standing back upright. "Her name is Vivian Baxter."

He puts down his sandwich and taps away on the computer keyboard. "Nope," he says, "no Baxter."

She wouldn't use her real name, how can stupid can I be?

I hold my palm out so high, "She's maybe five foot seven. But wearing heels. Sexy, you know, short skirt. Long red hair."

"Oh, yeah," he leers. "Red hair. She signed in as Lucille Balls."

I laugh. Good one, Vivian.

"What room number?"

"Seven. She said she had to have number seven."

I hold out my palm to him.

He jerks his sandwich back like I'm actually asking for a bite of it or something. "I don't want your sandwich, numbnuts. Gimme the keys to number seven."

"Lady, look..." he starts to protest.

"Gimme the keys or I bite your little dick off."

He hands them over. I walk to the door, then turn back around. "And if you wanna keep your dick, you never saw either one of us."

He holds his sandwich up and gives it a little shake in my direction. I guess that means okay.

I don't knock. I just turn the key and open the door. The room is beyond dark and the still air is stifling. I can make out Vivian's silhouette on the bed, but the air is so heavy, the stillness so deafening, I'm immediately filled with dread.

I flip on the overhead.

Vivian is sprawled on the bed, face down, with the covers bunched in a ball at her feet and the bags of money sitting on the table. Even though the harsh light makes me flinch, she doesn't move at all.

"Viv?" I whisper and ease the door closed.

No movement. Nothing. I stare at her back and can't make out if she's breathing or not.

I rush to her side and shake her by the shoulders. She doesn't move; she's just deadweight. I roll her over and take her face in my hands. "Vivian! Wake up!"

"Wha...?" she slurs and throws her arm across her eyes.

My relief is immediate and humbles me to my knees. I shake her leg and beg, "C'mon, Viv, talk to me. What's going on here?" When she doesn't answer, I crawl up on the bed with her. I point her face to mine and command, "Wake up! Tell me what's wrong with you!"

She opens her eyes to slits, sees me, and jerks her face away from mine.

I get back in her face. "What's wrong, tell me, Viv," I plead. "What's happening?"

She flings herself out of my arms and rolls to the far side of the bed, lying there limp.

"I'm calling nine-one-one, okay? I'm going to get help."

Suddenly, she's up on her knees in the middle of the bed all teeth and claws, screaming, "No! No, goddammit! Can't you see I want to be alone! I just want to be left alone! Why the hell can't you leave me alone!"

She swings at me with one loose fist, but I catch her wrist and wrestle her back down to the bed. She fights me like some kind of wild banshee, all sharp elbows and knees. I straddle her and hold her arms down with my knees and ignore her kicks in my back.

That's when I see it. Pills. Pills everywhere. Different colors, different shapes, must be a hundred or more pills strung around the bed and on the floor.

I scoop a few into my hand and show them to her. "What's this? Did you take a bunch of pills?"

She bucks me off, yelling, "Leave me the fuck alone!"

She kicks my hand with her bare foot and the pills fly across the room and ping off the far wall. Her voice breaks into gasping sobs, "Why can't you just leave me the fuck alone?!"

She curls up against the headboard and wraps herself around a pillow.

I gently grasp her shoulder. "How many did you take?" I plead. "Vivian? C'mon... How many did you take?"

She curls her legs up to her chest and sobs on her knees, "Just...go."

"I'm not going anywhere, Viv, I'm right here, okay? I'm right here."

"They always go," she sobs to herself. "They always go. Why should you be any different?"

"Yeah, well," I sigh, "they're probably a lot smarter than me."

I scoop her into my arms and carry her like a baby into the bathroom. "You're not gonna like this, princess, but it's got to be done."

I dump her into a pile in front of the toilet. She cusses and kicks and when she tries to crawl out the door, I catch her by her hair and drag her back to the toilet. I kneel on the floor behind her and hold her in a knee-lock so she can't escape again.

I force her mouth open with one hand and jam two fingers down her throat with the other. Thank God she has a good gag reflex. She heaves into the bowl while I hold her hair out of the way. I flush away the streams of bright pill colors that spew out of her belly.

I jam my fingers down her throat again and this time she bites me. I have to slap her across the face to get my fingers back. Fingers be damned, I do it again and again and again and I don't stop until all the colors have left her stomach and she's dry heaving.

We're both shaking and slick with sweat by the time I let her lay her head across the toilet.

I rip open the shower curtain and turn the water on cold. I kick off my boots and throw my jacket off. I pick her up under her arms, dangling her off the floor like a puppet. I drag her into the icy cold shower with me and her fight comes back full-force.

She twists and thrashes and tries every which way to get out from under the ice water. I lock my arms across her chest and let her just wear herself out.

She finally quiets and I stand a few minutes under the water with her limp body leaning back against me. When her muscles spasm and jerk involuntarily against the cold, I pick her up in my arms and walk with her into the bedroom. I lay her down on the bed and strip off her wet clothes. I shuck off my own clothes and crawl into bed with her. I hug her hard to my warm body and try to rub some warmth back into her arms and legs.

After a few moments, she cries, "Let me sleep, Lee, I just need to sleep."

"Sorry," I say. "You're not going to be sleeping for a while." I pull her off the bed and walk her around the tiny room. When her knees give out from exhaustion, I drape one of her arms across my shoulders and drag her.

I walk and drag and walk and drag. Then I get back in the cold shower with her and stand under the icy water until she gets her fight back. Then I walk her some more.

When dawn finally comes, I lay her back in bed, gather up every little pill I can find and flush them, then I spoon up behind Vivian while she sleeps. I place my palm on her belly so I can feel the motion of her breathing.

I don't sleep.

It's dusk when she wakes up. She bolts out of bed and and paces the floor like a caged animal.

"Lay down," I say. "You need to rest, Viv."

She looks at me directly for the first time since I found her and snarls, "Fuck you." She paces some more. Helpless, I sit on the edge of the mattress watching her.

Suddenly, she darts into the bathroom, slamming the door behind her. I follow her only to find out she's thumb-locked the damn door behind her.

I knock. "Let me in, Viv."

"Fuck you!"

"Let me in or I break down this door."

"Fuck you!"

I throw my shoulder as hard as I can against the hollow core door and it flies open, banging against the wall behind it.

Vivian stands over the sink with a handful of pills. A hairspray can is in the sink. Good Lord, she's been hiding pills in the lid of the hairspray can.

"Get the fuck out!" she screams. "Can't I even pee in privacy?!"

I wrestle her for the pills and am amazed at how much strength she has left. I finally get the pills and throw them in the toilet. She makes a dive for them, thrusting her arm down the bowl, but I manage to flush before she can catch any.

Screaming every obscenity I've ever heard and some I haven't, she heaves her body against mine and pushes me halfway out the door. She grabs the edge of the door and tries to slam it on me, but I manage to stop it with my foot. Defeated, Vivian plops down on the toilet lid and buries her face in her hands. "I just want to go. Please God, Lee, let me get out of here."

I kneel down in front of her and take her hands away from her face. "I can't let you do that."

She jumps up and is out the door before I can get off the floor. I stumble after her and for a scary moment I don't see her.

I hear her.

I crouch to my knees and look under the bed. She's squeezed herself under the bed and is frantically picking pills out of the dirty carpet nap. I reach under the bed and grab her by the wrist and hair and drag her out.

She shoves the pills in her mouth before I can get them out of her fist.

"You shouldn't have done that, Vivian," I say. "You really shouldn't have done that."

This time I don't even bother with the toilet. I bend her over the bed and shove my fingers in her mouth and scoop out several pills.

I'm working on no sleep and my nerves are shredded to a pulp, so this time when she bites me, I react and slap the shit out of her.

She slaps me back.

I push her flat on her back on top of the bed and grab her wrists. I pull her arms above her head and hold them there with my left hand and pin her to the bed with my knee.

I slap her across the face. "That's for slapping me!" I scream. I slap her again. "And that's for hitting me with your damn shoe all the time!"

She spits in my face. "You fucking dyke! Can't you see that I don't want to be around you?"

I let her spittle drip down my cheek.

"Yeah, well, sometimes I don't like you very much either. But I'm not trying to kill myself over it."

"Just like your mother!" she yells. "Don't you think that's more than a coincidence? All the women in your life trying to kill themselves? Gee, Lee, what's the common denominator, there?" she laughs.

I grit my teeth and choke back my anger.

"Are you getting mad, Lee? Mad enough to kill me?" She struggles against me, but I hold her tighter. "Too bad you don't have a gun, right? Then you could just erase this little problem, too."

"You're a real bitch," I say softly.

"Hell, I could've told you that," she says.

"I'm not going to let you die like this, Vivian. So you better just get used to the idea."

She bucks against me hard and it sends us both sprawling to the floor. Luckily, I end up on top of her so she can't get away. I lie prone on top of her with my whole body and hold her down.

"Go ahead, you fucking dyke," she says. "Go ahead and fuck me. Go ahead and fuck me and get it over with so you can just LEAVE!"

"I'm not trying to fuck you, you idiot! I'm trying to save your goddamn life! And as for calling me a dyke over and over... I take that as a compliment. If you really want me to leave, you'll dry out and calm down. But I'm not leaving until then."

She stops struggling, closes her eyes and turns her face away. I'm afraid she's faking, so I don't let her go for a long time. When

I'm sure she's really asleep, I lay down next to her on the floor with my palm on her belly.

I lie awake and feel the motion of her jagged breaths.

Time passes in fits and starts.

She claws at her own face. She rips at her hair. I pull her hands away and let her claw at me instead.

She cowers in a corner of the room, squatting in a puddle of her own piss, sweating and hallucinating. I throw her in another cold shower and wash her off.

The sun rises and bleeds through the curtains three times.

The fourth night I'm holding her in bed and I feel her body ease. Her muscles loosen and her breathing evens out. She falls into the blissful oblivion of sleep. I match my breathing to hers and am soon following.

"Wherever thou goest, I will go," I whisper.

I wake up to sunshine streaming harshly through the window and Vivian in just her all-together, straddling me as I lie flat on my back. "You saved my life," she says as soon as I open my eyes.

"Maybe a little," I say, not at all oblivious to the fact that it's not every day I wake up to a gorgeous naked woman sitting on me. I blink a couple of times to make sure she's real and doesn't disappear.

"I feel better than I've ever felt in my whole entire life and I'm awake and it's only eight-thirty in the morning. And I woke up naked. And you're naked. What have you done to me?"

"Nothing yet," I joke.

"Maybe you should," she says in a voice that doesn't sound at all like she's joking.

She leans over and her breasts lightly touch my own. Her long red hair trails over my shoulders and face. My nipples harden instantly.

Vivian looks into my eyes and holds my gaze. Her normally purple eyes are now blue like the color of the sky in a child's coloring book. She pins me to the bed with those unblinking eyes.

I know from my late-night viewing of the History Channel while caught up in insomnia, that somewhere out there is a parallel universe and in that parallel universe I am making mad, nasty, crazy, passionate love to Vivian. I decide to test the string theory and see if I can enter this alternate world.

Without taking my eyes from hers, I put my hand on her breast and let my thumb lightly graze across her nipple. She doesn't pull away or look away or blink or anything. So, I trail my other hand up the outside of her thigh and slide it under her butt.

She leans in to me a little more and confesses in my ear, "I don't know how to do this."

"You're doing an okay job so far," I whisper back.

I feel her warm breath in my ear and then her lips are on mine and she's kissing me. It's a take-all-the-time-you-need-type of kiss. Her tongue flicks across my teeth and teases my tongue. I follow her lead and revel in our first real kiss. She pulls an inch or so away and I'm hit with a sudden panic that she's changed her mind.

"You okay?" I ask. And when she doesn't immediately answer, I add, "We can stop. If you're not okay with this, we can stop."

She wraps her hand around the back of my neck, pulls my

mouth to hers and kisses me hard. She gives my tongue a sharp nip with her teeth and warns, "Stop talking."

I flip her onto her back. I'm on my knees in between her legs and I freeze to admire how absolutely beautiful she is. No makeup, no Wonderbra, no miniskirt or high heels and she is perfection in her natural state. I went to a museum once on a high school field trip and the paintings were so unbelievably beautiful that my fingers were twitching to just reach out and touch them. Of course, touching the paintings was forbidden.

But I'm not in a museum, am I?

I lie on top of Vivian and hold most of my weight on my elbows and let my body lightly graze hers. She wraps her legs around my hips and we move together, feeling each other's rhythm. Her kissing becomes more passionate, more intense. I reach my left hand under her butt and help her move with me. She sucks on my bottom lip as her fingers tease my nipples. I try to slow down the pace a little by moving my mouth to her throat, biting and nipping her neck and shoulders. I move down further and flick her nipples with my tongue, teasing. Her breath comes in short little gasps and when I suck a nipple into my mouth, she moans just the tiniest bit.

I'm reluctant to leave her breasts. Because, seriously, I could stay on them all day. And I would, too, but Vivian finally gasps, "...I want you...inside me."

I know what she just said, and I want nothing more in this parallel world, but there's no way I'm going to rush this. I slide my right hand down her hip and the outside of her thigh, caressing the length of her leg. I slowly move my hand up the inside of her leg and trace my fingers up her thigh. My fingers play across her warmth and I feel she's wet and more than ready.

I take my mouth away from her breast and look her in the face. She's staring at me expectantly, not breathing. I ease my fingers slowly inside her; she closes her eyes, arches her back and thrusts against my hand.

I pull back, testing her reaction. "Please..." she moans and grabs my hand, bringing it back fully inside her. I explore the inside of her with my fingers, moving slowly as she rocks against me. She knows what she wants and I'm content to let her set the pace. I move with her beat and her urgency.

She's breathing heavy now, eyes closed, wanting more. I scoot further down and while my fingers continue to move, I use my mouth and tongue to taste her.

She inhales sharply and I draw away for a second, but then she wraps her thighs around my shoulders, places her hands on my head and guides me back into place. Now I'm the one setting the pace with my tongue and hand and she moves to my tempo.

She tastes like sweet and sour together. She tastes like old-fashioned maple syrup and wild honey with just a dash of bitterness all at the same time. I feel like no matter how deep I am inside her, it's not enough. I want all of me inside her; I want all of her in my mouth; I want her to come all over me—my face, my hands, my entire body.

I look up the length of her body and watch her gorgeous face as she begins to climax. Her pink nipples are hard, she moves her hips in little circles and clutches the sheets in her fists.

She tightens, arches her back and moves back away from me a little. But I don't let up, I press into her; I move faster and harder and that's when she comes. She whispers hoarsely while her body spasms, "Oh God, Lee...Oh God..."

I keep my fingers deep inside her, feeling her muscles clench and unclench. I lie prone on top of her body and ride the waves of her orgasm. For a long time after she shudders, tiny aftershocks rock both her and me. When her body is peaceful again and her breathing evens out, only then do I pull my hand away.

"My God," she breathes into my neck, "I haven't come that hard since...ever."

I kiss away the wet tears at the corners of her eyes. I kiss and bite her breasts, sucking on her nipples. I can't seem to stop making love to her.

Vivian surprises me by raking her fingernails down my back, across my butt and then sliding her hand between my legs. She licks my ear and sucks my earlobe into her mouth. In a throaty voice, she asks, "Does that feel good?"

I don't even have time to say anything before her fingers expertly take me to the edge...but just before I fall off...

She stops.

"Don't do that," I plead. "Don't stop."

"Don't tell me what to do," she says, slapping my ass.

For chrissakes. I give up. I roll over and bury my face in the pillow. She's not like any woman I've ever met and I don't know how I feel about that.

The next thing I feel is her body pressed against my back and her tits and hair caressing me all the way from my neck to the soles of my feet. I feel like I'm floating. I feel like parts of my body don't exist until her breasts touch them, then they light up on fire.

She pushes my legs apart with her knee and rubs her tits down my ass and between my legs. She lifts my hips off the mattress with both hands. Then her right hand eases around my hip and under me and down and her fingers find the exact right spot. Her hips press into my ass and I can feel her tits on my back and...my God, I'm going to...

She stops.

"Vivian, dammit. Don't tease me."

"Beg," she orders.

She leans down and bites me kind of hard on my back and before I decide whether I like it or not, she uses her left hand to thrust her fingers deep inside me from behind and all I can do is gasp out loud and grab the headboard for support. Her right hand goes back to where it was and I'm filled with a need, a hunger, that there are no words for, and all I can do is hold onto the headboard.

And I beg. God help me, I beg just like she wants me to. "Fuck me. Please, God, Vivian...fuck me."

She doesn't stop this time. She takes me all the way and further. I explode from the inside out; it's like a flower blooms in the pit of my belly and opens wide and then completely devours me. I'm like Silly Putty or maybe Jello when I collapse back onto the bed.

I've just caught my breath when she spoons me from behind and playfully pinches one of my nipples, sending me into spasms all over again.

Oh, my God, this woman is most certainly going to kill me. And I mean that in a good way.

I sleep a thousand sleeps in the next couple of hours. Intertwined in Vivian's warm skin, my hand cupping her breast, I am oblivious to anything but my own contentment. I'm in a haze when I wake up. It's dusk and I can hear the sounds of a highway close by. I reach out for Vivian, but she's not there. I sit up and throw my legs over the side of the bed.

"Viv?"

She doesn't answer.

I walk to the bathroom and push open the door. I turn on the light. Nothing. I trip back into the bedroom and turn on those lights too. Nothing.

She's gone. Maybe, just maybe, she went out to get us something to eat. Or maybe to get a pack of cigarettes. I sit at the foot of the bed...and that's when I see it. A large heart is drawn in Viv's red lipstick on the mirror. I look around. That's all she's left behind—a large, lipstick-smeared heart.

She fucked me and left me and took the money with her.

I am numb from the top of my head to the tips of my toes for I have no idea how long. This curious little thought niggles at the edge of my brain. "I fucked a cheerleader," I say out loud. I start to laugh. The laughter rolls out of me in giant topsy-turvy waves. I slip off the bed and hit the floor, doubled over, holding my belly and flood the empty room with my laughter.

Without warning, my laughter abruptly turns to tears and I sob into my knees. I clutch desperately at the bedclothes and yank them off the bed and down on top of me. I bury myself in our smell and I cry.

CHAPTER FOURTEEN

Knock, knock.

I bound out of bed with my heart in my throat and throw open the door. I'm about to say "Vivian! I'm so glad you came back!" but my heart thuds back to my belly when I see it's just the maid. Her eyes glance up and down, and only then do I realize I'm standing in the doorway stark naked.

"Housecleaning," she mouths.

I shut and lock the door and roll back into bed.

Thirty minutes or so later there's another knock at the door. This time I open it with a sheet wrapped around me and much lower expectations.

It's the manager. He's balding and somewhere in his late fifties with pants pulled up way too high. Probably because he's wearing both a belt and suspenders. He has a little chili or something like it globbed on his tie. The glob totally missed the napkin he has tucked into his collar. He, too, looks me up and down and seems disappointed that I'm covered up.

"Checkout was an hour ago," he says, licking sauce off his mustache.

For one serious second I actually entertain the idea of pulling him inside and paying for the room the old-fashioned way before I realize I'd rather be homeless.

"I'll be out in a minute," I say, shutting and locking the door firmly between us.

I get into a steaming hot shower and scrub scrub scrub everything about Vivian off my skin. I don't want to smell her, think about her, talk about her, or any fuckin' thing about her ever again. It takes me until the water runs cold, but I'm pretty sure she doesn't exist to me anymore.

I put my dirty old clothes back on and feel a sizeable lump. There's a roll of bills in my right front pocket. I quickly count the money and realize I'm holding twenty grand in my hand. Thanks, Vivian, I've never been paid for sex before, but thanks for making me sink to new depths.

I'm planning on just walking out the door, but I don't make it that far. I catch sight of the lipstick heart drawn on the mirror and wild fury coats my brain and acid roils in my stomach. I ball up my fist and pound the mirror. I pound it over and over and over again, screaming, "I hate you! I hate you! Why the fuck did you leave me?"

Exhausted, I sink to my knees and cradle my cut, bleeding hand. I crawl to the bathroom and yank the roll of toilet paper from its holder. Panting like some damned dog, I wrap the toilet paper around and around my hand to stanch the bleeding.

"Bitch," I whisper through gritted teeth. "Look what you did to me."

I use the bathroom sink to pull myself to my feet. I crunch through the broken glass, open the door and step out into the bright sunshine.

The cab drops me off at WalMart and I am so fuckin' glad to see that my Harley is sitting right where I left it.

I zip up my jacket, put on my sunglasses, open the fuel cock, stick in the key and fire her right up.

This is why I love motorcycles more than people. They do exactly what you tell them to do.

The bike's loud pipes drown out any thoughts of my own, which is a nice break. I have no idea where I'm going. All I know is I'm going there at eighty miles an hour and I'm going feet first. It must've been instinct because when I roll to a stop, I'm parked in Ginger's driveway. Just here to pick up some of my shit, I tell myself. Just get my shit and leave.

I pick the house key out of the dead potted plant by the door and let myself inside. It smells stuffy and smoky and like stale alcohol. I flip on the kitchen lights to discover where the smells are coming from. The place is a mess. Dishes are piled shoulder high in the sink and ashtrays are overflowing everywhere. Instead of emptying the ashtrays somebody's just been stomping out the butts on the floor. Empty Wild Turkey bottles and beer cans and Margarita Mixer cartons are scattered around on every visible surface. Good. Maybe when she has to clean up by herself, she'll realize I was good for something.

I walk down the hallway to my room only to find the door open. Clothes are thrown about. The closet doors are open, the chest of drawers is tipped over, the bed sheets are off the bed and balled up in a corner. Looks like Ginger went on a little rampage. I don't really give a shit. I find three T-shirts and a couple pair of jeans that look less dirty than the rest and roll them into a ball. I get my stack of journals out of the ceiling panel where I hid them. I shrug at everything else. I guess that's all I really need.

Except food. I can't remember the last time I ate anything and my belly is letting me know about it. I go back to the kitchen and open the fridge. Good God. Condiments. Beer. And a leftover half-eaten Subway sandwich. I take out the sandwich and a beer. I open a cabinet door looking for a clean plate. The cabinet is bare. I open the dishwasher kind of hoping that maybe Ginger has actually washed some dishes. It's empty too. Except for...I pull open the top rack. Wow. It's a big neon blue dildo. Nine to ten inches long at least. I wonder if they ran it through a cycle already or if it's still dirty and just sitting in the dishwasher. I don't touch it just in case. I guess Ginger hasn't missed me too much.

I grab a chair and tip it over so all the shit that's on it dumps to the floor. I sit down heavily, pop open the beer and drain it all. Then I start in on the sandwich.

I'm only into it a couple of bites when the door opens and Ginger appears in the doorway. She's wearing some kind of spangly miniskirt. And, if I know Ginger, and I do, nothing underneath. She has on knee-high red boots and a black pleather bra. She takes one look at me, crosses her arms and leans against the doorjamb.

"Well, look what the cat drug in," she says. "What happened, Lee? You nail the little straight girl a couple of times and then she leave you?"

"Nope," I respond around mouthfuls of teriyaki chicken. "I just nailed her once."

Ginger smiles at me and I get a little queasy in my throat. Ginger smiling is not necessarily a good thing.

She swings right into my space bubble and looks down at me. "You miss me?"

"Nope." I take another bite.

"Not even a little bit?" she pouts.

"Nope." I swallow.

"I bet I know something you did miss." She reaches behind her back and pops open her bra, throws it across the room and straddles my lap. This position effectively traps me in the chair, puts her huge tits right in my face and now I can't finish my sandwich.

"I'm trying to eat here," I say.

Ginger squirms a little in my lap and pushes Bert and Ernie even further into my face, and if there's one thing Ginger knows, it's me.

"C'mon, baby," she coos. Her squirming becomes more insistent. "I need to relax. Why don't you relax me, hmmm?"

She sucks on my earlobe. That's not fair. That's not playing fair at all. She darts her tongue in and out of my ear and I drop the sandwich. Goddammit. When it rains, it fuckin' pours.

I relax Ginger in the chair. I bend her over the kitchen table and relax her again. Then I relax her once more on the floor.

I pull my pants back up, grab my cleanish clothes and journals and head for the door.

"Where you going, baby?" she asks.

"I don't know. I'll know when I get there," I say, slamming the door behind me.

Like a dog chasing its own tail, I ride in circles. And just like a loyal dog, I go back home to the same master that kicked it.

The blinking neon lights and smell of desperation hit me as soon as I pull into the parking lot of The Glitter Box. I got nowhere else to be, so I might as well be here. At least there's some girls to look at and nobody ever bothers me at the bar.

It hasn't changed from the last time I was in here with Vivian. Loud music, mostly naked girls swinging their tits, and Dixie's still slinging the drinks.

I nurse a beer for the next hour and think about how all tits start to look the same when you see so many of them. I pass the time by giving them all names: Fred & Ginger, Starsky & Hutch, Tom & Jerry, Sanford & Son, Adam & Eve... Even the dancer's names seem interchangeable: Tawny, Ebony, Brandi, Candi, Buffy and Kitty. And those are just the girls working tonight. I wonder if they became strippers and changed their names, or if they were born with those names and were destined to become strippers. I watch all the lonely men stuff their paychecks in the girls' G-strings and wonder how many of them are going home to their wives and how many of them are going home to jerk off in the shower. Or both.

Ginger comes out on the stage after awhile and I watch her work over a drunk redneck with a pocket of ones. She keeps glancing my way and I know she's dancing more for me than him. Or maybe that's just my ego thinking. After a couple of songs she leads him to the private room. She looks back over her shoulder and throws me a kiss. I feel absolutely nothing.

A woman sits down next to me even though there's at least

three empty barstools to either side. She orders a crantini. I study her in the mirror behind the bottles. She's probably closing in on fifty. She just looks real good for her age. She's got it going on strong. She's stacked pretty good and dresses to show off her Pamela Anderson's. (With tits that big you only need one name.) She glitters from head to toe in diamonds. She has expensive clothes, expensive hair, expensive jewelry and cheap taste in women if she sits down next to me.

I turn away from her when she catches my eye in the mirror. We both sip on our drinks and pretend to study the dancers, but I can feel her eyes on me.

Dixie points at my beer, but I shake my head. "Want another, Delia?" he asks the lady next to me.

"Sure, doll," she says. "And give her another beer too."

I look at this Delia for the first time straight on and say, "I can buy my own."

"Sure you can, sweetie. But why would you do that when Delia will buy it for you?"

I think it's a little strange when people refer to themselves in the third person, but I don't tell her that. I just shrug and look away.

Dixie brings the drinks back and doesn't collect any money. This Delia lady must be pretty important because I've never seen him run a tab before.

Delia swivels on her stool to face me and takes her sweet time looking me over. Normally, this would make me a little self-conscious, but I'm not in the mood. In fact, I'm primed for a fight. "See anything you like?" I ask.

"You have a very dark aura," she replies.

"It's the lighting."

"I've seen you in here before," she says, sipping her fancy drink. "You're Ginger's girl toy."

I think of about a million smart-ass remarks to make, but don't voice any of them. Probably because I know she's right. That's all I was. All I am. Somebody's girl toy.

I turn on my stool and look from her huge tits to her face and hear myself say, "Not anymore, I'm not. I'm totally available."

Delia picks up her rhinestone-studded purse, stands and

orders, "Dixie, you're closing it down tonight. Put the deposit in the safe and get all the girls out of here in one piece."

"Sure thing, Delia." Dixie nods.

"Come," Delia orders me, heading for the door.

I put my tail between my legs and follow her out.

Delia beeps her key and an orange Cadillac beeps back. I jerk open its door and hit the passenger seat and try not to think about what I'm getting ready to do. The inside is spacious and comfortable and smells like new leather. Delia scoots behind the wheel and sticks the key in the ignition. I snatch the keys out and hide them in my fist. I lean in and kiss her hard, but she places her palm in the middle of my chest and pushes me away. "You taste like cheap booze and stale cigarettes," she says.

I scoot back to my own side. I catch my reflection in the dark tinted window and ask out loud, "Why am I here?"

Delia seems to sense some deeper meaning to the question and doesn't answer. She holds out her hand and I give her back the keys. "Don't worry," she says, starting the car. "I'll have your motorcycle brought over in the morning."

I'm so fuckin' exhausted. I lean back in the seat and give in to her driving. I close my eyes, feel a left turn, then a couple of rights and the next thing I know, I'm back in prison.

I'd just turned eighteen, I was a convicted murderer and I was scared shitless. It didn't help any that I was the whitest person there.

I spent the first two months avoiding Teddy and everybody else. It wasn't too hard to do except during meals. All the white women sat at tables in the middle. The black women took up three tables to my left. The Mexicans were to my right and Indians claimed their space in the very front.

I grabbed my lunch tray and sat alone at a table in the back. I bit into my grilled-in-butter-flavored-Crisco cheese sandwich. I chewed and swallowed quickly so I didn't have to actually taste the food.

I finished my sandwich and started in on my soggy fries. The food tasted like shit, but I never got enough of it. Seemed like I was always hungry.

I glanced up and saw that all the Mexicans were staring at me. The entire table was staring me down and I had no idea why or what I did. The french fry lodged itself in my throat and I took a quick gulp of milk to wash it down. When I looked back over, Maria flashed her white teeth at me in a smile.

I had noticed Maria right off, like the first couple days I was in. She was impossible to miss. She had long, curly black hair and curves that made my mouth water and my palms itch. Every night I'd wait until Teddy was snoring, then I'd think of Maria and get busy under the thin blanket. One night I came seven times in a row just thinking about her tits, Frida and Diego.

I quickly looked away. I didn't dare smile back at her and the heat of my embarrassment lit up my face like Rudolph's damn nose. The Mexicans laughed at me. I forced myself to stare at my tray and choked down a few more fries.

A grilled cheese sandwich flopped down onto my tray. I looked up to see Maria looking down at me over those gorgeous chichis of hers and my heart lurched into my throat. Close up her eyes were black like a shark's. She devoured me with just one bite of those eyes.

She flipped her hair, turned and sashayed back to her table. All the Mexicans hooted and hollered and made lip-smacking noises in my direction. I picked up the grilled cheese gift and stuffed half of it into my mouth at once.

I looked at Maria while I chewed. She pursed her lips and blew me a sexy kiss. Her table went wild. I suppressed a grin and ate the rest of the sandwich without looking at them.

That night, after Teddy was asleep, I set a new personal best.

Shower time was my favorite time in prison. I didn't care if I was naked in front of the guard and I didn't care if I smelled like household cleansers when I was done. All I cared was that twice a week for ten minutes I got to feel halfway human again.

I rubbed the suds between my legs, up my butt crack and under my arms, getting all the important parts first. I rinsed that away under the lukewarm water, closed my eyes and lifted my face into the needles of spray and let it massage my head.

A wet hand reached into mine and grabbed the bar of soap. Maria. She stood before me in all her naked glory.

I looked around. We were alone except for the guard who stood at the doorway with her back to us. I wondered briefly how Maria pulled that favor in.

Maria let the bar of soap slip through her hands and drop to the floor. She pressed her body into mine and I took a second to savor the startling difference between her brown skin and my pale skin. She leaned down and wrapped her lips around my right nipple, nipping with her teeth.

She smiled up at me. "We have seven minutes," she said.

I pressed her back against the cold tile wall, buried my face in her long hair and Maria became the very first woman I ever fucked.

Seven minutes wasn't a very long time, but it was just long enough to violate several laws of the state of Oklahoma.

The next day I sat in my spot with my lunch tray and it only took me about ten seconds to realize something was up. I glanced to my right. The Mexicans were quiet, way too quiet. Even Maria wouldn't meet my eyes.

A chola stood up from the middle of their table and walked slowly and deliberately toward me.

Shit. I swallowed my spoonful of rice and it dropped to my belly like a hunk of lead.

The chola had a faded blue bandanna wrapped around her close-shaved head. She had teardrop tattoos under her right eye and letters tatted all up and down her arms. She was tall, not as tall as me, but she had a good fifty pounds of bulk on me. She had muscles ripped in places I didn't even know muscles existed.

I'd read that when you're about to be attacked by a bear, the worst thing you could do is run or act scared. You were supposed to stay calm, don't move, and look it directly in the eyes. I forced myself to look directly into the chola's sneering face. She edged up next to me, her hips touching my shoulder.

"*Gusta bajar al pozo*?" the chola asked.

I had no idea what she just said.

She laughed and her table laughed along with her. Encouraged by her own sense of machismo, the chola asked me louder, "*Chaca chaca Maria*?" She wiggled her hips back and forth, knocking into my shoulder and said it again, "*Chaca chaca*, huh?"

I was pretty damn sure what she meant by that so I answered with a clenched smile, "*Chaca chaca*, yeah, I *chaca chaca*'ed Maria."

The chola's smile melted. She reached out with one hand and deftly flipped my tray into my lap. I didn't wipe the slop off. I pressed both my palms on the top of the table and lifted myself to my feet, turning to her.

She called my bluff with a mighty chest bump that sent me stumbling backward and onto my ass. I was debating whether to get up and take my beating or let her just go ahead and kick the shit out of me on the floor when a big black shadow loomed over us. I froze and watched as Teddy moved her huge bulk between me and the chola.

Teddy was so immense that even the chola couldn't disguise the fear in her eyes. She spoke to the chola quietly, so quietly only her and I could hear: "*Chaca* with her and you *chaca* with me."

The chola took one step back. Two. Then three. She waved her hand in the air, dismissing me and strutted back to her table.

Teddy reached out her hand and I accepted. She pulled me to my feet, pushed me down into my chair and said, "Now sit yer scrawny ass down and keep your mouth shut."

She walked back to her table.

I glanced over at Maria. She winked at me.

That night during free time, I was lying on my bunk, reading aloud to Teddy who was lying on her bunk when Maria slithered into our cell. She began to unbutton her shirt. I glanced over to Teddy.

Teddy rolled her eyes and faced the wall, turning her back to us.

Maria stood in front of me and slipped out of her prison clothes like a snake sheds its skin.

I sat my book upside down beside me on the cot. Maria

straddled my lap and offered me a taste of her brown nipples. "You didn't answer Rosa's question. *Gusta bajar al pozo*?" Maria teased.

"I can't speak Spanish," I said around a nipple.

"...do you eat pussy?" she breathed in my ear.

I laid back and pulled Maria forward until she was sitting on my face. And since it's not polite to talk with your mouth full, she answered the question for me, "*Si...Oh, Dios mio, si...*"

I knew this wasn't exactly love, but it sure as hell was the next best thing.

When I wake up from the trip down memory lane, the car is parked in a big circular driveway in front of the biggest mansion I've ever seen in my life. The house looks like a movie's happy ending. Some guy in a suit is opening my door and beckoning me out of the car. I look over to Delia, but she's gone. "Miss Delia told me to take you to your room," he says.

I follow the little guy into the house and through a series of hallways and stairs. Finally, he opens a door for me and says, "Goodnight, ma'am, I hope you're comfortable."

Holy shit.

I've lived in entire houses that could fit into this room three times over. There's a monster bed and chests and fancy artwork and even a huge television set. I look at all the buttons and gadgets that make up the entertainment center. I don't even know where to begin. Plus, there's a huge bathroom all just for this bedroom. You don't have to share it with anybody. There's a separate tub and shower and two sinks and a toilet and one of those French bidet things.

I strip off my clothes and climb into bed. I don't know what Delia's game plan is, but I have a feeling she's just fattening up the pig before the slaughter. That's the last thought I have before falling asleep.

The next morning there's a knock on the door that wakes me up. For a minute I think it's the motel manager coming back, then I remember where I am. I sit up and go for my clothes on the floor—but they're gone. I jump up in panic and see some folded clothes on the foot of the bed with a note: *Lee Anne—I am having your clothes laundered. In the meantime, these should fit. Delia.*

My money! Shit! I had twenty grand stuffed into the pocket of my jeans! I glance around the room, already knowing the money's not there. I throw on the starched white button-down shirt she's left for me and grab for the pants. That's when I feel it. I reach into the pocket of the linen pants and there's my money. I quickly count it. Twenty grand minus the little I spent yesterday. Even my pocketknife is there.

What the hell? Twenty grand must be chump change to her.

I tippy-toe to the bedroom door (I don't know why, but tippy-toeing just seems appropriate) and open it a crack. There's a tray sitting on the floor. I glance both ways down the hall and bring the tray inside.

I lift the lid and get a whiff of the most mouth-watering breakfast I've ever seen. Eggs, bacon, toast, sausage, coffee, juice, and even some kind of green fruit that I have no idea what it is but I wolf it all down anyway.

My next stop is the bathroom and I pee and brush my teeth. Somebody left a new toothbrush and toothpaste out for me. I go for a bath next because I've never been in a tub this big before, and I want to give those jacuzzi jets a try. I slide down into the steam and watch my skin turn pink. Damn. The creamy soap feels so good on my skin I wash with it twice. I ease down into the bubbles and sink under the water, holding my breath for as long as I can. When I come back up, Delia is sitting on the toilet with her legs crossed, smoking a whopper of a joint and looking at me. I sputter away the bubbles and look right back at her.

She holds out the joint, offering it to me, but I shake my head. I need to keep all my senses about me for right now.

She speaks first. "I'm sending out for some new clothes for you. What size bra do you wear?"

"I dunno," I answer.

She bends forward a little and gives me the once-over. "Thirty-four B."

I really want to cover up, but I make myself sit still.

"Thirty-six inseam, I'm guessing?"

I answer with a question of my own, "What do you want from me?"

She takes a long toke and holds it in, never moving her eyes from mine, then exhales. "You're thirty-two years old. Went to prison when you were eighteen. Second-degree murder." She raises her eyebrows when she says the word murder. "Out at thirty. Held a few jobs over the past year and a half. Bartending. Convenience store clerk. Bartending again. You've lived on and off with a series of women. Ginger being the latest. You've got twenty G's in your pocket and I don't think you earned it bartending. Sound right so far?"

"You forgot that I'm a Gemini with Cancer rising. You know, it's hardly fair that you know so much about me and I don't know anything about you."

"Ask," she says.

"You own the strip club?"

"I do."

"You're rich, obviously."

"I am."

I can't resist the next question. "Thirty-six D?"

"Double D, smart ass," she laughs.

I rest my arm on the edge of the tub and balance my chin on my elbow. I study her for a moment, then say, "Tell me something about yourself I don't know."

She formulates her answer with another toke. "I used to strip in the club when I was young. I got out and married rich. Bought the club and a few other properties. I got older. I bought new tits. A new ass. A tummy tuck. Had my face done. My husband got a younger woman so I got my tits done again. Now he has a Viagra prescription and an even younger woman. He does what he wants, I do what I want, and we both look the other way."

"So you just pick up strays and bring them home."

"Something like that," she says.

"And..." I begin, "...I'm supposed to be your girl toy or what?"

"Or what," she says.

I laugh. A stray thought flickers across my mind. I haven't laughed since Vivian. "I still don't know who you are," I say.

She licks her thumb and forefinger, snuffs out the joint and does an eerily familiar thing—stows the joint down her ample cleavage. "That's the way I like it," she says. She winks at me and walks out.

I scoop up a handful of bubbles and blow them all over the bathroom. I take a deep breath and sink back under the water.

I stay inside my room for five days without leaving. That's not as bad as it sounds. Everything I need is either already there or delivered to my door. I write a lot. I watch a lot of TV and stare out the window. I see Delia coming and going in the orange Caddy. I see her butler or whatever he is, opening doors for her and carrying packages from upscale department stores. Sometimes when she's getting in her car, she glances up at my window, but I hide behind the curtain.

I think too much. Mostly about Vivian. I replay our one interlude together over and over in my head and wonder if that's what made her run. Or was she running from me? Probably. They always do.

My closet up here in my hidey-hole is brimming with new clothes. Men's linen pants and slacks and pretty damn cool tailored shirts. Delia let me keep my leather jacket and motorcycle boots, but got me a new stack of boxers. She bought me some bras too.

One day I see Delia leave and decide I'm bored enough to get out and explore a little. I open my bedroom door and step into the hallway. When nobody comes running at me shouting *Boo!* I walk in what direction I think will maybe lead somewhere. I get lost several times and have to retry. I pick out some landmarks to keep me oriented. Turn right at the naked lady painting, turn left at the blurry painting of the pond...

I find the stairs and walk down them and across a squeaky clean tile floor and find myself in a kitchen. There's two fridges built into the wall and a total of three stoves and I wonder who the hell she's cooking for that she needs that many stoves? As far as I can figure it's just Delia and the butler and a ghost husband that she alluded to but that I've never seen. And me, of course. There's one of those fancy island things in the middle of the kitchen. Copper pots and pans hang above it. There's another sink in the middle of the island and the faucet is drip drip dripping. I reach out and turn the handle tighter, but it keeps on dripping. All this money and she's still got a drippy faucet that a twenty-nine cent washer could fix.

I decide to fix it for her. It'll give me something to do for the next half hour. I don't have any tools, so I get out my trusty pocket knife and rummage around in all the kitchen drawers until I find a butter knife. That's all the tools I need.

I open the cabinet door under the sink and turn off the water supply line. It stops dripping. Yep, it's the cold water just like I thought. I use the butter knife and my pocketknife as a makeshift screwdriver and remove the knob assembly. I pull out the stem and wedge out the spring and cup. The cup's not in too bad of shape. Just a tiny little knick, but that'll make her drip every time.

I accidentally drop the spring on the floor. I'm down on my hands and knees combing the tile for that tiny little spring when a pair of animal skin high heels appear right under my nose. My heart fuckin' stops and I'm about to yell Viv's name when Delia says, "Lose something?"

I look from the shoes all the way up to Delia's smiling face and reply, "I was just fixing your faucet."

"You're good with your hands?" she asks without the slightest trace of sarcasm.

"I've never seen anything yet that I couldn't fix. With the right tools." I locate the spring right by the toe of her shoe and stand up and lean against the counter. I hand her the cup, saying, "You need a new one of these."

She holds out her key ring and smiles. "Go get it. There's a complete set of tools in the garage if you need them."

I take the keys and walk out the door.

I guess Delia figures I can start earning my keep now. Because the next day after I fix the leaky faucet, she leaves me a note on my breakfast tray. *Can you take a look at the tub in the master bath? It's dripping.* I fix that too.

The day after that her note wants me to fix the toilet near the foyer and the toaster is going on the fritz. I fix those too. Then the day after that I get a huge list of things to be fixed signed by Delia with a *P.S. Take your time.*

Months go by. I mark time by the weather change. Sleet and snow comes and goes. Christmas appears out of nowhere. Delia gets me a subscription to *Tattoo* magazine and I get her a deviled egg platter. She really likes it, go figure.

Time rolls on and I take my bike to the hardware store when it's a sunny clear day and when it's not I take Delia's Caddy. Sometimes Delia pops in when I'm fixing something and keeps me company.

I'm lying flat on my back with my head under a kitchen sink replacing the sprayer doodad and Delia's sitting on a stool smoking a joint. I ask her a question I've been thinking about lately, "What's it like stripping for a living?"

"What d'ya mean?" she asks.

"Did you find it demeaning? Getting paid to take off your clothes and sell yourself like that?"

She pauses long enough that I think maybe I've offended her. Then she replies, "Demeaning? No. Everybody sells themselves, Lee Anne. That's what makes the world go round. And selling yourself, whether you're a stripper or a prostitute or a trophy wife or a politician is powerful. You have all the power. It's the getting older that's demeaning."

"You look damn good," I say and mean it.

"I used to have a body just like yours," she replies.

I laugh out loud at that one. "Right."

"Before the boob job," she amends.

"Of course," I say. I finish tightening down the doodad and ask the next question on my list, "Did you ever have any kids?"

When she doesn't answer, I peek out from under the sink. She's already left the room.

Squeak, squeak.

I pause the DVR and listen. There it is again. A squeaky noise. A weird squeaky noise is coming from the room next door.

I get up off my bed and enter the bedroom next to mine without knocking. Howard, the butler, (that's all he'll tell me about himself, his name is Howard), kneels on the floor with a screwdriver in his hand. He's taken off an electrical outlet plate and is unscrewing the wires from the plug. He doesn't hear me as I walk up behind him. I look over his shoulder and watch him turn the screwdriver to the left. The wires look to me like they're hooked up right, but the dumbshit is turning the screwdriver the wrong way.

"Righty tighty, lefty loosey," I say.

He flinches and the screwdriver touches the hot wire. Howard throws it like he just got bit. "Damndamndamndamn," he says, sticking his fingers in his mouth.

"It's just a one-ten, Howard, you'll live. But you gotta turn off the main power before you start working with electric."

"Now you tell me," he says.

"Why're you doing this anyway?" I ask. "I can fix it tomorrow."

He shakes his head and murmurs, "Don't tell Miss Delia you caught me," before scurrying out of the room.

What a strange little man. I go back to my room thinking that at least I have some job security as long as Howard can't learn to fix anything.

In the morning I find a note that reads: *Lee Anne, the electrical outlet in the bedroom next to yours isn't working. Delia.* I go to the basement and am almost turning the main power switch off when clickclickclick sounds off in my brain. Howard was *unscrewing* the plug. At night. That's a weird time to fix something. And he told me not to tell Delia that I *caught* him.

I march back upstairs, head straight to the master bedroom and throw open the door without knocking. Delia is lying in bed reading a book, wearing some kind of black lace lingerie getup looking hotter than a woman half her age and I almost forget how mad I am before I find my anger and start in. "What the *hell*?"

"Lee Anne?" she says. She jerks her book toward the nightstand, knocking over a framed photo. She doesn't pick up the frame or even acknowledge that she knocked it on the floor. "What's wrong, baby?" she asks.

"Is this some kind of fuckin' joke?"

"What're you talking about, honey?" she asks. She grabs a matching lace robe and pulls it on.

"You have Howard break shit, then you have me fix it. Has he been breaking everything all along? Why? What the hell is that all about?"

"Sit down," she says, gesturing to a chair in the corner.

"You can tell me while I'm standing."

She throws her long legs over the edge of her bed and ties her robe. She looks back up at me and takes her reading glasses off. (That's the only concession to aging I've ever seen her display.) She sets the glasses on top of her book and looks at me again.

"I'm waiting, Delia."

"I didn't want you to leave," she explains. "It's that simple."

I look around the room while I digest this bit of information. I still don't get it. Why she wants me here bad enough to invent shit for me to do.

"I was afraid you'd get bored and leave. So I made things up to keep you busy. Keep you feeling useful," she says.

My eyes are drawn back to the book she was reading. Something's not right. I look at the framed photo on the floor by her feet. It's laying facedown. I reach down and pick it up. Delia grabs it out of my hands a little too quickly and lays it facedown on the bed beside her.

"Can I see it?" I ask.

She doesn't look to where I'm pointing. She knows exactly what I'm talking about. Suddenly, she ages about ten years in the next few seconds. I reach over her and and grab the photo.

It's a picture of me when I'm maybe nine years old. I'm riding my bicycle down the road in front of my house. I look like a wild child with uncombed hair and dirty clothes, but I have a huge smile on my face.

"How'd you get this?" I ask.

"You look so happy there," she says.

"What're you doing with this picture? Did you know my mother?"

"You wanted a bicycle so badly," she states.

"Answer my question."

"You know how your mother got the money to buy that bike?"

I shake my head the tiniest bit.

"She got it from me."

I digest this bit of information for a moment. It brings up more questions than answers them. "And you are...?"

She pats the bed next to her and this time I sit. She takes the photo out of my hands and looks at it. She inhales deeply and begins, "I ran away from home when I was sixteen. I ran away to be with a man I thought I was in love with. As soon as he found out I was pregnant, he left me. I gave the baby to my older sister to take care of. I was so young and stupid and...I was a stripper. I couldn't take care of a baby."

"What're you saying..." My voice sounds so far away, like it's coming from somebody else.

"That baby was you, Lee Anne," she answers softly.

I slam face-first into a brick wall. All I can see are stars and blinking geometric shapes.

"I'm your mother, your biological mother. I kept track of you, though, I watched you grow up, on and off..."

"What the fuck?" I yell. "What the hell is it with you people? Always leaving and shit?" I close my eyes and pinch the bridge of my nose to keep the hot tears back.

"Lee Anne, honey..."

I jump up, grab the framed photo from her hands and throw it across the room. It smacks into the far wall and splinters into pieces.

"You leave me! Mom leaves me! Vivian leaves me! Am I really that unfuckingloveable?"

"Who's Vivian?"

"And all this shit! All this shit and money and clothes you're trying to buy my feelings off with? Like that makes up for it? You can shove it all up your ass!"

I open the bedroom door and am so prepared to slam it, but Delia grabs it with both her hands and stops it midswing. "I'm not leaving," she says. "I'll never leave you again, Lee Anne."

I stare at her blankly for a second then stride down the hallway and out the front door.

CHAPTER FIFTEEN

After I realize I've taken the same exit the second time in a row, I pull over into the parking lot of an abandoned warehouse. I put the bike in neutral and rev the throttle, listening to the pipes roar and growl, roar and growl.

What the fuck am I doing?

I pull a cigarette out of my jacket pocket. This pack's been in my pocket for four months now. Ever since Vivian left. I light a cigarette and ponder my options. I've thought about it a lot of times. I've always preferred the overdosing route. That seems the least painful. Or drowning. However, I have no drugs or large bodies of water. I could hang myself, but you need rope to do that. I don't have a gun or even know where to get one quickly. I could crash my bike into or off something, but the chances of me living and being crippled are too great. A razor blade down my wrists? I could get a blade or even use my knife, but the sight of blood freaks me out. I'd probably just chicken out. I wish I hadn't flushed all those pills of Vivian's. I could just take them and go to sleep.

There's only one thing that is really stopping me from killing myself. I don't want to die. I didn't go through everything I have to give it all up now. I haven't even been out in the real world for two years yet.

Whatever happened to that feeling of invincibility, of a fresh start I had once? I think back and try to remember what it felt like.

I was sitting on a hard wooden chair in front of five people at a long table. They looked at me like I was a wild animal in the zoo. Baptists. They were all buttoned-down and slicked-back like Baptists. Four men and one woman. The woman kept looking at me, scared, like my tats were going to jump over the table and bite her on the ass.

Five people held my life in their hands. They could sign a paper and parole me or they could sign a different paper and keep me locked up.

"What was the question again?" I asked with a fake smile plastered to my face.

The man in the middle rephrased, "I asked, Ms. Hammond, why do *you* think we should grant your parole?"

"I don't know," I answered truthfully.

"You don't know," he repeated after me. He shuffled his paperwork and said, "We have a statement from the warden. She states that you're a model prisoner. You are well-liked by the general population here and even offer your services as a teacher. She goes on to state that at least twenty of the prisoners have received their G.E.D's under your direct tutelage."

I nodded. "They did it on their own. They just needed a little push."

"She also states that you've saved this institution thousands of dollars by repairing..." He scrambled through some more papers, searching.

I filled in the blanks for him, "Dishwashers. Washers and dryers. Plumbing. You name it, I can pretty much fix it."

He nodded at me.

"Might be a good reason to keep me here," I joked.

The woman stifled a smile behind her polished nails. The men didn't appear amused. This time the man at the end of the table spoke. "We have a letter from a Mr. Stan Baker offering you employment and a place to live upon your release."

Chopper. Chopper sent a letter to the parole board?

"Is that an opportunity that you would accept?"

"Definitely. Most definitely, I'd accept."

Middle Man leaned forward on his elbows and cocked his head at me. "Would you say," he began slowly, "that you feel remorse for the act of murder that put you here?"

"Remorse?" I asked. I looked at my feet and tried to put my thoughts in order. "I did what I did. I never made any excuses for it. I know it was wrong. But it was all I knew. You know, you back an animal, any animal, even a docile one, into a corner, they're going to fight to get away."

Middle Man set his jaw and leaned back in his chair.

I continued, "Do I wish I hadn't done it? Sure I do. I wish I'd known some other way. But all I can tell you is that since I pulled that trigger, that man hasn't beaten another woman and he hasn't raped another woman. And I'm glad for that."

He stacked his papers together and said, "Okay, Ms. Hammond, I think I understand." All five of them started making movements like they were dismissing me and ending the meeting.

"You asked me why I think I should be paroled," I said.

They looked at me again and I continued, "You all have looked over my paperwork and thought about my case maybe for the past two days. But I've spent twelve years thinking about it. I don't know how to put it into words exactly, but I have something inside me. I have something to offer. I'm more than a case file that's only two inches thick. I have something to offer and maybe I'm not sure what it is yet, but there's something out there...I just know that God would not have put me in this situation without giving me the ability to learn from it. I don't think this is the end of anything. I think the day I do leave will be just the beginning."

I stood up and smiled at each of them in turn. "Thank you for your time. And God bless."

I turned and walked out the door before they could ask any more questions. I felt guilty for pulling the God trump card out of my sleeve like that, but who knows? Maybe it was the truth.

And, it worked. Two days later, I'm processed and dressed in some state-bought chinos and a white button-down shirt and loafers and staring through the gates of Mabel Bassett at the road in front of me.

I had every right to be scared. I'd never had a job, rented an apartment, shopped for groceries, had a checking account, owned a credit card, a cell phone or paid a single bill. I'd never owned a car. I'd never gone on a date. I'd never been in love. That was a pretty long to-do list and I was late getting started.

But I wasn't scared.

I shoved my hands in my pockets and strolled through the gates of Mabel Bassett and kept on walking. I didn't look behind me. That was my past life.

I haven't been here since I was a teenager, but I have no problem finding the place. I steer my bike into the small gravel parking lot of Chopper's bike shop and let the nostalgia wash over me. The building looks like shit. Gray, fading paint and blacked-out windows. A lopsided closed sign in the door. There's a big For Sale sign hanging on a pole by the road. Judging by the curled edges and faded lettering, that sign has been there for quite some time. The place has definitely seen better days. Then again, so have I.

I put the bike in gear and follow the worn path around the building to the back of the shop. I kill the engine and kick her down. I walk up to the back door and jiggle the handle. It's locked. I kick the lump of cement sitting near the door. There's the key. Just like old times.

I let myself in but don't turn on any lights. After my eyes adjust to the dark I see that the place is a time capsule. The girlie calendar on the wall has changed to the current year, but that's the only clue that time has moved on.

I open the dilapidated old fridge. I can't believe the damn thing is still running. I grab a can of Bud Lite and pop it open. I drink half of it in one swig and wipe the foam off my mouth with the back of my hand.

I kick the fridge closed and take a tour. Looks like he's working on an old panhead Harley. It's standing like a ghost in the center of the garage floor with its parts spread out neatly on a tarp by its side.

I edge into his office and feel around in the dark until I find the small desk lamp. I turn it on and settle myself down in his cracked leather swivel chair. I drink my beer and have a look-see. Just like always, the place is filthy but organized. There's a couple of girlie rags on his desk, but other than that there's only a stack of invoices marked Paid or Payable.

Then I see it hanging in a cheap frame over the file cabinet.

I get up and take it off the wall. It's a yellowed newspaper article from the Tulsa paper. There's a black-and-white grainy photo of a skinny girl, handcuffed and being led into a courthouse. The headline screams in bold type: SEVENTEEN-YEAR-OLD, TRIED AS ADULT, TO BE SENTENCED.

The caption under the photo says: *Lee Anne Hammond, convicted of murdering her stepfather, is to be sentenced today.*

I don't read the article. I already know what happened.

I can't believe he cut this out of the paper and framed it. The oddest thing about it is that it's clean. There's dust and cobwebs and old grease marks everywhere. This is the only clean item in the whole joint.

I hang it back on the nail sticking out of the wall and drain the rest of the beer. I squish the can in my right hand and shoot it into the trash.

I mosey back out to the shop area, flip on the overhead, grab another beer and some choice tools off his shelf. I put a clean rag in my back pocket and settle down to the side of the panhead. I rub and clean all the parts he has scattered around.

It's like a puzzle. A puzzle that I'm damn good at figuring out. I concentrate on working on the engine with one side of my brain and let the other side roam and wander for a bit. Keeping my hands busy takes the edge off and it isn't long before—a steel-toed boot nudges me in the ribs and a gruff voice says, "'Bout time you showed up. What the hell took you so long?"

I look up and see Chopper. He's a little more grizzled and gray, but I'll be damned, I'd recognize him anywhere. He's still got a head full of thick wavy hair and that same old mustache, but now he's sporting a little goatee flavor-savor. The lines on his face are the good kind. Crinkles around his eyes and mouth from smiling. Or maybe they're from squinting into the wind when he's riding. Either way they're good.

"Heyya, Chopper," I say, lifting myself to my feet.

I was so busy with the bike I didn't even realize the time. Sun is leaking in through the front window where the edges of the black paint have peeled off.

"Hope you don't mind," I say, grinning toward the bike. "I was just fooling around. Don't think I did her any serious harm."

"Don't mind at all," he says. He takes a couple of steps back and looks me up and down. "You got a little taller."

"I was just thinking how much you shrunk."

"Nice ink," he adds, scanning my tats.

"Yours could do with a touch-up," I reply.

He allows a small smile. "I like 'em worn and faded. Just like me."

"You don't look all that faded."

"Grab us a beer," he says, walking toward his office. "C'mon in and have a sit-down. We got some catching up to do."

I notice that he's flying some colors on the back of his leather vest. The rocker spells out B.A.C.A. He must've ganged up.

I grab two beers and follow him into the tiny office. He sits in his chair and motions to a metal folding chair for me. I hand him his beer and sit.

"You an outlaw now?" I ask point-blank.

"Nah," he says, sipping on the Bud.

"Your cut says different."

"B.A.C.A.'s a gang, all right. But we're not outlaws. Kinda the opposite, in fact."

"You riding for Jesus?"

He laughs like I said something truly funny. "It's a nationwide organization. I'm the P of the Tulsa chapter. I started it myself some years back."

I ask the obvious. "What's B.A.C.A. stand for?"

He takes a slow drink before saying, "Bikers Against Child Abuse." He wipes the foam off his mustache with the back of his hand.

I sip on my beer. My eyes dart over to the framed news clipping on his wall.

"I knew a little kid once," he begins. "Had a wild streak in her a mile wide. Ornery as hell, but a good kid. I was even married to her mother for a while. I took the kid under my wing for a little. I ignored it when she stole my magazines. She even snuck in here and lived for a spell. I started stocking the fridge with bologna and bread and pop for her. I liked this kid, see..." He leans forward in chair and rests his elbows on his knees, talking toward me like it's the most important thing he's ever said. "...but I let her slip through my fingers. Her home life is none too good. And some asshole gets hold of her and she being who she is, the fighter type if you know what I mean, she takes the law into her own hands. She ends up having to pay for this asshole's..." he searches for the right word, "...depravity."

"Sounds familiar," I whisper.

"She does her time. But the whole time she's inside, I'm feeling guilty."

"You didn't do anything."

"That's just it," he sighs. "I didn't do anything. If I'd paid attention, I'd have known. Maybe I could've done something. Maybe not. But I'll never know... So, I brought B.A.C.A to T-town." He leans back in his chair and puts one big boot across his knee. "There's maybe twenty of us. Mostly men, a few of their old ladies. And we do what we can."

"What is that?" I ask. "What's 'doing what you can?'"

"Our crew looks pretty rough. We've got the bikes and the cuts and the tats. Some of the gang's done some time. We have sources out on the street. A couple of our guys are even cops. We hear about any child abuse happening...We stop it."

"How do you stop it?"

"You'd be surprised what little really has to be done. A gang of twenty bikers surround your house at three a.m. and knock on your door... Usually, we only have to talk to the son-of-a-bitch. Sometimes, we have to pack his bags for him."

"What if he doesn't leave?"

"I don't know," he laughs. "That's never happened."

I swallow all my beer and crush the can. "I like the sound of it."

He smiles at me. "I thought you would."

He gets up and walks out of the office. I hear his boots trudge across the shop. The fridge door opens and closes. When he comes back in he hands me an opened beer. "You got woman trouble?"

"How'd you know?"

He laughs. "I recognize the look."

"I'll get over it," I say. "Or not. But it's a done deal. Nothing I can do about it."

"You love her," he says. He doesn't ask, he just states it.

"Yeah. Against my better judgment."

"Does she know it?"

"I told her, but I don't think she believes it."

"Then tell her again so she'll believe it."

"Chopper...I don't know where she is. I think maybe she's got mixed up with an asshole. She's probably back with him. I just hope he hasn't killed her."

He perks up. "An asshole, huh? Them I know how to deal with. This asshole got a name?"

So I tell him everything I know. Everything. And I don't leave anything out.

Two beers and a slew of phone calls later to his cop friends, he tells me what I need to hear. "Crowne Plaza. Presidential Suite. He's got a pretty redhead with him."

"What do I do now?" I ask.

"Go get her."

Okay. I will.

Butch and Sundance, by God.

Five minutes later, I'm out the door and back on my bike. Chopper gave me a cell phone with a bunch of numbers plugged into it and I've tucked it safely into my bra.

"Remember," he said. "There's a whole gang of us. Nobody's more than ten minutes from wherever you are. Speed dial one if you need help. Even if you get scared, back out and let us handle it."

I rolled my eyes at him and lied through my teeth. "I won't be scared."

My heart's considerably lighter than it was last night. Sometimes God just reaches down and slaps you in the soul.

CHAPTER SIXTEEN

I put my on best swag and saunter into the lobby of the Crowne Plaza like I'm just another one of their fancy paying guests. I ease my ass down in an overstuffed chair near the front window where I'm hidden behind a big potted plant. I dig Chopper's phone out of my shirt and dial the number for the hotel (it's on a business card on the coffee table). I peek through the palm fronds as the phone rings. After a couple of rings, a swishy man at the front desk answers.

"Presidential Suite, please," I say in my best snooty accent.

The phone rings about ten times. I'm just about to hang up when Vivian answers, "'Ello?"

"Vivian! It's me."

Vivian's voice drops down to a barely audible whisper. "Lee? Is that really you?"

"Are you okay?"

I hear some rustling on the phone, then Vivian's voice calls out to somebody, "I've got it!"

"Vivian, just say yes if you want me to get you out of there."

"Yes," she whispers.

"Okay, then. Just tell him it's housecleaning or something and hang up."

"More towels," Vivian says. "We could use some more towels. Thank you." A few seconds later I'm listening to a dial tone.

I sit forward in the chair, bury my face in my hands and try to think this through. How the hell am I going to rescue her? Okay, the first thing I need to do is see the layout of this place.

I peer through the plant and wait until the little desk guy is absorbed in his computer screen, then I ease across the lobby, trying not to draw attention to myself. I jump inside the first elevator I see and punch in the very top button.

I press myself against the side wall and listen to the Beatles muzak. I can hear my own heart pounding above Ringo's drumbeat. The elevator stops, the doors whir open and I venture a small peek. There's one goon about fifty feet down the hallway standing guard outside the door. That must mean the other goon is inside.

I quickly shut the doors and press the next button. I get out on the floor below and don't have any better idea of what to do than I did five minutes ago.

All kinds of crazy-ass ideas zoom through my brain. I can do the room service thing. Disguise myself as a waiter pushing a cart. Or would it be better if I hid under the tablecloth and got pushed into the room? I saw that in a movie once and it worked great. No, wait, that was an *I Love Lucy* episode. Better not try that one.

I think through every action movie I've ever seen and realize that it looks so easy when they do it but in reality it's scary as hell. And what do I do once I get in the room? Try to overpower P.C.? He's a pretty big guy and the reality is that he'd probably take me out. Not to mention the damn goons. If I had a gun... But I don't.

I need to think outside the box. Instead of me going in, can

I get them to come out? That might just work. If I can get them all out and maybe...maybe get everybody in the hotel out then I could grab Viv and get lost in the crowd. Before I lose my nerve, I reach out and pull the fire alarm. I run down the hallway, madly pulling all four fire alarms.

Alarms scream and overhead sprinklers douse water everywhere. People in pajamas open their doors, peek into the hallway and shut their doors just like a game of whack the mole. I run to the elevators and punch the button.

The doors slide open and I find myself face-to-face with Prince Charles.

Oh, shit damn.

The two goons are flanking him and one of them has Vivian in a neck hold. They're all wet and mad as hell. But at least the element of surprise is working in my favor. P.C. looks even more surprised to see me than I do him.

I throw a big roundhouse punch and connect with P.C.'s perfect chin. I hit him so hard the shock wave of pain shooting up my arm almost sends me to my knees. Fortunately, the only one of us who actually falls is him and he crashes to the floor like a limp doll.

Vivian kicks out with her pointy shoes and lands a neat groin shot to the goon who's not holding her. He grabs his crotch, yelps like a puppy and falls across his boss's body.

That leaves just one more goon to deal with and Viv and I give it all we've got. She's elbowing and kicking like a wild woman and I'm punching anywhere I can get a clear shot...but the sumbitch just won't turn loose of her.

I'm grabbed from behind and wing-locked. Prince Charles rises up in front of me and muscle goon holds me. The last thing I see is a giant fist with hairy knuckles coming right at my face.

Fuck me, not the nose again.

When I come to it's pitch black and the only way I know I'm awake is because of the intense pain. I blink my eyes and even that hurts so much that I wince out loud. I run my tongue over my dry lips and taste the metal tang of blood. My nose is clogged with dried blood and snot and I have to breathe through my mouth. I try to sit up and after a few seconds of seeing stars, I realize that my hands are tied behind my back and I'm crammed into a very small space.

Son of a bitch, I hate small spaces.

I hear the roar of an engine in my ears and tires chewing and spitting gravel. Shit. I'm tied up and shoved into the trunk of a car. The car's a Mercedes from the sound of the engine. Knowing where I am doesn't make me feel any better.

"Lee?" I hear from behind me.

"Viv?"

I feel Vivian's warmth behind me.

"Please tell me this is all part of your plan to help me escape," Vivian says.

"This is all part of my plan to help you escape."

She doesn't laugh. I can't blame her.

"You okay?" I whisper.

The car careens to the right and we're tossed against each other. I grit my teeth against the sudden jolt of pain. When the pain subsides, I try to even out my breathing and will myself not to cry.

"I'm okay," she answers after a moment. "But they beat the shit outta you pretty good."

"Where're they taking us?"

"I don't know. Probably somewhere where they can torture us and kills us in private. But that's just a guess."

"You've watched too many TV movies."

"Yeah," she says. "They're probably just taking us to a surprise birthday party."

She's right. I know she's right. But I just don't want to think about being killed right now. If I'd known I was going to die this early in life, I would've done some things, lots of things, differently. But I don't want to make out a bucket list just yet.

"Maybe now's a good time to think about giving the money back," I say.

"Yeah, if I hadn't spent it all," she says. "They wouldn't let us go anyway. Not now."

"Half a million dollars!" I shout. "You spent a half a million dollars?!"

"Screaming at me isn't going to make it come back!"

"How in fuck's sake can you spend half a million dollars in just a few months?"

"Well, we can't all be dykes with simple needs!" she spits into my neck.

"So now I'm a dyke?"

"You've always been a dyke," she mutters.

"You didn't mind the dyke part that once," I spit back.

"Oh, great," she says. "You don't really think I enjoyed that."

"You can't fake that shit."

"Spoken like a true man. You're just in it for yourself and can't tell when a woman's faking it or not," she says.

"You are such a bitch," I say. "And if I remember right, you're the one who started it. *You* seduced *me*."

"Fer chrissakes. It was a thank you present."

"A THANK YOU PRESENT? If I weren't tied up right now, I'd strangle you!"

"I left you money," she says. "I'm not all cold."

"Yeah, well, I was faking it, too. How 'bout that?"

"You were not."

"Sure I was," I say. "You were a lousy fuck and I just wanted to get it over with. Thank God, you were gone when I woke up."

"You're such a lousy liar," she says.

"And to think I came back to rescue you," I say.

"Yeah. How's that working out for you?"

We're quiet for a long time. I feel her body shaking a little against mine and she sniffles into my neck.

"You're not fucking crying, are you?" I ask.

"No," she blubbers.

"Why the fuck are you crying?" I ask a little softer.

"Because."

"Because why?"

"Because you hate me," she says.

"Why do you care?"

She doesn't answer. She's crying harder now and getting snot and everything all over my back. I heave myself around until I'm finally nose to nose with her.

"Tell me why you're crying," I say.

"Because I'm going to die," she says. "Isn't that a good enough reason?"

"I've just never seen you cry," I say.

"Well, contrary to popular belief, I *do* have feelings. And I'm getting ready to be killed and you hate me."

"Okay, I don't hate you," I whisper.

"Really?"

"I love you. You're the best friend I've ever had. And that's the real truth."

"I love you, too. And..." she cuts herself off.

"And?"

"I seduced you because I wanted to. And I didn't fake it. It was all right and—"

"All right?" I interrupt.

"Okay," she laughs and sniffles at the same time. "It was fuckin' great. But I had to leave. I had to."

"Why?" I ask simply.

"I had to leave you before you left me."

"I wouldn't have left you."

"Sure you would. They all leave. And I know that and I get over it. But I don't know if I could get over you leaving me. How's that for truth?" she asks.

"As long as we're being honest," I venture. "I've realized since we've been apart that I don't really need you."

"You really know how to cheer me up, you know that?"

"Listen to me...I don't *need* you. But I do *want* you in my life. 'Cause I really missed my friend. I didn't know it was a choice, friend or nothing. And if it is, then...I choose to have my friend."

"Well, you could've realized that to begin with and saved us a helluva lot of trouble."

"I know, right?"

We both laugh. "I can't believe we're going to be killed any minute now and we're both laughing," I say.

That thought sobers us up good and we're quiet for a long moment.

"Lee?"

"Hmm?"

"Let's don't die today."

"There's my cheerleader." And as soon as I say that I have a knowing that if she cheers loud enough and long enough maybe we can get out of this alive. I'll do anything I can and maybe some things I can't, just to live long enough to make this right.

"Just one thing," I say.

"What's that?"

"You're Sundance. I get to be Butch."

"You're not nearly as butch as you think you are," she says.

"I am too."

"No, you're not."

"I am so butch," I say adamantly.

"I've seen you be pretty damn girlie. 'Fuck me, Vivian, please fuck me!'" she says in a high falsetto.

"Shut up!" I say too loudly.

Vivian laughs her ass off at my expense.

"Okay, then, you be Butch," I say.

BZZZZZ. BZZZZZ.

"Is that your phone?" we both ask each other at the same time.

"I don't have a phone," Vivian says.

BZZZZZZ.

"Oh, my God," I suddenly remember. "It's Chopper's phone. It's in my bra."

"Get it out!" Vivian yells right in my ear. She drops her voice to a harsh whisper and adds, "Talk to this Chopper person and get us out of this mess!"

"It's in my bra," I explain. "My hands are tied behind me. You're going to have to get it out for me."

"My hands are tied behind me too," she whines.

"Vivian..." I say, stifling a giggle.

"...you don't expect me to use my mouth," she mind-reads.

"Only if you want to live."

She sighs deeply. "Okay, but if you get off on this, I swear to God, I'll kill you myself."

"No promises," I say.

Vivian rips open the front of my shirt with her teeth and noses in between my boobs. After a few moments, she looks up at me with the phone between her teeth.

"Use your tongue to speed dial number one," I say.

"Ferchwissakes," Vivian mumbles around the phone. She sets the phone down and lowers her head over it. It's light pops on and the next thing I hear is it's ringing.

Chopper's voice answers, "Lee?"

"Chopper!" I shout. "They've got us in the trunk of a car. They're gonna kill us."

"Where are you?"

"I have no idea. We're on a gravel road so we must be in the country somewhere."

"Don't turn the phone off, Lee. I'm going to hang up and call the crew, but keep the phone turned on. Stick it in the trunk somewhere and hide it from view. I'll see how well the phone's tracking system works."

"Thanks, Chopper," I say.

"Lee?"

"Yeah?"

"I love you, kid. You know that, right?"

"Yeah, Chopper. I know that."

"Bye."

He hangs up.

"Bad news," I say. "Really bad news."

"Why?" Vivian asks softly.

"He told me he loved me. He'd never say that unless he thought he wouldn't ever see me again."

The car stops and the engine cuts off. I hear the doors creak open and close and footsteps crunching back toward us.

"You scared?" Vivian asks.

"Nope."

"Liar," she breathes.

The trunk lid opens and I twist my neck to see three dark shapes in the moonlight staring down at us.

"All cozy, are we?" the shape I think must be Prince Charles asks.

"Fuck you," I say.

"Still feisty then, are we?"

"Cut the 'we' shit. Just let us go," I say.

"Get them out," Prince Charles orders, stepping out of the way.

The two bigger dark shapes lean in the trunk; one grabs my feet and the other my shoulders and they lift me up and out.

As soon as my feet touch the ground, I head-butt the closest goon with everything I've got. I connect solidly and he goes down with a big thud. The other goon kicks my feet out from under me and I fall to the ground like a sack of potatoes. I see a glint of something metal and shiny arcing through the moonlight and then all I see is a billion stars dancing in my head.

CHAPTER SEVENTEEN

All this getting hit upside the head can't be too good for my brain. I open my eyes to slits and don't see anything but a wash of colors that don't make sense. At least my nose is unclogged and I can breathe through it again. Except when I do, I am overwhelmed by a god-awful smell.

"Chicken shit," I utter. "I smell chicken shit."

"We're in some kind of old vacant chicken factory," Vivian replies.

"We must be in Arkansas."

I blink my eyes hard a couple of times until I can see pretty good. Vivian's right. Chicken roosts are everywhere. Old feathers scattered about. It looks like I slept through a giant pillow fight.

Vivian helps me get to my feet. We both still have our hands tied, but now they're retied in front of us. I'm so shaky I have to lean against her in order to stay upright.

"They retied our hands," I say.

"I told them to do it so we could pee. Impossible to squat with our hands behind us," she whispers.

I throw her a weird look.

"It worked, didn't it?"

"Where are they?" I ask.

"Right here," Prince Charles says, stepping out of the shadows of a chicken roost scaffold. "The other chaps are outside digging your graves."

I stumble toward him a few steps, just to test this guy's mettle when he doesn't have his muscle flanking him. "Why don't you and I settle this," I say. "Just us. Man to man."

Prince Charles laughs in a relaxed kind of way like he's not nervous or scared at all. Like he's done this type of thing before. I get goosebumps up and down my arms and my nipples harden. Not in a good way either.

He unbuttons his jacket, reaches inside, pulls out a good-size gun and aims it right at my head, smiling all the while.

"You think you're big just 'cause you got a gun?" I ask in the calmest voice I can muster while he's pointing a fuckin' cannon at my face. "Let's see how big a man you are without it."

"Lee...back down," Vivian warns.

"He's a pansy," I retort. "He's one of those British fags who can't get it up without a fluffer."

P.C. glares at me, but swings his gun to Vivian. "Last time, Vivian dearest. Where's the money?"

"I told you. I spent it," she answers.

"Where?" he asks.

"WalMart," she smiles sweetly.

He raises the gun and points the business end at me. He walks toward me like he's Cagney in *The Public Enemy.* He presses the gun hard against my temple and smiles with his crooked fucking teeth and I actually throw up a little in my mouth. This is one cold mother.

"Vivian," he scolds. "Tell me where you've hidden my money or I'll be forced to shoot your lezzie girlfriend."

"How'd you know she was a lesbian? How come everybody but me can tell she's a lesbian?" Vivian asks, throwing her bound hands in the air.

"This is what you left me for?" P.C. asks, pressing the gun even harder against my head. "A dyke in some Hell's Angels gang?"

"You've been watching too much American TV," I say. "I'm not in a gang."

He continues, "You steal my money and leave me for this?" He traces the gun down my neck and across my chest, stopping it right at my left tit. "A dirty, ugly woman who dresses like a man?"

"She's not all *that* ugly," Vivian says.

I hope she's just buying time and doesn't really mean that.

"Did you have sex with her?" he asks me. "Have you been fucking my Vivian?"

I don't know how to answer that question. I could tell the truth, but he'd probably shoot me on the spot. I could lie and say no, but he'd probably shoot me anyway. I try answering by not answering.

"Depends on who you ask," I say.

"What does that mean?" he asks, perplexed.

"Some people, who shall remain nameless, thinks if there's not a penis involved..." I ramble, "...then it isn't really sex..."

I see headlights blink off in the distance. P.C. and Vivian don't see them because their backs are to the front windows. I hope it's somebody, anybody, coming this way. The headlights disappear and my hope for rescue along with them.

I continue my time-wasting ramble, "...that it's just more like heavy petting which doesn't really count. 'Cause of the no penis thing. Kinda like how, say you, for instance, could get a blow job from a really tall, black transvestite, but you wouldn't consider yourself homosexual or that it was really sex because you—"

He shoves the barrel of the gun in my mouth and yells, "Enough!"

I try to talk around the gun, "Iknoyheefyou."

"What?" he asks, removing the gun and placing it under my chin instead.

"I said, I know why she left you."

"Why is that?"

"I saw you naked, remember? My dick's bigger than yours."

He flinches just the tiniest bit. Good. I hit a nerve.

"Is it just you? Or do all Englishmen have tiny uncircumsized dicks?" Where is my courage coming from anyway? I remind myself that there's a thin line between stupidity and courage. Oh, well, I shrug and pile on more stupid, "I've seen bigger dicks on infants."

Headlights again. Motorcycle headlights? This time they're closer.

"Is the rumor true?" I ask. "Do all Englishmen sit down to pee?"

He pokes me hard with the gun and I stumble back a step. He closes in on me again, pressing the length of his body against mine. "I should fuck you," he hisses into my face. "And make Vivian watch."

"I've already seen her do that once," Vivian says loudly. "And, believe me, it's not pretty."

P.C. turns his head to look at her. In that split second, I seize my only chance. I bring my bound hands up, swiping the gun away and at the same time I bring one knee up right into his crotch with all the oomph I have.

He doubles over and crashes to the floor, grabbing me by my belt and taking me down with him. The gun falls about twenty feet away. Now we're both wrestling on the ground trying to get to the gun first. Vivian is in the mix, scrambling too.

P.C. and I both get a hand on the gun at the same time. Unfortunately, his hands are untied and he hits me across the face with one of them and comes up with the gun pointed right at me with the other.

We both jump to our feet, me much clumsier than him. He holds his balls with his left hand and has the gun trained on me with his right. Vivian has been thrown backward and is lying to my side with her skirt twisted high. My first thought is that she should've been wearing pants because miniskirts just aren't proper kidnapping and hostage attire. My second thought is that P.C. is now in a rage and is definitely going to kill me.

"Where's the bloody money?" he screams.

"You kill me," I say without inflection, "and I'll never be able to tell you where it is."

"Then I'll kill her," he says, moving his aim down and to my side.

I hear the thunder of motorcycle engines and time freezes solid. P.C. is too smart to look behind him, but I see panic register behind his eyes. He jerks his gaze to Vivian and one side of his mouth twitches. "Goodbye, dearie," he says to her.

I see his intention before he even finishes saying goodbye. I react entirely by instinct and dive headfirst in front of Vivian a split second before he pulls the trigger.

My head dive sends me rolling and I end up about ten feet from where I began and on my back. I look down to see a rose blooming across my chest. Damn. My new white linen shirt. The pain is suffocating and I can't breathe right. Getting shot hurts way more than the movies make it out.

I try to say something, I don't even know what I'm going to say, but all that comes out is a gurgle deep in my throat. From somewhere beyond my tunnel vision, I hear gunshots and yelling, but I can't sit up to help.

I offer up a silent prayer and hope all those Baptists are right about there being a God: Dear God, please don't let him kill Vivian. God, I know I haven't talked to you in a long time, maybe never really, but please God if you're there and you're listening, don't let him kill Vivian.

From out of the darkness, Vivian crawls on her hands and knees over to me and I'm so relieved to see her face looking down at me that I cry. I start to sob big ol' tears and I want to reach out and grab her, hug her, but my arms just don't want to move.

Vivian hovers over me and when I see the sheer horror on her face, I realize how bad off I am. She presses her hands on my chest and presses and presses...

"You're going to get all bloody," I think I manage to say.

Vivian's face is just inches from mine and she's crying real tears too. "Don't die on me, Lee. Don't you dare fucking die."

Then from out of nowhere Chopper's face appears beside

Vivian's. "Stay with us, Lee. Keep your eyes open and don't go to sleep. An ambulance is on the way."

"Chopper..." I gasp.

Chopper takes off his cut and wads it up behind my head. "Hang on, girl. Don't go anywhere, just hang on."

"I'm so sleepy," I say.

"Listen to me, Lee," Chopper begins. "You can't die now. You're a fighter, remember?"

Vivian rips open my shirt. She strips her own shirt off over her head and wads it up. She presses her shirt hard against my chest.

"Keep talking to her," Vivian says to Chopper. "Keep talking and don't stop."

Chopper takes my chin in his hands and points my face back to his. "Lee...I want you to know something. I know you've been through three kinds of hell. But the thing is, you went through it. And because you did, there's lotsa kids out there who don't have to go through the same thing. We need you to stick with us, okay? Your work's not done. Not by far."

"Shit, Chopper..." I say. "Don't cry."

He actually laughs a little. I look over to Vivian and lift my hand to her face. I place my palm on her cheek. She's so beautiful. Even when her makeup's all smeared and stuff. I drop my hand and watch her tears mingle with the bloody hand print I've left on her cheek.

"Viv...?"

"Uh-huh," she breathes.

"Remember...what I said earlier? About just wanting to be your friend?"

"Uh-huh," she says.

"I didn't mean it." And then I don't know if I tell her I love her or I just think it. I'm too tired to know the difference. My eyelids are too heavy...

"Open your eyes, Lee," Vivian sobs. "Look at me! Don't leave me, dammit!"

But I've never been so sleepy in my life.

CHAPTER EIGHTEEN

I'm flying. I don't have any wings and I don't even have to flap my arms. I soar above the rooftops and church steeples. Tulsa sure has a lot of church steeples. The air is warm against my face and I can fly anywhere I want with just a tilt of my head. I zip through clouds, which aren't nearly as solid as they seem from the ground. I nosedive down to a city park and circle the treetops, watching the children laugh and play. I zoom down a highway, passing all the cars in the passing lane.

I fly low over my childhood neighborhood. I see me, a nine-year-old wild child, riding a bicycle. I see a young Delia parked in her car down the street watching me. She's crying. When I pass her on the bicycle, she starts her car and drives away, swiping at her eyes.

I fly a few blocks over to my childhood house and get there just in time to see it surrounded by police cars and an ambulance. A gurney is wheeled out of the house with a sheet-covered body on it. It's loaded into the ambulance and it pulls away without its siren on. Two female police officers come out of the house escorting a tall, skinny girl with wild hair and wilder eyes. They load her into the back of their police car and drive away.

I follow the police car for a ways, knowing I can't do anything to stop it, but following it anyway. We pass by a cemetery and I stop. I see a handful of people standing before a gravestone marked *Margaret Hammond*.

It begins to rain and I fly to the opposite side of the cemetery to an open gravesite encircled by a lot of people. Vivian stands in the rain apart from the rest of the crowd. She's surrounded by so much pain and loneliness that nobody can get near her. I see myself standing under a tent wearing a leather jacket and motorcycle boots. Vivian flicks her cigarette away. She laughs out loud and walks over to me. There's a spark or a current or something that happens as we stand side by side. It's like a blue electric field of energy swallows us, *enlivens* us.

Next, I fly to Delia's house and find her sitting on her back veranda. She's wearing a fuzzy robe and no makeup and her hair is a mess. She's crying into her hands. Chopper walks out onto the porch and wraps his arms around her. She cries into his shoulder and he holds her tight.

I fly to St. Francis hospital and see Vivian outside on a concrete bench. She shivers against the cold wind. She sits in a tiny pool of sunshine and looks lonely and sad. People pass by and nod hello, but she doesn't see them.

I fly up to the hospital's second story and hover there, looking in one of the windows. I see myself laying in a bed. Machines and tubes and cords are everywhere. I am very pale and very still. One of the machines beeps with each one of my body's heartbeats while another machine does all the breathing for me. I hope to God nobody accidentally trips on one of those cords and unplugs it.

I bang on the window, trying to wake myself up. I bang and bang and bang, but it's no use.

Vivian walks into the room just then. She pauses at the foot of my bed and watches my body for a moment. Then she does the sweetest thing. She walks around to the side of the bed and kisses me lightly on the forehead.

She sits in a chair beside the bed and watches my body. I float through the windowpane and settle down next to Vivian. I know she can't see me or hear me, but I hold her hand anyway. We both watch my body try to breathe on its own.

Hours, weeks, days, seconds, Time is one big ball rolling into itself. I open my eyes and sometimes I catch glimpses of Delia or Chopper, sometimes it's a woman or a man in white, mostly I see Vivian's face staring intently at me. My eyes close immediately after opening them.

I open my eyes and this time I manage to keep them open. The sun is bright and hot through the window. White is everywhere and blinding. I have tubes hooked up in every orifice in my body and some man-made holes too. My whole body is one big, dull ache. My lips are dry and stuck together.

I turn my head and blink at a bright splash of color in a chair next to my bed. It's Vivian. She's sleeping and her arm is stretched out over the side of the chair like she's reaching out to me.

"Viv?" I croak hoarsely.

Vivian's eyes fly open and she rushes to my side with a big, scared smile on her face. "Oh, my God, Lee, you're awake!"

"I'm alive?" I ask, because it seems too good to be true.

"Yeah, you're alive. And you're going to be just fine. You got shot in the chest and it got one of your lungs and you'll have a really bitchin' scar."

"I told you that I'd never leave you," I say.

Tears spring to Vivian's eyes. "You sure didn't," she agrees.

"How long have I been in here?" I ask.

"Two weeks and three days."

Vivian is wearing old gray sweat pants and a baggy T-shirt. Her hair is pulled back in a loose ponytail and her face is clean and shiny.

"You look beautiful," I say.

She laughs. "You must have some brain damage."

"I wasn't too smart to begin with."

She hands me a glass of water with one of those little bendy straws and inserts the straw between my lips for me. "Thank you for saving my life," she says softly.

It's weird she thinks that. It was more impulse than thought. I don't know if you should get thank you's for impulses.

She adds, "That's twice now. The first time you saved my life, I slept with you."

I raise my eyebrows at her.

"But don't think it's going to happen again," she says. "I can't go around sleeping with you every time you save my life."

"Well, I wish you'd told me that before I got shot," I say.

We both laugh. God, it feels good to laugh. I'm so damn glad to be alive, I laugh a little too loud and a little too long. It hurts like hell, but even the pain feels good because it reminds me that I'm alive.

Then, as if cued by some magic button, people fill up the room. They're all wearing white and I assume they're doctors and nurses. One tall, skinny guy with glasses constantly sliding down his narrow nose, steps forward and examines me. They're all doing something to me: Punching buttons, looking at tubes, prodding me in different places. They all talk at once and ask me questions and all I want is a Dr. Pepper.

The doctor pushes his glasses back up his nose and talks directly to me. He speaks a lot of mumbo jumbo doctorese and I just hope Vivian understands what he's talking about. Then he says something that jerks me back to reality and sits my ass down hard, "...and your baby is going to be just fine."

I look at him and tilt my head to the side just like how dogs do when they hear a squeaky noise. "Baby?"

"You didn't know you're pregnant?" he asks.

I look to Vivian for help, but she's as floored as me, staring at the doctor with her mouth hanging wide open.

"No, sir," I say. "That's news to me."

"Well, congratulations," he says. "You're approximately four months along."

Everything else he says from that point on goes absolutely unrecognized by my brain. I push the rewind button in my head and realize that the one time with Houston is the culprit. I'm overwhelmed to say the least. The strangest part is...I feel this little ball of warmth in my chest. And it's getting bigger and bigger...

Finally, all the people leave the room and it's just me and Vivian again. She takes my hand and holds it in hers. Her eyes are all wet and shiny and she asks, "Is it mine? Is the baby mine?"

I laugh a little, then gasp out loud from the pain. "Oh, don't make me laugh anymore, Viv, it hurts too much."

She leans down and wraps her arms around me as gently as she can. "We're going to have a baby," she breathes. "A baby!"

The next time I open my eyes, Vivian and Delia and Chopper are looking back at me. I smile a little because I realize that everybody I love is standing right here in my room. Three people may not seem like a lot to anybody else, but it's three more than I knew about last year.

Vivian sits on the bed beside me and gently holds my hand. I note that Delia and Chopper are holding hands too.

Delia sits on the other side and lays her hand on top of my leg. "How you feeling, baby?"

"I feel good," I say.

They all three look at each other. Something unsaid passes between them before they all three look back to me.

"What?" I ask.

"We have to talk," Chopper says.

I feel good enough to walk, but the nurse insists that I leave the hospital in a wheelchair, so Chopper rolls me out the electric doors. I stand up on my own and am so not prepared—Hundreds of people, a whole mob of people, cameras and microphones surround me. A policeman and Chopper grab me by the elbows and escort me to a makeshift podium up some stairs.

Flashbulbs pop and blind me and microphones are in my face and cameras are thrust just inches in front of me and I wish I was anywhere else but here. I hope to God I don't faint or something. I search the crowd—

Suddenly, I feel a hand on my left arm and it's Vivian. She's standing right beside me smiling up at me and I know it's going to be okay. I'll get through this somehow.

I take a deep breath and say into the bouquet of microphones, "Uh, hi..."

I don't get anything else out before questions are hurled at me so fast and furious, I can't understand what anybody is saying. I speak into the mics again, "How about one question at a time? Just one at a time okay?"

I point to a lady closest to me. "How does it feel to be a hero?" she asks, then pushes her mic at me.

I grin. "I dunno, you'll have to ask a hero."

A man throws a question at me, "Did you know the three men you shot and killed? Did you know they were on the FBI's most wanted list?"

"Uh...no. I just knew they had kidnapped Vivian and, uh, I wanted to un-kidnap her. That's pretty much all I was concerned with."

"Tell us your side of the story," some reporter shouts.

"Well, it's all a little blurry, you know. I just knew that Vivian was kidnapped and I tried to help her, but that didn't work out so good. They threw us in the trunk of a car and dumped us at some old chicken plant. They said they were going to kill us. But when the main guy, I don't know his name, shot at Vivian...I kinda got in the way. Then we all...fought. I guess I got the gun. And you know the rest of the story." I nod that I'm finished, then quickly add, "It was a lot more exciting than that at the time. I guess you had to be there."

Everyone laughs.

I point to another reporter and he asks, "What precisely is your relationship with Vivian Baxter? How would you describe your relationship?"

Shit. I'm not prepared for that one. Especially since I don't really know what my relationship with Vivian is yet. I'm all prepared to say "No comment," just like Chopper coached me, but Vivian reaches out and pulls the nearest microphone to her and says, "I would describe our relationship as good. And if you really need to know more than that...I love her."

Holy shit.

I look at Viv and smile big. "You got some balls, you know that?" I whisper low.

"I told you I was really the butch one," she whispers back.

Chopper leans into the mics and says, "That's all for now. Thank you." He grabs me by the arm and a police officer parts the crowd so we can get through. One really pushy little reporter squeezes through and jumps right in my face with: "Have you sold the book rights yet?"

"What?" I ask.

"Have you decided which publisher you're selling your book to?"

"No comment," I mumble as Chopper pushes the nosy little guy away.

I look around for Vivian but she's gotten lost somewhere in the mix of people and reporters. Chopper pulls me to his truck and opens the door for me, but I push him away. "I got it," I reprimand. I climb into the truck and he gets behind the wheel. I wait until we get on the road good before asking, "Did I do all right? You think that went okay?"

"You did great. My guys at the police station are taking care of the paperwork and the details so we should be fine. Everybody's pretty happy this guy's gone, especially the British government, so nobody's going to throw too much of fit."

"What'd that guy mean about a book?"

"Vivian knows all about that shit. You'll have to talk to her."

I nod and ask another, "Where we going?"

He ignores the question by saying, "Delia and I have decided we're going away for a while."

"No shit?"

He smiles. "No shit."

"She's married, you know."

"For now."

"Where you all going?" I ask.

He shrugs one shoulder. "Wherever we want."

"Lucky you," I joke. "She's got nice tits."

"Don't talk about your mother that way," he scolds.

"Whoops," I laugh. "Yeah, that's going to take some getting used to."

"But you're right." He grins at me. "They are nice."

We laugh. And then I ask him the most serious question yet, "You ready to be a grandpa?"

His face lights up with the biggest grin I've ever seen. "Hell, yeah. I'm ready."

"Good," I say. "That's good."

Chopper pulls his truck up to his shop and parks near my Harley. I don't have a home, nowhere really to go. So, I'm grateful he's letting me stay here. And, I'm looking forward to keeping my hands busy with some work.

Chopper and I get out of the truck. He shuts his door and leans up against it. I walk around to him. "We going in?"

He looks up at the top of the building and I follow his eyes.

"What the hell?" jumps out of my mouth.

There's a new sign running the length of the building. Big blue cursive letters spell out "Lee's Bike Shop."

I squish my eyes shut and then open them again. Yep, it's still there.

"It's all yours," he says. "All of it. Tools and everything."

"You can't do this," I say, dumbfounded. "You can't just hand your shop over to me like this."

"Oh, I'm not giving you anything," he answers. "You bought it."

"I'm confused. I mean, I love it and all, but I didn't buy anything. How could I buy it?"

The answer to my question pulls up next to us in Hell Camino. It looks like Johnny Runningbear took pretty good care of her. Vivian jumps out and gives me a big, lingering hug. "What d'ya think? You like?"

"You bought this? But you said you spent all the money."

She laughs. "Oh, my God, Lee, I wasn't going to tell him I really had all that money stashed."

"Hot damn," I say. "Hot damn."

"Wait'll you see the house," Vivian says.

"What house?"

"You all bought my house too," Chopper says.

"It's so sweet, Lee, you'll love it. Two bedrooms and a great big kitchen. It even has a white picket fence," Vivian says.

"Two bedrooms..." I say, disappointment coloring my voice.

"Well, the baby has to have a room of its own."

I smile. A big wave engulfs me and I'm rolling in it and I start laughing. I guess laughter really is contagious because they join in and we're all laughing.

"Oh my God," I sputter. "I think I just peed my pants a little."

Vivian leads me around by the hand and my boots make clomping noises behind the soft pads of her bare feet as she shows me our new house. She proudly points out all the decorating she's been up to. New curtains and throw rugs in the living room with matching recliners and a TV that I personally think is way too big but I'm not about to complain.

The kitchen has old oak cabinets and countertops that Vivian says she loves and wants to keep. There's a new stainless steel fridge and matching dishwasher, though. And there's even a laundry room with matching washer and dryer.

Vivian pulls me into the back bedroom and proudly shows it off. She's turned an old spare room into a beautiful baby's room. Crib, dresser, books and toys and a rocking chair. Clouds and stars are painted on the ceiling and the wall facing the crib is a complete animal motif in bright colors.

"You paint that?" I ask.

"I did," she says, proudly.

Damn, I love this woman. Always full of surprises.

She leads me into the main bedroom and there's a nice king-size bed with an old-timey headboard and footboard. Vivian tells me she stripped it and refinished it herself. The sheets are new and they match the bedspread and the walls and even the curtains. Sitting on top of one of the nightstands is my huge stack of journals. I guess Vivian found them in my saddlebags.

I pick up the top journal and flip through the pages. "You read it?" I ask.

"Not yet," she says.

Her tits BZZZZ. I look at them, but she doesn't move. BZZZZ again.

"You going to answer that?" I ask.

"It's just another publisher," she says.

"Yeah, what's up with that?"

"You're a hero," she says. "The newspapers printed the story, then the news stations got hold of it, next thing you know you're on CNN and now publishers and producers are coming out of the woodwork. They want to pay you to write the book and then turn the book into a movie."

"Are you shitting me?"

"Hillary Swank's been calling. She wants to play you in the movie." Vivian smiles.

"No shit? For real?" I gulp.

"Okay, not really. The Hillary Swank part is a joke. But the other stuff's real."

"You got me," I laugh. I hand her the journal, the one that tells of our adventure, saying, "You can read it."

She accepts it from me and walks out of the room, already reading the first page.

I plop down on the bed. I feel dizzy. Too much shit coming at me at once. I take in a big breath and look out the window. I watch the big orange ball head for the horizon, leaving streaks of purple and yellow in its wake. I'm mesmerized by the descent of the sun and I sit and watch it until darkness spreads its blanket over my face.

I find Vivian in the kitchen sitting up on the countertop over by the sink, reading the journal. I lean up against the doorjamb on the other side of the room, stuff my hands in my pockets and just fill my eyes with her. She's barefoot and wearing faded jeans and a peasant blouse with some bangley beads hanging from the hem. Her hair is loose and windblown and she's the most gorgeous creature I've ever laid eyes on.

She laughs out loud at something in the journal, then looks up at me. "Sonny and Cher? And you really thought I was a hooker?"

I shrug and smile sheepishly.

She puts on her serious face. "You know, you never asked me where I went. Where I was that whole time we were apart," she says.

I shrug again. "I thought you'd tell me if you wanted to. I thought maybe I'd be better off not knowing."

She smiles. "I bounced around a while, going nowhere, just hiding. Finally, I checked myself into rehab."

"Oh, yeah?"

"Yeah..."

"How do you feel now?" I ask.

"Brand new," she answers. The corners of her mouth twitch into a smile. She holds out her hand for me and I walk over to her. She pulls me close, wraps her arms around my waist and holds me tight. I run my fingers through her hair and press my cheek against the top of her head.

She pulls away and her fingers undo the buttons of my shirt. She opens it wide and touches the tip of her finger lightly on my new scar.

"Does it hurt?" she asks.

"No."

She leans down and brushes her lips over the scar.

"We need to talk," she says, kissing my collarbone.

Uh-oh.

"Okay," I say.

She kisses my neck. "I'm not a dyke, okay?"

"Obviously."

She rubs her hands around my bare waist and tucks her fingers inside the back of my jeans. "And I'm not a lesbian either."

"I never thought you were," I say.

"I just love *you*, okay? Just you."

"I love you, too Vivian."

She sucks my earlobe between her teeth, forcing a shiver down my spine.

"Show me," she breathes into my ear. "Show me how much you love me."

I grab her legs and wrap them tight around my waist. "With pleasure," I say, kissing her on the lips.

I pull back a tiny bit and whisper, "But I want you to know this is going to take a *really* long time."

She laughs. "How long?"

"The rest of our lives."

"Okay," she says, gripping my hips and pulling me in closer. "I can live with that."

I place both my hands on her cheeks and look deep into her blue eyes. I swear, I can see my own reflection. And for the first time ever in my life, I don't mind what I'm seeing.

EPILOGUE

I lie back on the cold table and guide my bare feet into the metal stirrups. I tuck the green paper dress between my legs and press my knees together. Vivian stands beside the table looking down at me and smirking.

"You're going to have to spread your legs, you know," Vivian scolds.

"I know that. But I don't have to do it right at this very second," I say.

I know I sound bitchy, but I can't help it. This is something I've been dreading. It's not enough that my body is rebelling against me, but now I have to go and show my junk to a complete stranger. My belly is huge and my boobs have grown to tit status and I'm tired and hungry all the damn time. And when I get hungry, I get mean. I've been mean for the past month.

"She's a woman," Vivian soothes. "I made sure to get you a woman gyno. That way you'll be more comfortable when she sticks her fingers up your hoo-ha. You know?"

"Gawd, Viv, can you just not call it my hoo-ha?"

"I'm practicing not saying dirty words. I'm trying out substitute words. And a simple thank you for finding you a woman hoo-ha doctor would be nice," Vivian says and smiles.

"Thank you, Vivian, my dearest, who's always thinking of me. How can I ever repay such kindness and consideration?"

"No need to be sarcastic."

"You wanna trade me places?" I ask.

"Darlin', you know I only spread my legs for you."

I laugh. I can't help it. "Damn you, Vivian," I say. "You don't even let me get a good bitch on without making me laugh."

She lays her palm on my big belly. "I think it's a girl. Don't you?"

I shrug. "I think so. I hope so. I wouldn't mind a boy. It's when he turns into a man that worries me."

The door opens and the doctor walks in all smiles. She has long black hair loosely tied back in a knot and she has beautiful dark, almond-shaped eyes.

Vivian takes one look at gorgeous doctor lady and flashes her eyes back to me. Vivian reads my mind and doesn't like what's written there.

I shrug and whisper, "You picked her. Not me."

Vivian leans down to my ear and orders firmly, "You are not allowed to enjoy this. Do I make myself clear?"

"Yes, ma'am." I smile. But I must be smiling too big, because Vivian squints at me. I know what that squint means so I wipe the smile all the way off my face.

The doctor walks up to my side and smiles at me. "Hello, Ms. Hammond," she says. "I'm Dr. Drywater. But you can call me Gloria, if you don't mind that I call you Lee Anne."

"Lee," I answer her. "Call me Lee."

She smiles, showing perfect white teeth and because Vivian is still squinting at me, I'm real careful not to smile back.

"Okay, Lee," Gloria says.

"I'm Vivian," Vivian interjects. "Is Drywater an Indian name?"

"I'm Cherokee," Gloria says, setting her clipboard aside.

Vivian raises her eyebrows at me meaningfully. "She's Indian, Lee. In. Di. An. As in feather. And cheese," she wags her eyebrows up and down.

"I heard her, Vivian," I snap.

"Lee has a thing for Indians," Vivian explains. "And cheese."

Gloria gives her a perplexed smile and pulls a pair of plastic disposable gloves out of a box. She stretches the gloves, snapping them like a rubber band before she puts them on. She has really big hands.

I gulp and look away.

"Lee's a little nervous, Gloria. She's never had a girlie exam before," Vivian explains like she's my mother and I'm about five years old.

Gloria drapes a thin white sheet over the lower half of my body and sits on a stool at my feet.

"Really? You've never done this before?" Gloria asks.

"Not with gloves," I respond, then immediately grimace at my own feeble attempt at humor.

Gloria actually laughs and puts her hands on both my knees. I stare at the ceiling while she guides my knees apart. She slips a couple of fingers inside me and I try my damndest to think about anything but. She pushes and prods and I am not enjoying it at all.

Vivian says, "You know, Gloria, you and Lee have a lot in common. You work with girlie parts all day and Lee's a lesbian. You two share the same interests."

"Vivian!" I shout.

Gloria laughs out loud. "Good one."

I scold harshly, "What've I told you about just outing me like that?"

Vivian frowns at me. "You also told me lesbians don't go down the first time, but I know for a fact you've broken that rule."

I think I hear Gloria chuckle under the sheet.

"You can leave the room any time now," I say.

Vivian ignores me. "So, Gloria, Lee and I were just discussing, if the baby's a girl, what word we should use for her girlie parts. What do you think?"

"Hoo-ha's always a popular one," Gloria answers.

"Told you so," Vivian says to me.

"Okay, okay, hoo-ha then. I'm outnumbered."

Gloria slides that metal torture-looking device inside me and I gasp out loud. "Whoa...cold," I say.

"Karma, Lee. That's called karma," Vivian chuckles.

I start to get a little concerned with what Gloria's doing under the sheet, but she's all smiles as she cranks the thing open and talks to me, "So, tell me about yourself, Lee. What're your interests?"

"Interests?" I ask. It's really hard to concentrate right now.

"Small talk, Lee," Vivian says. "She's trying to distract you."

"Oh. I guess..." I think hard. "I like motorcycles."

Vivian interjects, "And tits. She loves tits. If you really want to distract her just whip out a tit."

"For chrissakes, Viv..."

"It's true." Vivian shrugs.

"Well, that'll cost more," Gloria jokes. Vivian and I both laugh. "So, you have a motorcycle?" Gloria asks me.

"Yeah," I answer. "And I have a shop. I fix motorcycles. Repair them, you know, and rebuild them and stuff."

"She's very good with her hands," Vivian says, then adds under her breath to Gloria, "really good."

I close my eyes and wish I could just disappear.

To her credit, Gloria looks more entertained than embarrassed. "What kind of bike do you have?" she asks.

Vivian leans a little to her left and looks at whatever Gloria's busy with under the sheet. "Looks like you're pretty good with your hands too," she says.

I hide my face in my hands and grumble, "Can you please make her leave the room?"

Gloria laughs. "She's not bothering me."

"Well, she's bothering me."

"What kind of bike?" Gloria asks.

"Harley. A Street Glide." I feel a big wave of relief as she uncranks that metal thing and takes it out of me.

Gloria looks at Vivian and asks, "Are you her partner?"

"Yeah," Vivian says, all smiles. "She fell in love with me at first sight and we've been together ever since."

Gloria laughs lightly. "I meant are you her birthing partner. Will you be there for the birth?"

I say, "Vivian thinks she's the father and I haven't told her any differently."

Vivian playfully slaps me on the arm and Gloria laughs.

"Now," Gloria says to me, "let's talk about you and your baby."

"Okay," I say tentatively. "Is something wrong?"

"Everything's perfect," she says. "I think you're progressing beautifully. I'll make you a list of vitamins I'd like for you to take and when you leave, ask the receptionist for an ultrasound appointment. And we'll have a look at your baby. You can get dressed now." She smiles and heads for the door.

She turns back to us. "It was good to meet you both. Lee, I'll see you again soon. You're going to make a great mother. Sorry," she corrects. "You're both going to make great mothers."

After Gloria leaves, Vivian turns back to me, smiling. "We are, you know. We're going to be fuckin' great mothers."

I close my eyes and shake my head. "Your little cussing problem still needs some work."

"It's all under control," Vivian says. "I've got a good year before the baby starts talking. I'm sure I can find all kinds of new words by then."

I sit up and grin slyly. "Wanna go home and play doctor?"

"You're so bad. You're a dirty, dirty girl," Vivian mock scolds, then adds brightly, "Sure. But I get to wear the paper dress this time."

The Beginning.

Publications from
Bella Books, Inc.
Women. Books. Even Better Together.
P.O. Box 10543
Tallahassee, FL 32302
Phone: 800-729-4992
www.bellabooks.com

CALM BEFORE THE STORM by Peggy J. Herring. Colonel Marcel Robideaux doesn't tell and so far no one official has asked, but the amorous pursuit by Jordan McGowan has her worried for both her career and her honor.
978-0-9677753-1-9

THE WILD ONE by Lyn Denison. Rachel Weston is busy keeping home and head together after the death of her husband. Her kids need her and what she doesn't need is the confusion that Quinn Farrelly creates in her body and heart.
978-0-9677753-4-0

LESSONS IN MURDER by Claire McNab. There's a corpse in the school with a neat hole in the head and a Black & Decker drill alongside. Which teacher should Inspector Carol Ashton suspect? Unfortunately, the alluring Sybil Quade is at the top of the list. First in this highly lauded series.
978-1-931513-65-4

WHEN AN ECHO RETURNS by Linda Kay Silva. The bayou where Echo Branson found her sanity has been swept clean by a hurricane — or at least they thought. Then an evil washed up by the storm comes looking for them all, one-by-one. Second in series.
978-1-59493-225-0

DEADLY INTERSECTIONS by Ann Roberts. Everyone is lying, including her own father and her girlfriend. Leaving matters to the professionals is supposed to be easier! Third in series with *PAID IN FULL* and *WHITE OFFERINGS*.
978-1-59493-224-3

SUBSTITUTE FOR LOVE by Karin Kallmaker. No substitutes, ever again! But then Holly's heart, body and soul are captured by Reyna... Reyna with no last name and a secret life that hides a terrible bargain, one written in family blood.
978-1-931513-62-3

MAKING UP FOR LOST TIME by Karin Kallmaker. Take one Next Home Network Star and add one Little White Lie to equal mayhem in little Mendocino and a recipe for sizzling romance. This lighthearted, steamy story is a feast for the senses in a kitchen that is way too hot.
978-1-931513-61-6

2ND FIDDLE by Kate Calloway. Cassidy James's first case left her with a broken heart. At least this new case is fighting the good fight, and she can throw all her passion and energy into it.
978-1-59493-200-7

HUNTING THE WITCH by Ellen Hart. The woman she loves — used to love — offers her help, and Jane Lawless finds it hard to say no. She needs TLC for recent injuries and who better than a doctor? But Julia's jittery demeanor awakens Jane's curiosity. And Jane has never been able to resist a mystery. #9 in series and Lammy-winner.
978-1-59493-206-9

FAÇADES by Alex Marcoux. Everything Anastasia ever wanted — she has it. Sidney is the woman who helped her get it. But keeping it will require a price — the unnamed passion that simmers between them.
978-1-59493-239-7

ELENA UNDONE by Nicole Conn. The risks. The passion. The devastating choices. The ultimate rewards. Nicole Conn rocked the lesbian cinema world with Claire of the Moon and has rocked it again with Elena Undone. This is the book that tells it all…
978-1-59493-254-0

WHISPERS IN THE WIND by Frankie J. Jones. It began as a camping trip, then a simple hike. Dixon Hayes and Elizabeth Colter uncover an intriguing cave on their hike, changing their world, perhaps irrevocably.
978-1-59493-037-9

WEDDING BELL BLUES by Julia Watts. She'll do anything to save what's left of her family. Anything. It didn't seem like a bad plan...at first. Hailed by readers as Lammy-winner Julia Watts' funniest novel.
978-1-59493-199-4

WILDFIRE by Lynn James. From the moment botanist Devon McKinney meets ranger Elaine Thomas the chemistry is undeniable. Sharing — and protecting — a mountain for the length of their short assignments leads to unexpected passion in this sizzling romance by newcomer Lynn James.
978-1-59493-191-8

LEAVING L.A. by Kate Christie. Eleanor Chapin is on the way to the rest of her life when Tessa Flanaghan offers her a lucrative summer job caring for Tessa's daughter Laya. It's only temporary and everyone expects Eleanor to be leaving L.A...
978-1-59493-221-2

SOMETHING TO BELIEVE by Robbi McCoy. When Lauren and Cassie meet on a once-in-a-lifetime river journey through China their feelings are innocent…at first. Ten years later, nothing — and everything — has changed. From Golden Crown winner Robbi McCoy.
978-1-59493-214-4

DEVIL'S ROCK: THE SEARCH FOR PATRICK DOE by Gerri Hill. Deputy Andrea Sullivan and Agent Cameron Ross vow to bring a killer to justice. The killer has other plans. Gerri Hill pens another intriguing blend of mystery and romance in this page-turning thriller.
978-1-59493-218-2

SHADOW POINT by Amy Briant. Madison Maguire has just been not-quite fired, told her brother is dead and discovered she has to pick up a five-year old niece she's never met. After she makes it to Shadow Point it seems like someone—or something—doesn't want her to leave. Romance sizzles in this ghost story from Amy Briant.
978-1-59493-216-8

JUKEBOX by Gina Daggett. Debutantes in love. With each other. Two young women chafe at the constraints of parents and society with a friendship that could be more, if they can break free. Gina Daggett is best known as "Lipstick" of the columnist duo Lipstick & Dipstick.
978-1-59493-212-0

BLIND BET by Tracey Richardson. The stakes are high when Ellen Turcotte and Courtney Langford meet at the blackjack tables. Lady Luck has been smiling on Courtney but Ellen is a wild card she may not be able to handle.
978-1-59493-211-3